HOLD ON TIGHT

RETURNING HOME BOOK 1

SERENA BELL

JMG
JELSBA
MEDIA
GROUP

To the men and women who have fought for my freedom

1

He didn't expect her to say yes. He asked on a whim, throwing the words out into the warm night as an experiment. "Let's go in."

They stood with their bare feet in the sand at the edge of the lake. The surface was a strip of glass—cool and mysterious, reflecting a row of spiky trees the moonlight had thrown between sky and water.

Pale light shone in her eyes. Her bottom lip was glossy and begged to be nipped. Her hair was something he wanted to get lost in, the way he wanted to get lost in her. He was out of time, and it made him brave. In a week, he'd be fighting in Afghanistan, and this—whatever it was—would be a memory.

This wasn't supposed to be happening. He wasn't the kind of guy who could meet a girl and feel things for her. He was the type who should've spent his leave drinking beer with his buds and longing to get the hell back to the war. Whereas this guy he'd become, this new version of himself, couldn't spend enough moments with his face pressed against Mira's hair, breathing peace.

She was eighteen; he was twenty. He'd picked her up in a Seattle bowling alley, where she'd come with friends, the first night of his leave. He'd been raring to burn off training testosterone. They'd made it as far as his car before she'd confessed how young she was and admitted she'd never been picked up by anyone in her life. He'd been planning to take her to a hotel room, but she was only a month past her birthday and obviously not that kind of girl, so they took a drive instead, the night air rushing by their open windows, the narrow roads hemmed in by trees. He found himself telling her everything in his head. Stories. Favorite books, childhood vacations, old friends, anxiety dreams . . . as if the pent-up thing in him had never been lust at all, but words, months' worth of thoughts he'd kept locked up tight.

At the end of that first night, she'd leaned over and kissed him, and he lost his mind in the softness of her lips.

Before he'd flown home, his fire team leader had gathered them together. "We deploy in a month. Don't get distracted. And for fuck's sake, whatever you do, *don't get married.*"

Jake leaned over and nudged Mike, his buddy, his teammate, and said, "No fucking chance." Because if there was one thing Jake knew, it was that he was never getting married. Never having a family.

When he first got home, he'd stopped in to see his folks. They were as miserable as he remembered, drunk when he arrived, snarling and snapping at each other. There were faded bruises on his mother's arms and circles under her eyes. It had always been that way: his father on disability since Jake's childhood, drifting through life since he'd fallen off a roof he was de-mossing; his mother using cheap wine and online shopping to drown the misery of a bad marital choice made worse by circumstance.

Jake had known at age twelve that he had to get out as soon as possible. And then at fourteen, the first plane had hit the first tower and he'd known where he was going *to*. He would take the fight to those assholes, wherever they were; he would rain destruction down on them like they'd rained it down on New York City. On his country.

He'd scoffed at the idea that he could be distracted. The month of post-training leave couldn't go fast enough; deployment couldn't come soon enough; he couldn't wait to put a bullet through the first motherfucker's head.

Except then there was Mira. Three weeks so far, nights strung together like shiny beads in his memory. Nights she told her parents she was with her friends, nights she stole from her life as a good girl. Movies, sitting side by side, the heat of her arm sinking into his skin and making it hard for him to sit still, a slow burn twisting in his gut. Nights at Dick's, splitting french fries and chocolate milkshakes and passing iPods across the speckled table to share songs.

In the car afterward, Mira setting the pace, her kisses bolder every night, their mouths sliding over each other's, slick and hungry, bodies tangled and sweaty, fighting the gearshift and the emergency brake, her kneeling over him, trying to press as close as possible.

Her hands gained confidence as they moved across his heated skin, as they unfastened the button and zipper of his jeans, as they slipped beneath the waistband of his briefs.

She'd never said she was a virgin, but he guessed she was because she'd seemed surprised when he'd flicked his thumbs over her nipples. When he'd tongued them. When he'd slid his hand down the front of her pants and worked a finger through the tangle of her curls to tap her clit. The first time, she'd come against his hand with a soft, broken cry.

That, like everything else, wasn't supposed to have happened. Nor was the tiny ping in his chest, a seed bursting through its tough shell to germinate, at the sound of her voice.

And now there were seven days left.

Not much time for what he wanted from her, which was all of her, under him, around him, over and over.

But it couldn't be more than that—not more than a week of sex. Because he was never getting married. Because she'd told him that first night that she'd deliberately chosen to get herself picked up by a stranger as an act of rebellion. Her father had just informed her that he wouldn't pay for her to attend art school, but would only give her money for "a real college." She'd been so pissed at her dad that night, she would have slept with a sixty-five-year-old hardened ex-con to get a rise out of him.

"My dad's a total control freak," she'd told him on their third date. She'd grown up on Bainbridge Island, college-bound before she'd popped out of the womb. Her parents were the same brand as his father, ex-hippies, but unlike his father, all whitewashed and clean living. She'd said, "My father would *kill* me. I never meant this to be anything other than a one-night thing."

"You and me both," he told her, but they didn't push it any further than that.

There was only *now*. The sand under their feet, the gathering mist over the water, her mouth curving into a smile. There was no future.

This is all there is. Now.

He willed her to feel it, too.

He listened so hard to hear her answer that he almost missed it, because she didn't give it in words. She unbuttoned the top button of her blouse instead. Long fingers fumbling with the pearl-white disk. No revelation at first, only that undoing. Then another button, and the shirt fell open, revealing her breasts mounded high in pink lace cups.

An ache bloomed at the base of his spine, the root of his dick, in his balls. His mouth ached, too. Before Mira, he hadn't understood that sex could make you crazy. That it could take hold in your teeth and knees and chest. That you could want something so badly you'd beg for it.

He'd kept the begging inside because he hadn't wanted to frighten her.

She undid another button and a sound came out of him he'd never heard before, something grating in his throat.

She smiled. "You like that?"

"Hell, yeah," he said.

Another button, and another, and the shirt hung down at her sides. He cupped her breasts in his hands. Now the ache was in his throat and his jaw and God, fucking *everywhere.*

With other girls, he'd kissed them because it was the thing to do, the time to do it. With Mira, he kissed her because he couldn't not. And he kept kissing her because it hurt to stop, played with her nipples and grabbed her ass and rocked her up against him because he wanted to have *all, fucking all,* of her; there wasn't enough of her, he *couldn't get enough of her.* That was how it was with Mira.

The way she got in his arms. Like something fierce, writhing and live. Like he could barely hold her. And that lit his craving worse. He wanted to trap her, wanted to rub his heat and need off on her, but she wouldn't be contained.

She wriggled out of his arms and darted a short distance away.

"Come back."

She shook her head and dropped her shirt to the sand behind her. She undid her bra and arched her back a little so her breasts swelled and her nipples tipped up. Something roared in him, but he stayed where he was because the visual was so fine he couldn't stop looking. Saliva rushed into his mouth, blood poured into his dick. And then her hands found the button of her denim shorts and slid them and her underpants down her long, white legs to the sand. The whole, perfect fantasy revealed in the moonlight.

He lunged, but she ran into the water, laughing at him. She gasped at the cold. "Get in here and warm me up."

He got out of his own clothes so fast he tripped over his jeans and got an arm tangled in his T-shirt. The cool water slid across his heated limbs. His body tightened and shrank, but his desire stayed sharp beneath the surface of his skin, like an undercurrent. He kicked and swam out, then back, stretching his legs and luxuriating. She treaded water and watched.

"C'mere," she said.

In the water, she was cool and slippery, heat hidden in the places where he buried his fingers and his face. They stood in water up to their shoulders, and her body warmed his until she pressed his erection between his belly and hers.

"Do you want to?" A gesture so vague she could have been

asking if he wanted to go to the grocery store, but even in the dim light he could see the flush rise in her cheeks.

He wanted to. So much he couldn't answer, couldn't choke out *yes, fuck yes, oh my God please yes.*

"I have two blankets in my bag," she said.

"I don't have condoms."

"I do."

She'd planned for it and—he wanted to believe—longed for it. *Jesus.* He kissed her hard and lifted her off her feet and tried to press up into her despite the mad impossibility of those logistics.

She laughed at him. "Hang on. Hang on."

He swept her into his arms and carried her up the beach. He squatted, balancing her across his thighs, ignoring the burn, grabbing the blankets out of the tote bag she'd brought and laying them out as best he could on the sand. He set her down on one and she spread the edges out, then reached for him and pulled him down so abruptly he lost his balance and fell beside her.

He crawled over her and dropped his mouth to hers. Her body was a dizzying contrast of warm and cool, her tongue a wild, aggressive thing. He couldn't catch his breath. She made senseless sounds, moving against his fingers, shifting to press her breasts up so he could duck his head and lick circles around her tight nipples. Her next noise was a definite moan. It swirled in his belly and made him so hard it hurt.

"I want you," she whispered in his ear.

His brain had shut down, and whatever part of him was in charge could only think: *In.* He moved over her and positioned himself, swollen and leaking pre-cum. He felt her wet heat give against his tip, felt her all over his head, and he almost came right then and there, almost blew his wad and ruined the whole fucking night.

"Condom," she said.

"Shit." He withdrew.

She tugged her bag over and found one, tore it open and reached for him. He had to use all his self-control to hang on. He made a choked sound, and she hummed her approval as he got between her legs again and she lined him up against her wetness. He thrust forward. An inch, and he wouldn't have thought it possible but he wanted her even more, her fierce heat squeezing him, and he pressed farther, farther, until he noticed she'd gone still beneath him.

He was so crazed with lust that it took him a moment to catch on. She'd turned her face away, too.

"Mira," he whispered.

"Ow," she whispered back.

"Oh, Christ, I'm sorry," he said, and drew back, which elicited another squeaked noise of—he now recognized— pain. "I'll go slower." He dropped a hand between her legs and began to slick his thumb lightly back and forth over her clit.

"That feels good," she said, but as soon as he tried to move again, she made another noise of distress.

He kissed her, hard, and her mouth opened to him, got wetter against his, but her body got more rigid. She drew back. Some nasty animal part of him wanted to grab her and refuse to let go, but he was stern with his lust and it subsided. His erection was doing the same. Shrinking away from her misery. In a few seconds, he'd slip out of her. The thought filled him with despair. *This is all there is, the now.* A few minutes ago, it had seemed like infinite space, unlimited promise. Now it was the end.

He withdrew and rolled away.

"I'm sorry." She had tucked her face under her arm and her shoulders shook. Crying. He felt it, a hollow pain in his chest.

"Don't be. We'll try again." He tried to soothe her with a hand on her hair, but she didn't soften under his touch.

"There's no time. We don't have enough time."

"We have a week," he said, but he felt desperation lock around his ribs.

"I'm an idiot," she said.

"This wasn't your fault. It was your first time, right?"

She nodded.

"It'll be better next time. I'll make it better."

Because he wanted to leave her with something that mattered. Something she would always have. In case she met assholes in college who took advantage, who didn't know what they were doing, who didn't see how amazing she was, how she deserved the best he could give her. Not like this, not halfway and awkward, but the way he would do it next time, as much a revelation as the first time she'd cried out and arched in his arms.

But she was shaking her head. "I'm not an idiot because of that. I'm an idiot because I didn't see this coming."

"What?"

"How I would feel—"

His chest got tight. Tighter.

"That I would fall—"

"Don't say it," he said.

She turned away. Her shoulders slumped. He ached to

reach out and pull her in. To be a different guy with a different life, to say, *We have all the time in the world.*

"I was trying to prove something. To my father. To myself. But this—Do you think—" Whatever she was trying to say, it was costing her something. "Do you think there's any chance I could see you? Next time you're home? That we could—I don't know—try to be together?"

Don't get distracted. He could see his fire team leader, Sergeant Trebwylyn, in his mind's eye. Buzzed hair, big as a Hummer, perpetually pissed off, warning them that he'd known way too many guys who'd come back from leave married. Dads-to-be. Entangled, distracted, bullet magnets.

He'd given them one job, *Don't get distracted,* and Jake had managed to screw it up. He hadn't even set foot on Afghan soil and he was already a fuckup (*like your father,* said that particular voice in his head). And what she was asking him for led him straight to what he'd vowed he'd never do. *I will never be like my parents.* The only way he knew for sure to avoid that was to never become part of a family. He'd already let himself get pulled way too far down this path. There was only one answer he could give her.

When he looked into her dark brown eyes, a stark contrast with her blond hair and fair skin, he wanted to kiss her. But if he kissed her, he'd want more of her, and if he took what he wanted, he'd be in deeper. They'd both be in deeper.

She heard what he hadn't said into the silence.

"Okay," she said. "Okay."

But I didn't even answer yet. He wanted to take back his non-answer, wanted to beg her for another chance.

The words were there, pressure in his chest, like that first night when he'd found himself telling her so much, for no reason other than that she was Mira, that she listened, that she *heard.* A pressure stronger than lust, the need to tell her how he felt. He wanted her to know everything. He wanted her to be the only person he ever told anything to.

Don't get distracted.

She turned away.

"I can't," she said. "I can't do this."

2

Mira Shipley watched her son, Sam, through the window of the physical therapist's office. He was frowning as the PT explained something. His seven-year-old forehead was wrinkled under too much hair, his skinny body stork-like in shorts and a T-shirt. He needed a haircut and socks that fit and probably, as usual, to have his fingernails cleaned and trimmed. When she'd lived with her parents, she hadn't fully appreciated how much they took care of. Now all the tasks of a single mom were hers and hers alone.

She wished she were in the office with him, but the physical therapist had asked her to stay in the waiting room. Watching Sam from a distance made Mira feel deeply, peculiarly, tender, some vestige of the way she'd felt when she'd stood outside the newborn nursery and watched him through the glass. *That one's mine. I made him. And now I have to keep him safe.* She'd been alone with him in the world, terrified—having no idea how to change a diaper or administer a bath or soothe that overstimulated crying he'd launched into at five p.m. on his fourth day of life, a pattern that would continue for ten solid weeks.

She could smile now, thinking of it, of walking the halls of her parents' house with Sam swaddled tightly to her chest. Of the small, exhausted sighs Sam emitted when he finally dropped into sleep. Of the way he'd nestled against her on the bed as he'd nursed in the early morning. They hadn't done so badly, she and Sam. Not at all. They were a good team, and they'd get through this crazy summer, too.

Of course, she hadn't felt at all tender toward him in the car on the way here as he'd griped about physical therapy. She wanted to say, *You should have thought of that before you climbed that spindly tree. What did you* think *was going to happen?*

Even if Sam *had* been able to predict that the branch—half the diameter of his absurdly thin wrists—would snap, he wouldn't have been able to foresee all the consequences of his risk-taking. He'd hurt his shoulder, arm, and knee, earning himself a couple of weeks of physical therapy. And disqualifying him from going to summer camp.

Now she had no place for him to go while she worked.

She and Sam had just moved out of her parents' house in Florida, where they'd been living for the last seven years. Under their roof, she hadn't had to work. They'd paid Sam's medical bills, supported them both. Now she and Sam were living in Seattle, where she'd been born and raised, and they had no one to depend on but themselves.

That was how she wanted it.

Or so she'd thought.

Behind the plate-glass window, Sam stretched a giant red rubber band while his therapist, a thin woman with gray hair pulled tightly back in a ponytail, corrected his form. Mira was supposed to have started work Monday, but they'd granted her an extra week to find childcare. Now it was Friday, and she was due to plant her butt in her office chair on Monday, but luckily, yesterday she'd finally interviewed and hired a sitter. Penny had been charming, articulate, and a big hit with Sam, who wasn't always the easiest kid to win over. For the first time since Mira had unrolled sleeping bags on the floor of their new house, she felt like she had all the pieces of her new life—her fabulous, independent new life—in place.

The door of the office swung open and a man stepped in. He went to the check-in desk and spoke in a low voice to the woman there, then came into the waiting area. The slightest hesitation in his step drew her eye downward. One of his legs was prosthetic—an expensive gray running shoe was fitted with a slim shank of metal ankle that thickened to a robotic calf and knee. She tried not to stare—at either the prosthetic or his flesh-and-blood calf, which was lean, well-muscled, and covered with golden curls.

Nice.

She made herself look away, feeling vaguely guilty for wondering what had happened and how he felt about it. Even though she wanted to look again, she wouldn't let herself.

But she peeked. He wore nylon hiking shorts with a red plaid short-sleeved shirt, untucked. Slim hips and waist, nicely sculpted posterior, broad chest and hunky shoulders.

Very, very nice.

He made his way over to a chair and sat down on a diagonal from her. Even in her peripheral vision, she could see that he'd taken over the seat like an alpha male—knees apart, leaning back casually. *This is what I've got to offer, baby. I'm so good, I don't even have to convince you.*

Sadly, the posture worked on her. But it was somehow at odds with her expectation, and she chastised herself. *What? He's not allowed to be cocky because he has a prosthetic leg?*

Her phone buzzed in her back jeans pocket. Penny Dawson. Her life-saving babysitter.

"Hello?"

"Mira? It's Penny. I'm so sorry to do this to you—"

Oh, shit. Mira's breath stopped. She couldn't lose Penny. In her last conversation with her new boss, Haley had been patient but firm: "We can give you till Monday, but we need to know that we can depend on you. We need to know childcare isn't going to be an ongoing issue."

Mira had moved across the country. She'd pulled up stakes, broken her parents' hearts, and bet everything on herself. She needed her job.

"I'm so sorry, Mira. I just got a permanent, full-time offer teaching at Broadview Montessori. Summer and school year."

A collection of desperate thoughts went through Mira's head. Bribes, extravagant promises, a willingness to prostrate herself and beg.

"Any chance you could watch Sam just next week?"

"I'm sorry. I asked. They said no. They said they had another candidate who could start right away if I couldn't." Penny sounded wretched.

So Mira would have to go back to the drawing board on babysitters. Maybe, if she was lucky, she could still find one for Monday. She swallowed hard. "It's okay. That's great about the new job. I'm really psyched for you. Of course you need to take it. You wouldn't happen to have any ideas about who else could watch a smart, well-behaved seven-year-old for the summer—or even just next week—would you?"

"I'm really sorry," Penny said. "I wracked my brain this morning to try to think of someone who could do it. I even called a few friends. I swear if I think of *anyone*, I will let you know."

"Thank you. I really appreciate that."

"It was really nice to meet you. And Sam. If you ever need an evening sitter, or weekends—"

"I'll definitely call."

"And meantime, I'll keep my fingers crossed that you find someone, and I'll call you if I think of anyone."

"Thanks."

Mira let the phone drop into her lap and took a deep breath.

On the other side of the room, the cocky guy with the prosthetic leg shifted in his seat, drawing her gaze. Brown hair, on the longer side of short, uncombed. A couple of days' unshaven scruff. Not her type; she liked professional men, clean-shaven. Her mind was about to dismiss him—*a guy I ran into in the physical therapist's office and wasn't attracted to, but not because he was an amputee, just because he wasn't my fantasy.* But something made her look again.

Holy shit. She knew that face. The strong jaw, the well-formed upper lip, the deep groove that ran vertically between his brows—

She'd memorized his features in the few weeks they'd been together, the quick three-quarters way he smiled, like he couldn't quite fully commit to happiness, the all-in truth of his smile when he gave himself over. The creases that formed when he frowned, the way his jaw set when something bothered him. That night at the lake—*the last night*—the look on his face when she'd taken off her clothes. Gratitude and longing and *Who, me? For real?*

The night came back to her in sharp contrasts, pairs of impressions. The coolness of his wet skin and the heat of his body. The softness of his mouth moving over hers, over her breasts, and the hard tug of his suckling, the yank of desire she'd felt. The rich summer smells, green and overripe, and the clean soap scent of him. How open she'd felt, how boundary-less, melting, flowing, willing—and how her body had betrayed and frustrated her.

How good he'd made her feel, better than she'd ever felt in her life, and the way he'd hurt her. The way they'd dressed, packed up, and driven home in silence. How hard she'd cried, and for how long.

Jake.

His eyes caught hers, caught and held and held and held. Sam's gray-blue eyes, Sam's full lower lip, Sam's absurdly long eyelashes. Jake's face.

Would Sam someday have a jaw like that, square and strong? Would his nose, which was still a little boy's pudgy upturned nose, be as bladelike as his father's?

How many times had she promised herself that if this moment ever came, she wouldn't hold the truth back from Jake?

But she'd never pictured it happening in a setting like this. Public. Awkward.

"Mira." He said it slowly, as if he were pulling the name from the furthest reaches of his memory.

"Hi, Jake."

Her voice was splintered, thready. There was no pretending this was a no-big-deal moment. Not for her. And he wasn't trying to play it cool either. He scrutinized her, jaw set, expression serious. There was grief in every line of his face. Something she thought might be anger. A darkness behind the surface of his eyes that she'd seen only once before, that night by the lake, when she'd asked him for a future he couldn't give.

She was feeling too much, and she couldn't put it all together. When he'd been a stranger with a prosthetic leg, she could manage the sympathy, the curiosity, the faint survivor's guilt. But he was *her Jake*, a man she'd been intimate with, and he'd lost part of the body she'd worshipped. He was *her Jake,* and he was here, in this room, and she was so glad to see him, so glad she wanted to hurl herself at him, but also terrified, because what was she supposed to do or say now?

She had promised herself she'd tell him.

But he had never really been *her Jake*, had he? And now—

Now he really was a stranger. Even if her body was trying to tell her he wasn't. Insisting it hadn't forgotten the scent or the heat or the weight of him, hadn't forgotten what he could do with his hungry mouth and skilled fingers.

She wasn't eighteen. She wasn't free to indulge herself, to throw herself open like a book. She had Sam to think about.

"You look good," she said, because the silence was spreading and someone had to say something.

For a fraction of a second—she might have missed it if she hadn't been so hyperalert—he looked down at his leg. Then back up at her face, his eyes empty.

He didn't say it back. *You look good, too, Mira.* She hated herself for wishing he had.

She had no idea what to say next. How to make small talk with a man who was all the things he was to her: a summer fling gone wrong, the hottest not-sex she'd ever had, the father of her child. How to make small talk with someone who so obviously wanted nothing to do with her.

"You look like you're doing great."

The look in his eyes, pure scorn, told her how absurd he thought that was. "I do all right."

Every word she said that was not *I have a son, and he's your son, too* felt like a lie. Like postponing the inevitable. But could she just . . . do it? In the waiting room of the physical therapist's office? They were the only two people here, but surely there was a better time and place. Someplace quiet, someplace private, someplace . . . intimate.

But how would she get him alone like that? How would she explain why she needed to?

So many times, she had imagined a chance meeting, this opportunity to finally say, *Jake, I have something to tell you. You might want to sit down.*

Well, here he was. Sitting.

"That's my son," she said, pointing through the window. "Sam."

Her heart pounded so hard she thought she'd be sick.

She waited for a flicker of recognition, something to indicate he'd made the connection, but there was nothing. Only his blank, grim expression. Was he still in there somewhere, behind that mask? Was it the loss of his leg that had made him like this, or what he'd seen in the war? She'd read somewhere that the army was requiring longer and longer commitments from soldiers, pushing them to the outside limit of what they could endure, physically and mentally. Who knew how damaged he was?

Who knew if he was someone she would choose to let her child spend time with, let alone love?

"Could I—could we—get coffee?"

Maybe if she sat down with him, if they could talk, if she could find out who he was and where he'd been.

"What?" he asked. "Chat and catch up?"

"Yes. Chat and catch up."

"I fill you in on what it's like to be down a limb?"

He was angry. Not at her, or at least not at her for any good reason. At his fate, at the world. And she couldn't blame him for that. She couldn't imagine—couldn't fathom—what it would be like to have to relearn everything, to start from scratch with walking and balance and all the things she took for granted.

"I don't think so," he said. "I'm not much for coffee talk these days."

"Ms. Shipley?" The physical therapist, Joanne, had poked her head into the waiting room. "I want to go over Sam's homework with you."

Okay, what did she do now? Walk away? Despite his curtness, she couldn't imagine turning her back on him and writing him off. Sam's *father*.

If she walked away now, if she let him walk away now, she'd have no way to get in touch with him. It would be as good as if they'd never had this chance meeting.

Was that what she wanted?

She'd *promised* herself. *If I ever see him again, I will tell him he's Sam's father.*

"Sure. Can you hang on a second?" she asked Joanne. "I'll be right there."

"No problem. I'll show Sam one more thing on the ball while we wait for you." Joanne disappeared again.

"Just—please," she said to Jake. "Coffee, a drink—I don't care. I'd just like us to get a chance to talk."

"Do we have something to talk about?"

His words found their way into her old, half-healed hurt. The part of her that had tried for months—years—to understand how she could have been so wrong about what he felt for her.

But there was no room for pride now, no room to care if he thought she was desperate or throwing herself at him, hoping for a reprise of the good old times. She just didn't want to lose this thread, this chance. She would *not* let her cowardice cheat Sam out of the chance to have a father in his life.

"Yes," she said. "I have to tell you something I think you'll want to hear."

Nothing. No curiosity, no glimmer of the old Jake. It was like he wasn't in there at all.

"Jake?" The receptionist had poked her head into the waiting area. "Linda says you can head back there as soon as you're ready, and she'll be with you in two."

Jake used the arms of his chair to pull himself to his feet and shook his head at Mira. "I don't think it's a good idea."

He crossed the room, then paused and turned back. "Nice to see you, Mira."

"Wait. Wait." Her heart pounded like crazy.

He hesitated.

Half a room separated them. She crossed the space and

stood next to him. "Sam. He's seven." Her voice had slid to a whisper.

"Good age," Jake said.

Was he being deliberately dense? Subtlety wasn't going to do it; she'd have to blurt it out. After all these years, it was no easier to say the words. Her heart beat hard, her stomach clenched tight, her hands and feet were numb. When she opened her mouth, she didn't say what she'd meant to say.

"I should have called or written right away, once I knew, but they said—everyone said—that I should wait. Till you were home on leave."

Something moved behind his eyes, just enough of a shift that she was sure he heard the urgency in her voice.

They—mainly her friend Polly, who had a brother in the army—had said it would be dangerous to give the news of her pregnancy when he was deployed. That he'd lose his focus and get himself killed.

"And you'd said you'd be home for leave in six months, so I waited, and then I called. Did you get my texts and messages?"

He shook his head. Slowly, his eyes wary.

"I didn't know how to find you, other than the cell number. I tried to find your parents, but—"

"Their number was unlisted."

"I kept thinking you'd get in touch. That you'd see the texts and messages, and then you didn't, and then—I wanted to tell you."

"Tell me what?"

"Sam's yours."

If she'd expected a reaction, if she'd expected drama, she would have been thoroughly disappointed. His jaw might have tightened a notch, but otherwise, she couldn't see any evidence that he was moved by her revelation. Her life might have been remade from scratch, but she could have told him there was a donut shop opening in town, for all the emotion he'd showed.

Just when she was pretty sure he wasn't going to say anything at all, he said, "We didn't have sex."

Oh, fuck you, *dude.*

In all her fantasies about what it would be like to tell Jake that he had a son, he had never denied responsibility. It had never crossed her mind that he would deny responsibility. She guessed that made her ridiculously naive.

"We *did* have sex." The word "sex" sounded particularly loud in the empty waiting room. Mira looked over at the receptionist, but she was making calls with a headset on. "Just because it was *bad* sex doesn't mean it wasn't sex."

That got more reaction from him than the news that Sam was his son. She saw a muscle jump in his jaw. *Just telling it like it is, baby denier.*

"I wore a condom."

"You put it on too late. I was shocked, too, believe me. My OB said the odds are low, but it definitely happens. Look. I'm telling you Sam's yours because I thought you might want to know. I thought you might want to know that there was a person walking around on this earth with half your DNA, doing stuff he probably inherited from you. For all I know he got all the asthma and allergies from your side of the family, because he sure as hell didn't get them from mine. But whatever. We don't need anything from you. We've done perfectly fine without you up to this point. I didn't tell you so you could argue with me about whether he's really yours."

No reaction, other than a few blinks and a swallow. As if they weren't fighting about a *child*. What was *wrong* with him?

"If you guys are doing so fine, what was that phone call a few minutes ago all about?"

She shut her eyes. *Seriously?* He was going to refuse to admit Sam was his son but then get all up in her business about her life? She took a deep breath. He was damaged. Something had happened to him. He needed her—her sympathy. Her patience. "I have some childcare issues."

"Some," he repeated. "Your babysitter bailed on you."

"What are you doing, volunteering?"

She wasn't sure where the snark had come from.

"You wouldn't really want that, now, would you? Near stranger, gimpy leg? Not exactly the best raw babysitting material."

"You forgot grumpy asshole," she said.

Again, a flicker of something behind his eyes. "I was about to get to that," he said.

"You know what? Forget it." She reached into her purse and pulled out an old credit-card receipt and scribbled her cell number on it. "If you change your mind about getting to know Sam . . ."

She held it out. He hesitated a moment, then took it.

She felt Jake watching as she walked away.

3

He held the piece of paper, still tightly folded, and looked through the window at the boy and his mother.

She was still beautiful. Butter-yellow hair, pink-cheeked fair skin, and a milkmaid's voluptuousness. He could remember how much he'd wanted her, wanted big handfuls of her, the satin feel of her naked body. How much he'd wanted to bury himself in her.

For weeks now, for months, nothing had penetrated his sexual deadness. His doctor had said to be patient, that the cocktail of medications he'd spent weeks taking on and off could mess him up for a while. That, and survivor's guilt, and the depression that tended to go with it. Whatever the reason, it had felt as if nothing could reach down to where the real impulse lay, as if the neurons that had once connected his vision and his desire had been snipped.

Now those same neurons sparked and his dick stirred like something coming out of a long hibernation.

I want to fuck her. Still.

It had been so long since he'd wanted anything, it caught him off guard. And as if that realization had propped open a door, it let in the darkest of all the dark thoughts: *Mike will never do that again. Not that. Not anything.*

He squelched it—the desire *and* the reminder that his friend was dust.

He wanted to look away, to break her spell. But he made himself look at Mira because then he wouldn't have to look at the boy. Because as much as he didn't want to still want Mira, he *really* didn't want to know how it would feel to look at the boy.

He unfolded the piece of paper she'd pressed on him. Her name, first and last, and cell number. And then one more word: *Sam.*

He'd wondered if she'd written something more. *You're his father, asshole. Get with the program.* But it was only the series of neatly printed numbers, separated with little dots instead of dashes.

He should have known Mira wouldn't do anything the ordinary way. She was a girl who'd done a gutsy—if risky— thing when she'd taken her clothes off at the lake all those years ago. She was a woman who'd raised a seven-year-old boy by herself. *We don't need anything from you. We've done perfectly fine without you up to this point.*

She was a woman who wasn't afraid to call out a guy who was treating her like crap. She'd called him a grumpy asshole. *Guilty as charged.*

He remembered, with a pang, how he'd rejected her plea for a relationship. When she'd gotten out of his car in front of her house, he'd almost jumped from the car and run after her. Called her back. Begged her forgiveness, begged for another chance. Begged to have back that last week he'd forfeited.

She snuck a look in his direction, and he cast his gaze away from hers and crumpled the paper so she couldn't see that he'd opened it.

Even if that boy in there was his, there were good reasons for Jake to stay away from them. The time he'd spend in physical therapy this morning was the only plan he had for himself today. If this day stayed true to form, he'd spend the rest of it sleeping. Or not-drinking. Not-drinking was an activity that now occupied huge portions of his life, the legacy of watching his father drink himself to death and his mother rebuild her life afterward, stone-cold sober. Jake, for his part, doled out Gentleman Jack whiskey to himself as if he were a stingy, hostile psychiatrist prescribing medication. Watching the clock as the numbers gathered themselves toward 5 p.m. Allocating doses at regular intervals through the evening. Carefully cutting himself off before he could become a drunk ex-soldier. A drunk *gimpy* ex-soldier.

He was all *ex*. There was nothing to him now, no present, no future.

He'd once heard some football players interviewed about what they'd do if they injured themselves and couldn't play anymore. They'd been smart, articulate guys who'd given plenty of good answers to the other interview questions, but when the reporter asked that question, they'd gotten deer-in-the-headlights looks on their faces and gone silent. There wasn't a good answer. What would you do if your reason for being, the thing you were both mysteriously good at and most loved to do, wasn't there for you?

When he'd decided that he could make something positive out of his life, that he could do something that *meant* something, it had been an impulse more than a reasoned decision. It had been a goal stitched together from other pieces of knowledge about himself. He was a tough three-season high-school athlete—football, basketball, baseball—not a superstar at any of them, but strong, varsity, a contributor. Coaches commented on his tirelessness. On his discipline. On his ability to step up and lead or blend as a team player, depending on what the situation called for.

He'd been sent home from school on 9/11, and he sat in his parents' living room and watched, transfixed, as the planes hit over and over again in repeated news clips. As people jumped, like insects, like toys, improbably, impossibly. As paper floated up like some terrible reverse rain. As the towers collapsed under their own weight. He'd sworn he'd do something. Not just hand wringing and mourning, but something concrete, something big.

Even when he'd enlisted, he hadn't known for sure that it would feel like he'd found his purpose. That being a soldier would feel like *him*. But once he fought, he knew. He was meant for it.

That part of him was dead now, a much neater and keener incision than the mess that the bomb blast had made of his foot and lower leg. He'd lost his sense that there was meaning in what he was doing, his conviction that he was doing the right thing, his willingness to trade lives for lives. The man he'd fought beside was dead, and he would never again be certain that what they'd done was worth what they'd lost.

The thing was, when you killed the part of you that knew your purpose, that possessed that sharp, youthful certainty, there was very little left. Numbness. The sick acid panic that he could never shake. The world through a fog of purpose-lessness and, when he permitted himself, Gentleman Jack.

He squeezed his fist tighter, crushing the paper into a hard knot.

He didn't want any kid to have him for a father. *Ex-soldier. Ex-person.* A guy, like his own father, who occupied a chair and sucked the life out of a room, out of the world. And in some ways, he feared even more finding something to fill the hours, to kill the time, something that was a shadow of purpose, a substitute for meaning.

His good leg ached like a mo-fo. Sweat had pooled between the silicone sheath of his prosthesis and his stump —because that's what it was, not a "residual limb" in the politically correct parlance of all the do-gooder doctors and prosthetists and physical therapists, but a fucking dead, aching, battered stump.

Mira was laughing and brushing the boy's hair off his forehead as she chatted with the PT. Jake tried not to, but he let himself see the boy's face.

The ways he felt and didn't feel surprised him.

There was no wave of recognition. Or even a ping. Sam looked like Mira, but not so much like Mira that Jake would have found him familiar if he'd met him on the street. And he guessed it was hard to see yourself in a child, because he didn't. Not himself and not his father, mother, sister, or brother. Sam was just a kid. A good-looking kid, with some baby left to his face, and big eyes, whose color, admittedly, was an exact match for his own.

What he did feel was curiosity. The sensation was unex-pected, because aside from the numbness and fog and God, the irritability, the sense of needing desperately to escape his own skin, he felt very little these days. Certainly not a tug, an impulse, toward investigation. Certainly not any wish to know more about *anything*, let alone something big and complicated, a whole unexplored and deeply fraught territory.

I wonder if he has trouble falling asleep at night. If he's afraid of the dark. If he hates nuts and beans.

I wonder if he wishes he had a father.

The physical therapist said something and Sam smiled, and Jake took it like a soccer ball in the groin. That smile. Mira's smile. If the color of Sam's eyes was his, the way they crinkled and shone was all Mira. The slight asymmetry to his mouth. The dimple in only one cheek.

He had no right to be affected by her smile, whether it was on her face or someone else's. No right. He'd given her up, walked away from her. And he sure as hell didn't deserve her now.

But whether he had the right or not, her smile got under the first layer of the numbness and niggled like a splinter.

He told himself he hadn't walked away yet because he was waiting for his appointment, because he needed this one hour today when he'd know what he was doing. When he had a sense of purpose, even if it was small, even if it was constrained, even if it was dictated by someone else. But he knew he was still sitting here, watching them, because he couldn't walk away.

"Jake?" Linda, his physical therapist, stood in the doorway to the waiting room. "Thanks for meeting me here. We'll be back at the VA Tuesday—there was just no way for me to teach Pilates here and get back there in time today."

"I need one more minute," he told her.

She nodded. "I'll be in back."

Linda was a patient woman. She'd hung in with him through a lot of bad sessions. Sessions where he'd sweated and come close to tears, where "agility" had meant tripping over hula hoops and yoga blocks. He'd sworn and yelled and blamed her for the slowness of his progress. And she'd told him to take his time and not worry, that "agility" would come.

"We'll have you running."

"Fat fucking chance."

"And biking."

"No way."

"And swimming."

"I don't think the hydraulic knee would appreciate that."

"They make swim prostheses."

"What about carrying a fifty-pound pack and forty pounds of weaponry over rough terrain?"

"It'll come, if that's what you want."

Now she said, "Take your time." Her mantra.

Mira and Sam were coming toward them. Sam's hair was dark and shaggy. His ankle was wrapped.

Jake's ghost foot throbbed.

He was still here. Because there was some small, not-yet-dead part of him that wanted to be useful, and that part recognized an opportunity when he saw one.

And maybe, as much as he didn't want to admit it to himself, because it felt good, feeling something again. It felt good, *wanting* her. Letting himself think about what it would be like to crave, to grasp, to bury himself—fingers, tongue, dick—in her. To get himself back and give himself away again, in one swift purge.

Mike can't. Not that. Not anything.

I'm alive. He's dead.

For weeks, he'd let that dark thought make decisions for him. He'd turned away from anything that could remind him.

But now? It felt as if someone had shone a thin beam of light into a dark mine shaft. It wasn't enough to navigate by, but it shoved the darkness back to the corners.

"I'll watch him Monday. If you want."

Mira shook her head. "I can't do that. I don't *know* you."

"In the biblical sense—" His body roused again at the memory.

"Haven't we already been over this? You're the one who denied that we knew each other in the biblical sense. The point is, I can't leave my son with a guy I don't know anything about."

He didn't like it that her words erased all the intimacy of those few, luminous weeks, but he couldn't blame her, especially because of the way he'd ended things. What she meant, he was pretty sure, was that she couldn't leave her son with a grumpy asshole with a gimpy leg, but he didn't say that. He just said, "Right."

"I mean, I don't even know if you're married. Have other kids."

He shook his head. "Just me," he said. "What about you? Is there a man in the picture?"

That wasn't what he really wanted to ask. What he really wanted to ask was, *Have you ever had real sex that was as good as the not-sex we had? Because I haven't.*

What he really wanted to ask was, *Who's the lucky bastard who gets to put his hands all over you?*

But he didn't ask those things, and his brain fed back, swift as an echo, *Someone who deserves her.*

She was shaking her head. "I had a boyfriend in Florida, but it's over. Look. What if we meet at a park and you could toss a ball around with him?"

"I'm not much for catch these days. Still working out all the balance issues." He gestured at his artificial leg.

She reddened. "Sorry."

"You know what? It was a dumb idea. Sorry I suggested it. Can we forget this whole thing happened?"

Her mouth tightened, the skin around it whitening. "This 'whole thing'?"

She'd been about to say more, but then she'd looked down at Sam, who was watching them both intently. "Look. You do whatever you need to do. Forget it happened, remember it happened, whatever. You have my number. If you want to get in touch, call me. Otherwise, good luck with the physical therapy, okay?"

She grabbed Sam's hand and practically hauled him out of the physical therapist's office. As they passed through the glass front door, he heard Sam ask, "Who was that guy?"

Her response was muffled, but he was pretty sure it was, "Some jerk."

4

S he tossed and turned and consulted the clock nearly hourly. At seven a.m., she let herself give up on sleep and get lost in memory.

Jake.

After Sam had come, she'd—yes—selfishly longed for someone who would take turns rocking him after her parents had conked out, who could cry with her nights when the baby wouldn't sleep. Someone who would be with her and Sam against the world.

And maybe Jake wouldn't have wanted to be that man. She didn't know. But she'd *used* him to fill the role in her head. She'd plugged him into the fantasies, made him her knight in shining armor.

She'd wanted Jake so badly that when Sam was three months old and she had enough energy to do something other than nurse him and sleep, she'd defied her friends' advice and her parents' wishes. She'd called his cell phone again, but a recording said it was out of service. So she launched a secret search for him. Because she felt he had a right to know that Sam existed, even if her parents didn't think so. Because at barely nineteen, she believed that the truth came first and everything followed neatly from it. And, after all, how hard could it possibly be to track down a soldier, even one with a common name like Jake Taylor? How many of them could there be?

Quite a few, it turned out. Google was monumentally unhelpful, and if her particular Jake Taylor had a Facebook account, she couldn't find it.

She'd started from the assumption that since she'd met him in a Seattle bowling alley, he had to be stationed somewhere in the area. She cursed herself for never asking. They had talked about the most intense, most intimate things, but apparently not the things that mattered.

She began with Joint Base Lewis-McChord and fanned outward. She visited JBLM and Yakima, called the others.

"Hello? I need to find a guy named Jake Taylor. Or Jacob Taylor, maybe."

"Infantry?"

"What does that mean?"

"He's not Special Forces, is he?"

"I don't think so."

Sometimes she got laughed at. Sometimes people made genuine efforts to assist her but came up empty. Sometimes she got to talk to soldiers named Jake Taylor, but none of them were her Jake—although every once in a while, one offered to stand in for him. Once a base operator said, "Honey. Before you waste the JAG's time making him hunt down this guy—do you really think that's even his name? 'Jake Taylor' is like 'Mike Smith.' A name you tell a woman when you want to disappear."

She'd hung up.

If she had reached him, she would have told him about Sam; she would have asked him to be her baby's father. She would have consulted him about his wishes for how Sam should be raised. She would have encouraged him to visit. She would have negotiated with him about the terms of their strange new engagement. Money might or might not have been exchanged. He could be only a name on the birth certificate or a parenting partner. They could get married and be the kind of husband and wife whose vows were paper, not flesh and blood or heart and soul.

Except in many of her fantasies, he played that role, too. He kissed away her tears and smoothed her hair back from her brow and relieved her from childcare duties so she could get a massage or have a drink with a friend or take a shower. And when Sam had been tucked back in, Jake had lain beside her in the big empty bed, slipping wordlessly and without effort into her, moving inside her, whispering her name.

She had let go of the idea of Jake little by little, but he never went away entirely. He reappeared at odd intervals, at pivotal moments. When Sam smiled for the first time, when he laughed for the first time, when he reached out and grabbed her nose, when he rolled over. No matter how much her parents celebrated with her, Jake was there, a presence, an absence.

Only not *Jake*. Some guy she'd made up. A hopeful, naive dream.

She got out of bed, sat at the desk she'd set up in her bedroom, and checked her email. She'd emailed work the night before to beg for another week to find childcare. There was a new message from her boss. It said only, "We need you Monday."

Her stomach started to hurt. Bad.

"Mommy, is it Saturday?"

Sam was in the doorway, so skinny, his face eager.

"Hey, bud. Yeah, it's Saturday."

"Can we call Grammy and Grampy?"

It was their Saturday morning tradition for Sam to call her parents. Early morning was the best time to talk to her stepmother, Lani, who lived in Fort Myers, Florida, where Mira had moved with her parents when Sam was a year old. That was one of the things she couldn't get used to about living in Seattle again—having three time zones between herself and her father and stepmother. By the time she got Sam settled in bed, her parents were sound asleep.

She wasn't eager to call them this morning. She knew they'd hear her troubles in her voice and want to help. And she'd moved clear across the country to get away from her father's brand of well-meaning but suffocating help.

"Maybe later, Sam."

"But they'll go out and get busy, and then it will be too late."

He was echoing words she'd said on many other occasions.

"You're right," she said.

She let Sam dial and talk to them, hoping they wouldn't ask to talk to her, but Sam handed her the phone after only a few minutes. "Grammy wants to talk to you. Can I play on your iPad?"

"Go ahead, bud," she said, and he trotted off.

"Hey, baby. I miss you so much!" Lani said, distant but clear.

The sound of her stepmother's voice made Mira's throat tight. "Hi, Lani. Miss you, too."

Mira's stepmother was the only mother she'd ever known, the best mother she could have imagined. Mira's biological mother had ditched her infant daughter and joined a commune—or, as Mira's father usually said, with some bitterness, a cult. She'd visited infrequently after that—sometimes less than once a year. She had breezed in, bestowed gifts, then disappeared. She'd died ten years ago in a skiing accident.

Mira hadn't mourned. Her life had always been her dad and Lani.

"You okay, sweetheart?" Lani asked.

Three seconds in, and her stepmother knew the score.

"Mira?"

Mira sighed. "I saw Jake."

"Honey?" Alarm rang in her stepmother's voice.

"I took Sam to physical therapy and he was there."

In the background, her father demanded, "Is everything okay?"

She heard her stepmother's muffled voice. "She ran into Sam's father. In the physical therapist's office."

"Oh, for fuck's sake," her father said, clear as day.

"Hang on," Lani said. "I'm putting you on speaker."

The phone beeped and her father said, "What happened?"

She was glad to hear him, and for a moment, she thought, *I could be there. I could be with them. Instead of here, swimming upstream—*

She cut off the thought. This was what she wanted. To make her own life. A life where she made decisions, solved problems. She wanted to be sure she knew who she was. That was why she was here.

She gripped the phone tighter and listened for any sound from Sam's room, but it was quiet. "He showed up in the waiting room at physical therapy."

"Did you tell him about Sam?" her father asked.

She instinctively recoiled from the concern in his voice. She'd traveled three thousand miles to put some space between her father and his love, which was deep but rarely tidy. When her father found out she was pregnant, he'd accused her of being irresponsible and stupid. He'd told her she'd ruined her life and theirs and that she would pay for the mistake for as long as she lived. He'd called her selfish and told her she was worse than her mother.

Lani had reasoned with him, pleaded with him, and of course ultimately Sam had brought him around. It was impossible to hold Sam, to smell the clean baby smell of the crown of his head, to feel his trusting weight in your arms, and still believe him to be any kind of mistake. Or see anyone's life as ruined.

But Mira's father had been against her trying to contact Jake. The situation was bad enough, he'd said, without adding another complication. A man none of them knew, a man foolish enough to engage in unprotected sex during army leave with a barely of-age girl who was almost a stranger.

With the phone clutched to her ear, her parents waiting for her to answer, she felt a peculiar twist of defensiveness on Jake's behalf.

"Yeah. I told him."

"Do you think that was wise?"

She took a breath. "I've always believed that if I ever saw him, I would tell him the truth. No matter what the circumstances. I've always believed it was the right thing to do. He's Sam's father."

"How did he react?" her father asked.

"He didn't believe it."

"Oh, *honey,*" Lani said, which was somehow way worse than her father's "Mira, I think you need to be more cautious."

Why was she surprised every time he demonstrated how little he thought of her judgment? Why did it still hurt that he didn't think she could manage to run her own life without screwing it up?

"How did he seem?" Lani asked.

"He has a prosthetic leg."

"Oh, honey." Ten thousand subtleties to the way those words could come out of her stepmother's mouth.

"Yeah."

"Christ," said her father. "Do you know anything about the circumstances? Where was he? Iraq? Afghanistan?"

When she didn't respond, he sighed. "I think you need to call a lawyer."

"Why?"

"What if he wants to have some kind of relationship with Sam?"

"What if he does?" For a second, she let herself fantasize about it. About what it might mean to Sam. *A father.* For so many years, he'd been stoic about his fatherless status, but that didn't mean that it didn't bother him.

"Mira, I think you need to think these things through more."

She had to take several deep breaths.

"A lawyer could help you anticipate potential consequences. The best defense is a good offense."

"Defense against what?"

"What if he wants visitation? Custody?"

"Why would he?"

"He might. Now that he knows. You could spend the rest of your life negotiating the terms of where Sam will be, when."

"Hon, stop, you're going to upset her," Lani said. "I don't see how a lawyer changes things, anyway. There's nothing she can do to keep him from seeing Sam, if he's the father."

"She can put more distance between them."

"How?"

"Move back."

"Dad, come on."

"Don't be ridiculous," Lani said.

Her father had hated the idea of the move. *Hated* it. Lani had done her level best to help him understand how important it was for Mira to make her own life, and what a great opportunity the job was. How important it was for Sam to see different parts of the country. "Plus we'll be able to have time together. To travel," Lani had told her father.

When her father had stayed adamant that he believed Mira was making a mistake, Lani had helped bolster Mira's determination to go anyway. "I love him to death," Lani had said to her. "But it's time for you to do this. If you stay here—"

She hadn't had to finish the sentence. They both knew

Doug wouldn't give Mira the space to grow up as long as she was under his roof.

The job *was* a terrific opportunity. It turned out that Mira had an unexpected talent for programming, which she'd discovered while taking an online coding class whose teacher turned out to be Seattle-based. Mira had written an app for the class, trying to find something that would take the sting out of a finals period spent in solitude in her bedroom, online, instead of partying with friends on a college campus. She'd been half brainstorming, half shoe shopping, and she'd thought to herself for the ten thousandth time that she'd be ever so much more likely to buy shoes online if she could see them with one of her outfits. She lost a week's sleep writing code, but when she was done, she had "If the Shoe Fits." If you took a barefoot picture of yourself in a particular outfit, the app would show you what you'd look like in a given pair of shoes—more or less.

A lark. A homework assignment.

And, it turned out, the ticket to gainful employment. Her professor worked full-time for an e-tailer that had acquired an online shoe-seller. The group was hiring, and he'd connected her with Haley, who loved Mira's app and was looking for people in Seattle who had both technical talent and people savvy.

At first, Mira hadn't wanted the job. She'd listened intently to Haley's job description and sold herself dutifully in phone interviews, but she'd thought, *I'd have to be crazy.* Because in Fort Myers, she had everything queued up for her: a safe, warm, comfortable home, people who shared the cooking and cleaning tasks, free childcare. A built-in family for Sam. A safety net. If sometimes it felt more like a wet blanket, well, that wasn't such a high price.

And then, twenty-four hours before she owed Haley an answer, she'd been out with her boyfriend, Aaron, and they'd driven up to an espresso shack. He'd tossed his wallet in her lap so she could restore his money to the leather folds, and she'd seen it. Nestled in there. A check. Her father's handwriting.

She hadn't thought. She acted on instinct. She pulled the check out. "What's this?"

He glanced over, then did a double take. "Oh," he said. Only that. *Oh.*

"Aaron?"

She was having trouble catching her breath. In the lower left-hand corner of the check it said, *Dinner for two.*

"Why is my father writing you checks?"

"Just—some money he gave me."

"Dinner for two?"

"He wanted me to take you somewhere nice."

"That's—that's kind of weird, Aaron. Has he done that before?"

"A couple of times."

"You never mentioned it. You should have told me."

His expression told her exactly why he hadn't. Because he'd known it would make her uncomfortable. "Aaron. You have to tell him you can't take his money like that."

Silence.

"Aaron?"

"It's not such a big deal, is it, Mir?"

"You don't want to tell him you won't take it."

"I don't want to hurt his feelings."

"You don't want to hurt his feelings, or you don't want to tick him off?"

"Either. He's my friend."

Of course she knew that. Aaron and her father had hung out before she and Aaron had started dating. They were woodworking buddies, and Aaron worked occasionally for her father as a weekend-and-evening apprentice. And then he'd started sticking around for meals, and then sometimes her dad had encouraged her to go out with Aaron alone . . .

"Which is it, Aaron? Are you his friend? Or my boyfriend?"

"Can't I be both?"

"I guess so," she'd said.

But it rankled, and then it rankled more, until it was like a splinter under her skin.

She *believed* Aaron cared about her. She believed her father's motives were pure. But that wasn't the point. The point was, she was starting to see that there was nothing that was hers. No piece of her life she could make without her father's "help."

There had been other moments like this, and they had all piled up on her. The day her father had told her he wouldn't pay to send her to art school because art wasn't a real career. Because it wasn't practical.

The night he'd found out she was pregnant.

She'd gone off to college and waited until it was too late to terminate the pregnancy before she'd told her father.

"Why?"

He'd asked it over and over again. *Why* had she let this happen, *why* hadn't she told him, *why* had she waited until it was too late?

And she couldn't answer the questions. She couldn't explain why. *Because I can't. Because . . .*

Because one night she'd painted *it,* the not-yet-him, a bean in an ocean in her belly, and she'd used her tiniest brush to put intricate details on his little bean face. And she'd known she'd keep him.

The bean in her belly felt like a secret. It felt like a rebellion. It felt like the best decision she'd ever made. "Why, Mira? Why didn't you tell me? Why didn't you consult us?"

Because she'd known he'd poke and prod and *doubt.* She'd known that he would erode her certainty, that he would question her conviction that carrying the baby to term was the right thing for her to do.

That was why.

But she hadn't said any of that to her father, because she knew he wouldn't understand.

Not telling her father she was pregnant until it was too late for him to influence the outcome had been the only way she knew to make sure the decision was *hers* and hers alone. But it had been like whispering in the wind, because he'd come to school and packed her up and brought her home to live with them again, and there was nothing she could do about it. Without his help, there was no way she could give her baby the life he deserved.

For seven years, she'd bided her time. She'd fought the good fight, when she could, when it mattered. She picked her battles with her father, and she won the piece of territory that mattered most to her: *She* decided where Sam should go to preschool, how much time he was allowed to spend on the computer, whether refusing to eat vegetables was an action subject to discipline, what time bedtime should be.

In doing so, however, she lost the big fight. She took her father's money. She listened to his advice. She gave up the right to build her own life from scratch, her way.

For a long time it had been worth the trade-off. His love, the security of his household, for a little autonomy.

Until she saw the check in Aaron's wallet. Because she *knew* her father had the best of intentions, but she was drowning in his good intentions. In his love. She had to remove herself. She had to retake, remake, her life.

She accepted the job. She took Sam and she went to Seattle.

It was the first thing she'd ever done as an independent adult, and she loved it. Even the hard and complicated parts. Even the canceled sitters and Jake's unexpected appearance. Because it was hers.

Her father was talking again. "I think this situation calls for extreme caution. He's been badly injured. As far as we know, he's been fighting the last eight years. I've been reading about this. They're giving soldiers these long deployments, more engagement with the enemy than in past wars. More consecutive deployments. They're coming back with much more serious mental issues, and that's setting aside the fact that we know he's lost a limb, which has to be incredibly traumatic in and of itself. This is a guy we don't know, who's been exposed to we-don't-know-what, who is potentially going to be involved in my grandson's—"

"Dad?" Mira said. "I can handle this."

"Huh?"

"I can handle Jake. You can relax over there."

She heard a sound on the line that might have been Lani snickering.

On the kitchen counter, her iPhone buzzed. She crossed the kitchen to pick it up. The text said: *It's Jake. What's your email?*

Her heart pounded. She hesitated, then tapped, mirashipley@mailthang.com.

I'm sending you things.

Shld I be scared?

No.

Her father sighed. "Just—"

"I know, Dad. *Be careful.*

"I'd better go," she told her parents.

"Just promise me you won't—"

"Love you, guys," she said, and hung up.

She went to the computer and waited for Jake's email.

Back when she was pregnant, back when Sam was little, she hadn't challenged her father's view of Jake. *Stupid. Hotheaded.* She and Jake *had* been stupid, both of them. And hotheaded.

At eighteen, she'd been willing to see the world through her parents' eyes. You had to be at least a little bit hotheaded to sleep with an eighteen-year-old girl you'd known only a few weeks. To go off and fight a war.

It had been okay for her to accept her father's version, back then, because there was nothing at stake, not really. Jake was far, far away, both geographically and emotionally, out of their reaches. They could believe whatever they wanted about him, whatever prejudices, whatever half-truths. But now he was here. In Seattle. And he was Sam's father. Not some abstract concept, but a man who might, depending on what they did next, play a role in how Sam came to see the world. It wasn't enough to just accept what she'd been told about him.

For Sam, she needed to know who Jake really was.

For herself.

Her computer pinged its acceptance of new mail. From Jacksontaylor@mailthang.com.

Jackson Taylor.

No wonder it had been impossible to track him down. It hadn't occurred to her that Jake was a nickname for something other than Jacob.

I'm sending you some references, the first email said. *Watch your in-box.*

Her heart gave a little squeeze. He was wooing her. On Sam's behalf, admittedly, but—he was pursuing them. Her and Sam.

She did a web search on "Jackson Taylor," and there he was. An article in the *Tacoma News Tribune.* Jackson Taylor was an Army Ranger—God, that would have been a helpful piece of info, too. How had she conceived a child with someone she knew so little about?

According to the article she was reading, his leg had been mangled by an IED. The article was full of praise from his teammates and superiors: *Impeccable judgment. Strong, agile, a leader. Loyal, brave, kind, cool under pressure. Great guy. The best. Working his butt off to walk again.*

Not a grumpy asshole. At least he hadn't been, back on the ground in Afghanistan, where, apparently, he'd saved a badly injured teammate's life by carrying him to safety and medical care under a rain of PK fire, whatever *that* was. It sounded horrifying. And a lot harder than keeping even a challenging seven-year-old safe for nine hours.

Her email pinged again. The attachment turned out to be a partial scan of some kind of hospital admission notes. The email's subject line was: *Officially: A sane asshole.*

She laughed aloud in the silent room.

Clean, neatly dressed . . . no visible psycho-motor agitation . . . no obvious evidence of PTSD . . . psych consult not warranted at this time.

The third email was a video. Subject: *Not always this grumpy.*

Jake, leg still intact, playing soccer with several other men —teammates, she guessed, from the fact that their bodies echoed Jake's ridiculously ripped physique—and a horde of kids, ages toddler to teen. He was grinning, joking with the kids, passing them the ball. Punching a shoulder here and there, shouting instructions. Gently. He looked amazing. Strong and virile, and those white teeth in that brilliant grin of his did something all wrong, and all right, to her. Had he smiled at her once yesterday? She didn't think so.

At a picnic table in the background, women—wives and girlfriends?—laid out food.

With a pang of loss, it occurred to her that in a different life, she might have been there.

The fourth email. Subject: *For what it's worth, my mom likes me.*

A forwarded email from his mom. *Hey, hon. Hope you got the care package. As you asked, no nuts in the cookies. Stay alive. That's my request.*

Her eyes filled with tears. There was no explicit apology here, no acknowledgment that he'd rejected or hurt her, but still, there was something so tender and vulnerable about this gesture. It said, without words, that he'd been thinking of them since he'd seen them yesterday. That her dilemma was on his mind. That he respected her fears, wanted to help, understood what she needed.

That he wanted to know Sam badly enough that he'd be willing to expose himself for a chance.

That he understood what it meant to have, and be, a mother.

A fifth email dropped into her in-box above the others.

I can babysit Monday if you still need me.

5

S unday morning, Jake took the 29 bus from Belltown, his downtown Seattle neighborhood, to Mira's house in Ballard.

Her reply text had said, *Thanks for the emails. Do you want to come meet Sam tomorrow? I can't just leave my kid alone with you because he happens to share your DNA and your mom loves you. I think there are some serial killers whose mothers staunchly defend them.*

He hadn't been able to argue with that. He could only be glad the recipient of his DNA was being cared for by a woman with a good head on her shoulders.

Still, riding the bus to the address she'd given him was an ordeal of step-climbing and enduring the stares of fellow riders. Weeks ago, he'd made the stubborn decision that he wouldn't try to hide the fact that he was an amputee. He never wore pants to cover his prosthesis if the weather called for shorts, and he almost never wore his dress leg. None of that molded flesh-like silicone for him, thank you very much. He thought it looked more eerie than his mechanical leg, because for a moment your eye would be fooled before it realized no one's skin was that peach-colored, that smooth, or that flaccid.

The trade-off for not hiding his prosthesis was curiosity and pity and, occasionally, unwanted conversation with someone who was bold enough to ask what had happened or who had an uncle or a brother with an amputation. He didn't mind that latter category so much, because those people mostly understood—that his life wasn't over but profoundly altered, that a prosthesis wasn't a smooth path back to normalcy but more like a rickety rope bridge.

That was what he was supposed to be doing now on his Temporary Disability Retirement, getting back to normal. If he did a good job of it, he could head back to a job in the army, where he belonged.

Or where he'd once belonged. Now he didn't know.

It was a long, hilly walk from the bus stop on 15th Avenue to Mira's house back in the residential grid. His leg ached and sweated. Maybe he shouldn't have sent those emails after all. Maybe he should have stayed home and ticked the hours off in his mind.

Friday night, after he'd seen Mira, he'd stared into the empty lowball and thought about his rules. Another hour before he could pour another glass. A night of hours, one after the other, Gentleman Jack the only punctuation between sentences. All the hours of this night lined up next to all the empty hours of tomorrow and all the hours of tomorrow night, of all the days and nights into the foreseeable future.

Who's that guy?
Some jerk.

Effectively, he had three choices. He could choose not to live. He had thought about it many times—most often in the earliest days, before he'd seen that he would be able to walk again. But he still thought about it, occasionally, when the calendar day clicked over, 12:01, and nothing had changed—not time's plodding pace; not his persistent, raging anxiety; not his deadly boredom.

He could choose to live like this, yield to the way the hours followed one from the next with no true distinction, no meaning. If he did that, it would also mean he accepted what she'd said about him. What *he'd* said about himself. *Grumpy. Gimpy. Asshole.*

Or he could believe that Sam and Mira had turned up in his path yesterday for some reason he couldn't fathom yet. That he hadn't merely stumbled across them; he had stumbled straight into their need, a need he was perfectly positioned to fill. Sam needed to be watched; Jake needed something to do.

Of all the unexpected emotions he'd felt yesterday in their presence—attraction to Mira, curiosity about Sam—the most unexpected of all had been the pure *will* he'd felt to claim this new possibility that had presented itself. Jake was so distant from the notion of *wanting something* that he almost didn't recognize it at first. The words had to come out of his mouth— "I'll watch him Monday"—before he knew the impulse was there. But after he'd offered himself and she'd turned him down, he'd wanted to fight—for the right to be with Sam in a way that would be *useful*. And he recognized *that,* that will to fight. He recognized it as the purest core of himself. A notion worth guarding. A goal he regarded so highly, he'd be willing to slough off his numbness to have it back in his life.

A goal that would reassemble the endless collection of hours into a life.

Purpose.

But maybe that was only whiskey's special form of delusion. He was so tired now, so unsure that he could handle what he'd signed himself up for, that he wanted to turn around and go home.

Instead, he gathered his strength and made himself walk up to the dumpy little Roman brick single-story house that he assumed was a rental based on the unloved appearance of the yard. The grass was dull and dry, the gardens overgrown, the front steps broken concrete.

The cast-iron railing on one side of the too-high steps wiggled when he grasped it. *Fine.* He gave it a mental fuck-you and turned his body a quarter turn so he'd have to bend his robo-knee slightly less as he climbed.

It wasn't a natural-looking way to climb stairs, but it was how things worked now.

The door opened a split second before he could raise his hand to ring the bell, and Sam stood there, looking at him suspiciously. He couldn't blame the kid. Who wanted some guy—some *jerk*—as a babysitter? He suspected Sam's former babysitters were young and female, with soft hair and soft hands and soft other stuff that would look like a hell of a lot better substitute for his mom.

"Hi," Jake said.

"You're not *really* a babysitter, are you?"

"Not really," he admitted.

"Who *are* you?"

He hadn't expected to have to confront that question so quickly. He knew he might have to answer it eventually, but he'd hoped he'd have at least been admitted through the front door. He should have asked Mira what she was planning to do about telling Sam the truth.

"Who did your mom tell you I was?" He hoped Sam wasn't old enough yet to get pissed at Jake's caginess.

"She said you were a friend. But I didn't exactly believe her because she also said you were a jerk."

"Sam," Mira said from somewhere behind the front door. "I said I shouldn't have said that and neither should you."

"I was just *telling* him," Sam protested.

"You don't need to tell him that," Mira said. "He already knows."

But she was smiling as she held the door open for him. "Sam, do you want to help me give him a tour?"

She wore a pair of jeans and a tight tank top with skinny little straps that were loose on her shoulders. They looked in danger of slipping down. It wouldn't take much—the brush of a hand, a finger hooked underneath. Teeth.

Jesus. If this continued, he was going to be wishing he were still sexually dead. Nothing like interviewing for a babysitting position with a boner.

"This is the living room," Sam said unnecessarily.

In contrast to the shabby feel of the outside of the house, the interior felt neat and cozy. Light flooded in through a huge front window, illuminating a white room with a pastel, geometric rough-surfaced rug, a comfy gray couch, a matching armchair, and a glass coffee table. There was a game spread out on the rug, something with tons of teeny-tiny plastic pieces that looked complicated. Jake wasn't sure

how he felt about playing board games. He'd always avoided
doing it with his niece and nephew, but that had been *before*.
When his soccer-ball-kicking foot had been made of flesh
and blood and hitting a baseball wouldn't require several
dedicated physical therapy sessions to work out the logistics.

There were books all over the coffee table, more than one
left facedown and open. Mostly kids' books, fat-chapter
books he would have guessed were too difficult for a seven-
year-old. Apparently his son was an advanced reader. He felt
a peculiar, unwarranted sense of pride. He'd done nothing,
other than make his unintentional and (if you considered the
volume of fluid involved) piddling genetic contribution, to
deserve any pride, but he figured maybe that was one of those
things you couldn't help. *That's my boy*. Not that he'd been a
great reader himself, not until high school, when he'd begun
gobbling up nonfiction, mostly war histories.

"You like to read?" he asked Sam.

"Yeah."

"What are these books about? Warriors?"

"About clans of cats who fight each other."

"Oh, yeah? Like mountain lions and stuff?"

"No, like cats. You know, like pet cats, but these ones don't
live with people."

"That is seriously weird, dude," Jake said. "Warriors are
wolves and lions and soldiers in Black Hawk helicopters, not
fluffy house cats." Any son of his should know that.

Son. His.

It was starting to get through to him, starting to penetrate.
He had a *kid*.

"They're not house cats. They're wild."

Sam glared at him, his gaze never faltering, not even when Jake leveled a glare right back at him.

That's my boy.

My boy.

Holy shit.

He had a son, this miniature *man* who was meeting his challenge without flinching.

"Maybe you can read that to me later."

"Or you can read it to me."

Stubborn son of a bitch. A good trait. "Or we can take turns."

"Maybe," said Sam, but Jake thought he might be smiling.

Mira was watching him. He could feel it. He snuck a glance at her, at the scoop of her tank, the beckoning V of cleavage. He could seriously deal with taking some quality time with that top. He could just make out the bump of her nipples under the fabric, and he speculated that it would take just a touch to bring them to attention. She'd been so responsive.

You don't deserve—you have no right—Mike can't—can't— not that, not anything.

Was it his imagination, or was that chant getting softer, the clamor in his body louder?

Mira was watching him with a look on her face that he couldn't interpret.

"Show me the rest of the house?" Jake asked Sam.

Sam led him into the kitchen, which was small but serviceable, with wood cabinets painted white and speckled Formica countertops. The appliances were newer, and there was a small round kitchen table that still held breakfast dishes. "The snacks are here," Sam said, and opened a cabinet at knee height.

"Very important," Mira said. "Sam has serious nut allergies, so he needs to have snacks from the house. He can't go out for ice cream and donuts and treats like that, because most of that stuff isn't prepared nut-free. He can safely eat anything in this house, though, so you don't have to worry about anything you feed him here."

She was talking now like she was leaning toward leaving him with Sam.

"You said he has asthma," Jake said. "Is there an inhaler?"

"I'll get it." Sam dashed off.

"He likes you." Her arms were crossed, but her expression was the softest he'd seen it. So soft it moved something behind the cage of his ribs. So soft he could feel it sinking into the base of his spine.

"How can you tell?"

"I just can. He's slow to warm up, but he likes you. He doesn't usually engage this fast."

He likes me. It was an unexpected boon, a sudden, strange, sharp almost-pleasure. He caught himself feeling something that, if it were indulged, might be called *happy.*

Then he remembered. That there were kids in the world whose father would never come home again, because of him. That there was a father—one who had been a real father, who had wanted to be one—who would never see his kids again.

Sam came back with the inhaler in the palm of his hand.

"Do you know how to use it?" Jake asked Sam.

"Yeah," he said. But Mira took it from Sam anyway and demonstrated it to Jake. "Inhaler in the spacer, like this." She showed him how they fit together. "Squeeze once, breathe in and out five times. Squeeze again, five more breaths. He hasn't had an asthma attack in more than a year and a half, though. Kids do sometimes outgrow it. I remind him not to overtax his system, though. If he's running really fast, or whatever, I remind him to take it down a notch."

"Really?" Jake asked, before he could think better of it.

Her face darkened.

Okay, that had been a dumb thing to say. But *really*? A seven-year-old kid who hadn't had an asthma attack in over a year, and she was discouraging him from realizing his full potential? It went against everything Jake believed about people, everything he'd been taught in training and in war. You pushed yourself to the limit and you saw what your limits were. You saw that everything you feared at the furthest edges of your capabilities wasn't to be feared. That there was nothing to fear in yourself.

Until you weren't yourself, because the thing you'd believed made you you was gone. Then it was appropriate to be scared shitless.

There was a dark rut in his mind where he used to be sure he knew what he was doing. Sometimes, when his thoughts went there, he had trouble pulling them back. *Maybe if I went back to war, I'd find it again. The rhythm, the reason. The thing that made me feel like fighting was worthwhile.* It was as if he were watching a jerky filmstrip of his life as a soldier, the rah-rah, the gung-ho, then the early edge of doubt, how the first thing he'd thought the first time he'd seen Mike hesitate under fire was, *That could be me. That's what happens when you aren't sure anymore.*

He could feel the groove worn in his brain by this line of

thinking, and he could get stuck there for hours. *Could be me, should have been me.*

She was watching him carefully. "Sam has to be cautious about physical activity right now, anyway. He's a lot better than he was, but he's supposed to take it easy for a few more weeks. The reason we were at PT is he fell out of a tree. That's the whole reason we're in the fix we're in. He was supposed to go to this tennis and golf camp all day the last two weeks and the next two until I could work out sitting arrangements. But he's too banged up."

"He seems pretty good now." He hadn't seen evidence of a limp or any other injury.

"He's a lot better. That was probably our last PT session. But like I said, with the asthma, anyway, I want him to take it easy."

There was nothing, per se, wrong with tennis and golf. It just rubbed him the wrong way, somehow. There was more to life, more to being a boy and a man, than hitting little balls at a country club. Not that Sam had to love football or hockey or riflery or archery. But he deserved a chance to figure out for himself what he did love, what his body could do.

"Take it easy" wasn't a credo Jake knew anything about.

"You'll bring your phone, right, if you sit?"

He nodded.

"So we have each other's numbers."

"Yeah."

"I also have a landline in case the power goes out." She showed him. Above that phone, she'd listed emergency numbers. Her home number, cell, and work. Her parents' number, with the note "long distance, but knowledgeable." The pediatrician, 911, poison control.

"Can I show Jake my room?"

Mira looked at Jake, and he shrugged. "Sure."

Sam led him down a short hallway to a small bedroom littered with Legos and other building toys. Jake's first impulse was to kneel and begin playing with the toys, but kneeling wasn't easy for him. It still involved an embarrassing amount of effort and the potential loss of balance. He didn't want that to happen to him in front of Sam and Mira. So he stayed standing. "I like Legos," he said.

"Can we do Legos? If you babysit?"

He looked at Mira, not sure how to answer. Was he going to babysit?

"Sure," she said. Answering both Sam's question and his, with a tight nod, as if to say, *You're on probation, buddy.*

And that was just fine with him. They'd all try this out. See what happened.

"I'm trying to think if there's anything else you need to know," Mira said. "If you're still game to do it tomorrow?"

"Sure," he echoed her.

"So if there's an emergency—"

"I'll call 911. Or patch him up myself. I've done that a time or two. All Rangers have some medical training."

"I guess you're a little overqualified for this job, huh?"

"My dad's a soldier," Sam reported.

The room suddenly shrank, closing in on them. Mira's face drained of color.

"You don't say," Jake said. "Where is he now?"

Mira shot Jake a hard look.

"He was my sperm donor."

Holy shit. He felt like he'd been hit in his chest plate with a round. He guessed it should have occurred to him, before

this moment, that Sam had some mythology about his father
—about *him*—that wasn't the truth, the whole truth, and
nothing but. But *sperm donor*?

Jesus.

He opened his mouth to speak, but Mira grabbed and
pinched his arm. "Can I talk to you a second?"

He followed her without protest. He wanted to hear how
she'd explain this one.

"I'm sorry, okay?" she said. "I'm sorry I told him that, but
—you tell me if you can think of a better way to explain it to a
little kid. Why his dad isn't anywhere around, why he
shouldn't be out on a campaign to find him. I'd already
looked for you. I'd already called bases. I knew it would be
hard, if not impossible, to track you down. I didn't want him
to turn it into a quest."

"You could have told him I was dead," Jake said quietly.

She turned away. When she turned back, there were tears
in her eyes. "I couldn't," she said.

He didn't ask her why not. He was already reeling, already
feeling more than he'd felt in months. Years, maybe. He didn't
want to know the answer behind the tears.

Sperm donor.

Yeah, that was about all he was good for, these days. And
on bad days, not even that.

"Look," she said. "I know this is weird. I know it's—hard
to believe. If—if it would help, I could do a paternity test."

Her offer helped, oddly enough. It eased something. Not
that he'd ever really doubted her, not even when he'd been so
grumpy and difficult in the PT's office. The world was full of
women who would lie to ensnare a guy, but he just couldn't
make himself believe Mira was one of them.

But the fact that she'd offered, and how vulnerable she'd made herself in doing so—it soothed him.

"I think we can wait on that a bit," he said. He'd leave it open. Maybe at some point he'd feel like he needed to know for sure, some evidence beyond those too-familiar blue-gray eyes of Sam's. But he couldn't see himself demanding a cheek swab.

Not now, not when he wasn't even completely sure what, if anything, he wanted from them, or what, if anything, they were asking of him.

6

WhHen Mira opened the door the next morning, she wore tailored gray slacks and a matching blazer over a silky-looking scrap of pale-blue fabric. The slacks and blazer were all buttoned up and professional looking, but that scrap of blue was as insubstantial as tissue.

Like a sexy nightgown. It would feel good to her, against her bare skin, cool and light. You could tease her with it.

No hesitation this time, only a surge of blood, powerful in his veins, the chain of neurons all the way from the images burning into his brain to the quick tightening of his dick. She'd woken something up, and it wasn't going back to sleep.

Bloody hell.

It felt good.

It felt urgent.

It felt extremely inconvenient. Why now? Why wake from the dead *now*?

She wasn't some random woman he'd met in a bar. She was—

God, he didn't even know *who* she was. The mother of the

son he hadn't known he had. A fling that hadn't even been consummated. She wasn't anything, except she *was,* which made it totally fucked up for him to be thinking about—

He shouldn't be thinking about her at all. It was so out of place with the moment. Out of place with her outfit, which was a Professional Lady Camouflage Uniform. Her hair was pulled back into some kind of twist behind her head, her face made up; it was the first time he'd ever seen her with makeup. She looked tightly wound and slightly scary.

And she'd caught him looking, and thinking, her head tilted, her gaze quizzical and—

Was that interest in her eyes?

Then Sam was running down the stairs. *Sam.* The reason he was here. Because he sure as hell wasn't here to mess with Mira's head and expose her to the bad shit that lurked just under the presentable surface of his skin. He'd hurt her bad enough once, and he was done hurting people. *And maiming and killing,* the darkest voice said, before he could squelch it.

"Anything else I need to know? Any particular time he needs to eat?"

"Lunch around twelve thirty. I made you guys sandwiches for lunch. They're in the fridge."

"You didn't have to make my lunch." The fact that she had done so made him feel peculiar. It was so domestic and wifely, something his mother might have done before she'd had it scared and beaten out of her. It made him aware that the woman and the child in this room were the components of what, to another man, one who hadn't seen what he'd seen, would be *family.*

Even if he'd once had a remotely loving notion of childhood, even if he'd thought that a man and a woman living in

a house together could make the kind of magic you saw on
TV or in the movies, he'd given that dream up when he
decided to become a soldier. He didn't believe you could do
both well. It wasn't fair to taunt death on a regular basis while
people at home were counting on you.

The therapist who'd worked with him briefly at Walter
Reed had asked him if he wanted a family someday.

"No fucking way," he'd said.

"Why not?"

"You need me to list the reasons?"

Anyway, it was moot. He didn't want a family, and neither
did he have any reason to believe this family wanted him as a
bona fide member. Sam didn't know Jake was his father, and
Mira hadn't given him any sign that she saw him as anything
other than a potential drop-in father figure for Sam.

"Snacks not too close to meals," she was saying. "I'll give
him dinner when I get home. I'll bring takeout with me." She
hesitated, as if she'd been about to offer to include him, but
she didn't say anything more.

Just as well, right? Having dinner with her wasn't going to
help any with his inconvenient attraction to her. "Go," he
shooed her. "We're fine."

Mira looked doubtful.

"We're fine, right, Sam?"

"Mom, we're fine," Sam said, sounding more like seven-
teen than seven.

But as soon as she was out the door, Sam's shoulders
slumped. The bravado he'd displayed when he reassured his
mother had apparently been all bluster. You had to give it to
the kid for acting skills.

"Should we go up and build with Legos?" Jake asked.

"Don't feel like it." Sam threw himself onto the couch and looked in imminent danger of tears.

"What do you like to do with your friends?"

"Nothing." If possible, Sam seemed to be sinking deeper into the couch.

"You sit around and do nothing?"

"I don't have friends. We moved here after school was done. I don't know anyone."

"Well, what did you used to do in—where did you guys move from?"

"Fort Myers, Florida."

"What did you used to do in Fort Myers with your friends?"

There was a long silence. Then Sam confessed, "I didn't really have friends there, either."

Apparently it was make-Jake-have-emotions week around here, because that delivered a chest smack on par with the sperm donor comment. It was all part of the great cosmic unraveling of Jake's world. With each new blow, he felt like there was nothing more absurd that could happen to him. He'd lost his leg and nearly his life. He'd said goodbye to a close friend, to his vocation, his sense of meaning, his friends and colleagues, the world he'd grown up in, his whole adult life. He'd come back here to escape from Walter Reed, where the constant ebb and flow of army life reminded him of what he'd lost, only to be slapped with a new piece of absurdity: his son. Sam. Seven. Here in Seattle.

In the scheme of things, discovering that Sam thought his father was an entry in a sperm bank shouldn't be a huge additional injury. Nor should finding out that his son had no friends. But *Jesus*.

He sat on the couch next to Sam. "What do you mean you didn't have friends? Did you play with anyone at recess?"

"Not usually. I usually played by myself. The other kids played with each other outside school at playdates and did soccer and baseball and stuff, so they knew each other better. I didn't know them that well." His little face was pinched and grim. He had a crusty spot at the side of his mouth, probably dried milk from breakfast. It made Jake remember, with disgust, how his mother had licked her fingers and cleaned his face when he was a small child. He'd hated that, squirmed away.

Now he wished his mother would look at him with that same critical eye, instead of with pity and concern. He wished he could believe she called him twice a week for some reason other than that she was terrified that he'd fallen and couldn't get up.

His mother. He was going to have to tell her about Sam at some point. She would—God, he had no idea how she'd react. With joy, he supposed, which he hoped would overcome the pain of the lost years. His sister, Susannah, too. And his brother, for that matter—Pierce would think it was the best thing ever. Two single-dad brothers—because Pierce was on his own now, since his marriage had imploded. Pierce would be all *Let's take them to the zoo.*

He and Pierce had been close, but Jake had been avoiding him. *Since.* He hadn't liked the sympathy or the awkward silences.

"Didn't you do soccer and baseball and play outside school?"

"I didn't have that many playdates."

"Why not?" Jake recognized that his question had been

dodged, but he stuck to hearing Sam out. He had the feeling that this was the most delicate interrogation Special Forces had ever undertaken.

"Grampy didn't like to have them. And Mom said we couldn't ask him to very much because Grampy and Grammy were already doing so much."

Oh. Poor kid. And poor Mira, because he bet Sam had been close-mouthed about his friendship woes.

"Did you tell your mom you didn't have any friends?"

"No."

"Why not?"

But Jake thought he might know the answer. He thought it might be buried in the scene he'd already witnessed. *Mom, we're fine.* When Sam was feeling anything *but* fine.

Sam had clamped his mouth shut.

"It's okay," Jake said. "You can tell me."

"I'm not supposed to talk to strangers," Sam said.

Fucking wiseass. He was old enough to know Jake wasn't a stranger. He'd said that because he knew it would wound.

"I'm not a stranger anymore," Jake said.

"You have a fake leg. That's strange."

Trust a seven-year-old to get straight to the heart of the matter.

"True enough. But that makes me more trustworthy. I can't run and tell anyone else what you tell me."

"You can't run?"

"Not really. I just learned how to walk."

"If you practiced, could you run?"

He knew guys who were doing it. Training to run, even prepping for the Paralympics.

"How 'bout you answer my question, then I'll answer your question?"

Sam considered that carefully. "Okay. What was your question?"

"Why didn't you tell your mom you didn't have any friends?"

"Because stuff like that makes her sad, and she worries too much already."

That was what he'd suspected, that Sam protected Mira. Damn it, a seven-year-old boy shouldn't have to do that. He shouldn't have to think about anything other than Halloween and baseball practice and feeding the dog.

"Now me. If you practiced, could you run?"

"Yeah," Jake said. In fact, he knew from hearing it talked about at Walter Reed that there were runners—Oscar Pistorius, a double amputee, was an infamous example—who ran faster on prostheses than they could on their own legs.

Sam was sitting up now, his face lit. "I'm a good runner. My mom doesn't like it when I run fast, but I'm good at it."

Why the hell did Mira make him hold back like that?

"Do you want to see me run?" Sam asked.

"Your mom said you hurt your shoulder and arm and knee."

"I did. But they're better now."

"So let's see it."

"I won't run super hard."

A spark of rebelliousness made Jake say, "You can run as hard as you want. That's why you have an inhaler."

"Oh." Sam frowned.

She's going to kill me, Jake thought, and then, *Really? I must have left my balls in Afghanistan.*

They went out front. There were cars parked here and there on the street, but otherwise it was empty. "I'm going to run from that red mailbox to that fire hydrant."

"Okay," Jake said. Today the Seattle summer weather was perfect, a slight fog lifting away as the morning wore on, the sky vivid blue behind the scrim of gray. "Do you want me to time you?" He got his phone out and selected the stopwatch app.

"Yeah." Sam got into a runner's starting stance and almost made Jake laugh, he was so earnest and *coiled*.

"Twenty-five seconds," Jake reported, after Sam had collapsed, panting, on the mostly dead grass.

"Is that good?"

"I think so."

"Will you race with me?"

Jake hesitated. He wasn't sure what would happen. In PT, he'd done some of the early jumping, hopping, and skipping exercises that would eventually translate into jogging, but he'd only run once. The street was reasonably flat and even, but even small irregularities could trip him up.

The time he'd run had been on a track, under the watchful eye of his physical therapist. There had been no joy in it, only frustration. He'd heard that walking—forget running—generated eight times the amputee's body weight in force at the point where prosthesis met body. *Eight times his body weight.* Slamming his prosthesis into his residual leg. Jarring dead meat and bone, jamming his aching hip, stunning his miserable brain. He'd only wanted it to stop—the impact, the pain, his PT's eyes boring into him.

And then he'd taken a spill, skidded across the red

rubbery composite surface. Sprained his wrist. Set himself back another week and a half.

He hadn't run since.

He wanted to say no to Sam. *I don't run. Running is hard for me. I'm slow. You'd beat me.*

I'm afraid to fall.

Not words he wanted to model for a seven-year-old boy. *I won't even try. Things that are hard aren't worth working at. I've quit trying to get better. I've given up on myself.*

I'm afraid.

Sam had it hard enough with a mom who was asking him to hold back for his own health and safety. He didn't need other voices in his head working against him. The least Jake could do was to do no harm.

"Sure," Jake said.

They stood together on the imaginary starting line suggested by the red mailbox. Sam got back into his runner's crouch. Jake thought about what he knew about his prosthesis. It was an all-purpose leg, meant at best to allow for a casual jog around the neighborhood. It wasn't a sprinter's leg, but it would let him run. He just *hadn't* before. There hadn't been any *reason* to. There hadn't been any reason to do anything, and he'd been used to reasons being supplied to him for so long, he'd forgotten that sometimes in life, you had to make them up yourself.

Just because.

Or more accurately, as Sam gazed at him expectantly, *Because it'll make his day.*

"Ready, set, go," he said, and Sam took off.

He'd meant to take it easy, but when he pushed off, he stumbled and he had to hop and skip a few paces hard to get his balance back. Then it was easier to keep going than to stop.

Today felt so different from that day on the track. Maybe because of how much he'd been walking, maybe because of the work he'd done in physical therapy on the treadmill. He had to use far more of his brain than he wanted in deliberate decisions—*right leg, left leg. Knee up. Push off. Push, push, push.* It was more like skipping than running.

But there was a rhythm, an alternating thwack of artificial and natural limbs against pavement. Not the feel of two good legs, earth moving away beneath his feet in a steady, even pulse, but something you could cling to, something you could almost lose yourself in—*step-step, step-step.* More like jazz than rock, but still.

He could feel Sam beside him, could feel the pavement under his real foot. His residual leg ached, but bearably.

Air rushed past his ears, and he felt—

He felt good. Strong.

He pulled ahead of Sam, lurching but moving fast on two legs, and beat him.

"Mom lets me win," Sam said.

Jake was panting. Sweaty. His heart pounded, because despite all the work they'd done to get him on an exercise regimen, he hadn't been able to motivate himself to walk or swim regularly. There had been no *reason* to.

Sam was pissed, struggling hard to keep the tears back. *Damn,* he was a competitive little guy. He'd wanted to win, and he'd wanted it bad.

Jake liked that in a man.

"Well," Jake said. "First lesson. I'm not Mom."

7

"What kind of pizza do you guys want?"

Mira was stuck in traffic on 15th Ave, talking on her hands-free to Sam. Sometime on the drive, Mira had made the snap decision that she was going to invite Jake to join them for dinner, even though earlier that morning, she'd been pretty sure she'd find a way not to. But she'd had a beast of a day. Her boss had told her, kindly but firmly, that she was out of second chances. She'd battled a programming language she barely knew, a twisted syntax that had pried its way into the smallest reaches of her mind. And right now, it just seemed easier to slap some pizza on the table than to do the active work of getting rid of Jake, since Sam inevitably wanted his friends and babysitters to stay as long as possible and would kick up a stink to get Jake invited to dinner.

Or that's what she was telling herself. Deciding to ask him to stay for pizza had nothing to do with the way he'd looked at her this morning, or the stirred-up, liquid feeling it had produced in the pit of her belly. It had nothing to do with the impulse she'd almost indulged, to draw her hand across his shoulders, just to see if they still felt as hard and alive with muscle as she remembered.

She'd texted him a few times to check in on them, and she'd gotten an inappropriate thrill out of it. Not the way she normally felt when keeping tabs on a new babysitter. More the way she felt when she was engaged in text flirtation. Nothing flirtatious, though, about "How are you guys doing?" or his response, "Great." Maybe it was "Hey. I've got this"— his response to her fourth text—that had spiked her pulse. Made her think about the way he'd swept her off her feet and carried her up the sandy beach at the lake.

"Jake, what kind of pizza do you like?" That was Sam's little voice, which always sounded younger than she expected on the phone.

There was a rumble of male response in the background, and then Sam said, "He wants to talk to you."

Jake's voice in her ear was deeper than she remembered, surprisingly intimate, and her nether regions gave an appreciative squeeze. "Sam and I will pick up dinner," he said.

"I'm out anyway," Mira protested.

"We need the exercise. We haven't done anything for hours except play Ticket to Ride and bowl with your lipsticks."

"*Excuse me?*"

"We needed pins. Sam said the only thing he could think of that were all the same size was your lipsticks."

"You're fired," she said, but she was laughing. It was possible there'd been laughter in his voice, too, when he'd told her about the lipsticks. She couldn't swear there hadn't been.

"Let us get dinner," Jake said again.

"I'm on the road. It's ridiculous for you guys to go out. You'd have to walk, and it's a long way."

Would he think she was implying that he couldn't do it, with his prosthetic leg? *Oh, hell,* she didn't want to go down this road of worrying about every little thing she said to him. She had to treat him like any other guy. He *was* like any other guy. She'd pretty much forgotten he was missing most of a leg, which was why she hadn't thought about the implication of her words until they were out of her mouth.

"If you tell me it's easy for you to stop, that it won't slow you down, that's one thing. But if you have to go out of your way, and get out of the car, and sit and wait—"

Her chest felt tight. Since the moving van had pulled away from the front of her parents' house, she'd been on her own with Sam. When they first arrived in Seattle late at night, Sam had been sleeping so hard she'd carried him inside, warm and weighty in sleep, and she'd thought: *We're really doing this. Sam and me.*

It would be so easy to let Jake and Sam get the pizza. Because it would slice half an hour off her commute, get her back with her boy sooner, remove a layer of stress from her evening.

She took a deep breath.

"Mira? You still there?"

"Yeah, still here. Just—thinking a sec."

In the weeks after she'd first met Jake, she'd taken courage from his conviction. He'd said, "If you know what you want to do with your life, you should do it. You want to go to art school? Go to art school. Tell your father he can pay or not pay but you're going. Find a way." She'd gone home, stood up, told her father she was going to art school. She applied for financial aid, took out loans, got a job.

And then—

And then she'd discovered she was pregnant, and the whole enterprise had been put on hold for eight years.

This project she'd undertaken, of becoming an adult, a stand-on-my-own-two-feet woman, meant learning to help herself. Even when she was tired. Even when the thought of sitting on a bench and waiting for takeout pizza made her feel like curling up in a ball.

She'd spent a good chunk of time at work today lining up a sitter for tomorrow. Penny had a friend whose sister was visiting this week. She could do the rest of the week, to give Mira more time to find someone permanent. Which she'd have to do, fast, before she lost her mind over this piecemeal, strung-together situation. The sister was coming tomorrow, 7:30 a.m., and the rest of the week, too.

Jake wouldn't be here other nights and no babysitter would order and pick up pizza for Mira. She would have to get in the habit of drawing on her own reserves, of finding what was left after she'd exhausted all the obvious stores of patience and energy. The sooner she learned her depths, the more she trusted herself, the better off she and Sam would be.

"It's easy for me to stop," she told Jake. "It won't slow me down."

He didn't try to argue with her. "Okay," he said. "Sam and I will play another game and wait for you."

And she had to try not to like that, either, the thought of the two of them playing together, biding their time until she came through the door to greet them.

JAKE FOLLOWED Sam into the kitchen as Mira set two large pizzas and two six-packs on the counter and slung her messenger bag over the back of a chair. She looked tired, her eye makeup slightly smudged, her hair wilder than it had been this morning. Wild the way it would be if he'd just rumpled the hell out of it kissing her. The way it had been that night at the lake, spread out on the blanket under her.

"That's a lot of pizza and beer. You expecting someone else?"

"You're a big guy," Mira said. Then she blushed.

Jake's pulse picked up.

Her gaze found points around the room, anywhere but his face.

"Guess I am," he said mildly.

Interesting, how pink her cheeks turned. She couldn't meet his eye. She pushed her hair off her shoulders. He bet he could count the number of people on earth who had hair as soft as hers.

He imagined burying his face in it. Two strides would bring him close enough to do it. Would put her shoulders under his palms and her mouth under his.

He could make a muddle of the only good thing that had happened to him since his truck had been blown to bits. He could guarantee the simple pleasure he'd taken in Sam's company today would be a much harder thing to come by.

He stayed where he was.

"I figured between you, me, and Sam, we'd manage to finish most of this," she amended.

He was about to say he hadn't had much of an appetite for

food since coming back from Afghanistan, but then he realized he was ravenous.

"I could probably put away a good amount of pizza," he said carefully.

"Me, *too*," Sam said.

Maybe it was the running. He and Sam had found a yardstick, measured out a fifty-yard dash, and done it a whole bunch of times. Until he was in a fuckload of pain, his thigh chafed from the socket of the prosthesis.

Maybe he'd make an appointment to see one of the VA prosthetists. For the last couple of weeks, things had seemed good enough—at least for the good-enough existence he'd been living. But there were some prosthetists who were supposed to be geniuses. They'd take a mold of your residual leg and craft a socket around it that would cleave to you no matter how much you sweated, no matter how much the temperature varied. Those were the guys you saw if you were serious about being a parathlete.

He wasn't. But maybe someone at his VA knew what they were doing and could tweak things a little. Couldn't hurt. Might help.

They ate at the round kitchen table off paper plates, drinking beer from steins she'd popped in the freezer for a few minutes. A couple of times he caught himself watching her mouth as she ate. He could still remember the feel of her full lower lip between his teeth.

Not relevant.

"So what'd you guys do all day?" Mira asked.

Jake hadn't told Sam not to tell his mother about the running. He didn't think that was fair, to ask a seven-year-old who already kept too many secrets to keep one more. So he was curious to see what Sam would and wouldn't tell Mira.

"Played games, ate lunch, bowled with your lipsticks, went to the park and played on the play structure. That was just me. Jake didn't climb."

Sam had chosen to leave out the running. They'd both shaved a few seconds off their times. Jake had fallen, but only once, and Sam had helped him back up. They'd clapped high-fives, and Jake could tell it had killed Sam not to sulk about losing, but the kid had done it anyway. *Good man.*

"That sounds like a lot of fun," Mira said, smiling at Jake. Her teeth weren't perfectly straight. Her eyeteeth were set forward a tiny bit, and one was crooked.

He had *not* just contemplated the way her teeth would feel against the skin of his throat. Because that would be absurd. It would be especially absurd if that thought had actually given him yet another Mira-induced hard-on.

"Grampy called," Sam offered.

And Jake had answered. The guy had been barely civil to him, asking point blank what Jake's intentions were—"to babysit your grandson, sir"—and whether he had any idea how much trouble he could cause, because Mira was "fragile" and "vulnerable" and didn't need a "horny hooah" messing with her life. That had pissed Jake off enough that he'd said, between clenched teeth, "Sir. It doesn't bother me if you want to call me a 'horny hooah,' but Mira is not fragile, and she's not vulnerable."

"I know what 'fragile' means, but what's 'vulnerable'?" Sam had demanded when he got off the phone. And Jake had said, "Your mom is a smart, tough woman—that's the important thing to know."

Mira shot him a look over the top of her beer glass. "Did you talk to him?"

"We had a brief exchange."

"Was he...?"

"He was—curt." Jake could handle himself; no need to give any extra power to Mira's dad and his rudeness.

Mira sighed. "He's a piece of work."

"Jake's the best babysitter," Sam said. "Can he come back tomorrow?"

Jake tried not to be pleased by that, but damn, he was. Even if it was only the overachiever's impulse to feel good about a job done to spec. It wasn't as if he actually wanted to come back tomorrow.

"I got a new sitter for tomorrow," Mira told Sam.

Oh. Maybe that twinge of disappointment meant he *had* wanted to come back tomorrow. The truth was, he'd loved his time with Sam. Figuring out who he was, helping him find his way, teaching him how to give his all or lose graciously. It had made Jake feel *alive*. All-the-way alive, and like maybe, maybe there was a reason to be glad he was.

"I want Jake." Sam screwed up his face, preparing for a tantrum. Jake felt an odd twinge of camaraderie.

"You'll like this sitter."

"Who is it?" Sam demanded, through a mouthful of pizza.

"Chew with your mouth closed, please. She's Penny's friend's sister."

"Is she a teenager?" Sam looked intrigued.

"No. She's a grown-up."

"I don't *want* her," Sam insisted. "I want *Jake*."

Okay. Sam was fighting for him. For *him*. Even if he didn't understand what he was fighting for, or why, Jake couldn't hang him out to dry.

Sam wasn't looking in Jake's direction. Jake mouthed over his son's head, *I could do it.*

She hesitated. *Are you sure?*

Sam's head swiveled back and forth between them, just short of *Exorcist*-child. "Jake, Jake, are you gonna do it?"

"Until you find someone else," Jake told Mira. "I mean, no point in having all these changes, right? You'll find someone permanent in a couple of days."

"Totally. I'm sure I can find someone. But I don't want you to feel like you're on the hook indefinitely. We could say you'll do the rest of the week, and then I'll figure something out for after that."

Short term. That was good. Because he wanted to be useful to them, but he had to draw the line somewhere. Keep things casual. This was too crazy of a situation to let the lines get all blurry and weird. Sam didn't even know who he was. And he probably should get himself out of the way of temptation before he did something he'd live to regret.

Mira was relieved, he could tell. But uneasy, too. She had a nervous habit of running her thumb across her other four fingernails. He'd seen her do it in the physical therapist's office. Well, if she was nervous about this whole setup, that made two of them.

He grabbed another slice of pizza. That was probably more food than he'd eaten the rest of the week combined.

"So Jake's going to come tomorrow?"

He looked to Mira, who nodded. "Yeah," Jake told Sam.

"Awesome! We can race again!"

"You guys raced?" Mira's eyes narrowed.

Jake looked over at Sam, who appeared to be sinking in his chair. "It was Jake's idea," Sam said hastily.

Jake would give him a lecture tomorrow on not selling out your fellow soldiers. In the meantime, fine, he was the grown-up here. He'd take the blame. "Yes, we did."

Mira's jaw hardened. "Sam. Are you done?"

Sam had begun tearing his uneaten pizza crust into tiny pieces. He nodded.

"Clear your place and go get in your pajamas, brush your teeth, and get in bed. You remember the rule?"

"If I stay there, you'll come up and snuggle me for a long time. If I come down, only a hug and a kiss?"

"That's right. Your *Dragonbreath* book is on the night table. You can read till I come up."

Sam went.

Mira's anger creased the space between her brows and tightened her jaw. "I told you straight out, totally clearly, that he has asthma. That he was injured. I told you I ask him not to run flat out. I told you I ask him to take it down a notch if he's overtaxing his system. And you decided it would be a good idea to *run races with him*?"

"I'm sorry," he said. "I didn't mean to freak you out. He was fine. He said nothing hurt anymore. I kept a close eye on his breathing, and I only let him do short runs, with lots of breaks."

"That's not the point. The point is that you knew I don't let him do that, and you let him do it! The point is, he has asthma, and he could have had an asthma attack." She got up and began clearing the table, her motions jerky with anger.

He couldn't sit here and watch her clean up, so he got up and helped. "We had his inhaler."

"That's not your decision, Jake. You're his *babysitter*. That's it. His *babysitter*." She jammed a paper plate into the trash. "And you're not even his babysitter anymore, because I'm firing you."

"No. Mira, please don't. He wanted to show off a little for me, and I wanted to let him. He seemed like he could use the confidence boost. And he wanted to see me run on this damn thing." He gestured at the leg.

Some of the starch went out of her posture. She took a step back and touched her fingertips to her temples. He became aware of the ticking of a clock, of the hum of the refrigerator, of the sound of a car starting on the street outside. Of her breathing, rapid and shallow.

"He loved it." He had to make her understand, that running wasn't a danger to Sam. That *he* wasn't a danger to Sam. Because he wanted this. Wanted another day with Sam, another evening with Mira.

She put her hand over her mouth.

"You should have seen him." Sam, legs pumping as he powered across the finish line, the expression on his face. "God! He was so psyched. He was running as hard as he could, and loving it. Smile as big as a barn, and—he's a tough kid, Mira. He's a great kid. He's a great kid, and I took good care of him, I promise."

Not trying to convince her anymore. Only saying it because it mattered to him. "He's a great kid. And I want to spend more time with him. If you don't want me to run with him, I won't run with him."

She lifted her chin, and he thought maybe she was about to kick him out, but she nodded instead. "He *is* a great kid. And I get it. I get why you did it. It makes sense to me. But if you want to spend time with him, you have to respect *my* boundaries. And that means asking before you let him do stuff like that."

Jake nodded. "Got it."

"Sounds like it was good for him."

"It was definitely good for me. First time I've really run on this sucker."

Her eyes took him in, a slow survey of his face. The flush of anger that had risen earlier in her cheeks covered her throat and extended to the smooth fair skin above the curved neckline of that insubstantial silk shell she wore.

He became aware that the adrenaline that had fueled him through their exchange had transmuted into a much more familiar feeling. Balls tightening, dick hard. Every soldier knew about this. You got scared or pissed, and then you were so fucking horny you had to jerk one out silently under the feeble cover of your sleeping bag, or in the shower and hope you didn't get walked in on.

That high-emotion arousal meant nothing. This hard-on wasn't *for* her. He didn't have to act on it.

And yet he couldn't stop thinking about grabbing her and pushing up her shirt and sucking her breasts and unfastening her Professional Lady Pants and getting his hand in her panties so he could see if she was ready. Somehow, years of combat, of death and destruction, hadn't managed to eradicate the memory of her wet heat against his fingers that night by the lake. Or the sounds she'd made into his mouth when he'd kissed her.

He wanted to get it right this time. He wanted to be buried in her so far she could taste him.

And his dick was totally, completely, 100 percent on board.

It just went to show that dicks were stupid, stupid, stupid.

He'd been staring at the smooth expanse of her skin above where the silk flirted with her breasts, and when he lifted his eyes, they met hers. She stared back. Curious. Watching him watch her.

For a long, frozen moment, he couldn't look away.

Finally he forced himself to look down at his hands, which, he discovered, were in fists.

Fuck.

This wasn't a place where he could afford to mess around. This wasn't a part of his life where he could make dumb mistakes. This was a situation that called for him to be a grown man with big balls who stuck to the program.

The exact opposite of how he'd been three days before he got his leg blown off, in fact. The exact goddamned opposite.

"This is too complicated," he said.

"I know." But she stepped closer, close enough that she violated some magic boundary line, and his chemical world shifted, every hair on his body rising to attention. Along with some other things.

"We need to keep it simple." But it was possible he'd taken a step forward, too. More than possible. There was almost no distance between them now, and he could smell her shampoo. It reminded him of new leaves.

"I know."

"This is a bad idea," he told her. Then he gave up, let his fingers find the thick softness of her hair, and lowered his mouth to hers.

8

H is lips were cool and soft, but the rest of his mouth was hot, and something about the contrast lit Mira up.

It was too much, all at once. And there was the unfinished business in their far-off past, which was part of her excitement, twined up in it in a way she couldn't untangle. Way back then, at the lake, she'd made him want her so badly he'd forgotten caution. And she had too, because no one had ever made her feel quite like that. Nothing before him had given her that sense of possibility, that rashness, that raw, sweet achiness.

The way she felt now, all eagerness and daring.

And here they were, his mouth not demanding but *suggesting. Here are a thousand lovely, dirty things I would like to do to you. I will start here with this slide of tongue over tongue, slow and sure.* As if he had all the time in the world to get that one caress exactly right, as if they weren't grumpy asshole, injured soldier and beleaguered mom, woman in search of herself. His kisses were long and sweet, came to an end, began again, blurred together.

"You taste *exactly* the same." He said it so close to her mouth that she felt his breath, his words, on her lips.

She pushed her mouth against his, trying to get closer, to fall into what he was telling her. That he felt it, too, the connection to that weird, splintered moment in the past, one long thread, her desire and willingness, his response.

He made a dark sound into her mouth and kissed her harder. He drew her lower lip in, sucked on it. The sensation pulled deep, tugged at her core. Caused heat to pool, to rise, to spread in her limbs.

She whimpered.

"Shh."

He was kissing her jaw now, her throat, the hollow between her collarbones. His hair tickled her chin. She clutched his arms as his mouth brushed the curve of her neckline. "Jake—"

"Shh," he said again. He drew back, his eyes dark, his mouth red and slightly slack, his breath quick. "Sam will hear. And how would you explain it to him? Can you imagine at school? 'I saw Mommy kissing the babysitter.'"

Was that what this was? Just Mommy kissing the babysitter? If so, it should be easy to stop, to make the right decision and pull away. But her body refused the idea. It was begging for more, liquid heat between her legs, her breasts tight, her breath still searing her throat. Even parts of her that by all rights shouldn't be involved felt jacked up. The backs of her knees. Her earlobes. The skin all over her body, hyper-activated, wide awake.

"What is this? What just happened?" she asked.

"I don't know."

He didn't say it like he was cutting off the conversation. He said it like he wanted more information. Like he wanted her to give him the answers.

"Just crazy chemistry?" She tilted her head.

"It feels crazy."

"Crazy good," she said.

He was looking at her that way again. Like he could barely keep himself in check, like he was thinking about every possible thing he wanted to do to her. It did terrible things to her self-control. It overrode caution and common sense and the absolute conviction that, yes, this was too complicated.

"Sam won't come down," she said. "I promised him snuggles if he stays up, and snuggles are important to him."

He kissed her again. Slid his mouth over hers, his hands down her body, over her breasts, to her waist, up again. He pulled her close and sealed her mouth with his. He licked her and bit her lip and made her moan. Loudly. He found her earlobe and sucked the heat there to the surface, and her hands got out of her control and started wandering all over him. Over the hard muscles of his back, into his soft hair, across the rough landscape of his face.

Her thumbs described his pecs, and then she slid one hand down across the ridged plane of his belly and grabbed the waistband of his jeans. Held it in her fist. Her hands didn't feel like hers. They felt like they belonged to someone else and like they might do something she'd have to apologize for afterward. Also, she thought she might bite him, right there, where a thick cord of muscle connected his neck to his shoulder—she did it, and he groaned, deep in his chest. He

grabbed her ass, hard, as if to tug her against him, but he lost
his balance and fell backwards, barely catching himself with
a hand on the counter.

"Motherfu—" He put his head in his hands.

"Jake—"

"No, don't. I sometimes forget. My head was somewhere
else, I forgot who I was, I thought I could do something the
normal way for fucking once. My bad."

Her heart hurt, and she reached out to offer him comfort.

He drew back. "This is a dumb fucking idea," he said. "In
every way. I can't even catalog all the ways this is a dumb
idea."

It was, she knew, and yet this thing, whatever it was, with
Jake felt different from anything she'd ever known. Definitely
a whole different ball game from what she'd felt for Aaron.

Aaron, despite whatever weakness had compelled him to
accept her father's money, had been a terrifically nice guy. He
played games with Sam, he got along great with her parents,
he treated her right without fail.

In bed, he was attentive, creative, and energetic. They had
a lot in common—they enjoyed going to the movies together.
Reading similar books. Hiking, kayaking, biking, either alone
together or with Sam in tow.

If she had stayed in Florida, she was pretty sure he would
have proposed. Even after their fight, even after she'd broken
up with him, he'd insisted he wanted to earn back her trust.
He said he'd keep an eye out for jobs in the Seattle area,
because he'd miss her like fury. He said he'd find a way to
show her how much he loved her, that her father's money
had meant nothing to him.

She'd expressed doubt, but his pleading had softened her

and she hadn't told him not to bother trying. Because the truth was, Aaron would make a good husband and a good father.

Even if he had sometimes bored her to tears.

Kissing Jake had been, as Jake had so eloquently put it, a dumb fucking idea. But the furthest thing from boring. It had woken her up—not just the eager dampness between her legs, not just the tight demand of her nipples, but something else. The way it had been that night at the lake, the physical connection reaching deep into her, grabbing at some emotional truth she wanted to but couldn't hide. How much she liked him. How deeply she *felt* him.

He took a step toward the living room. "I should go."

She should let him go. She should let him walk away, for so many reasons. And yet her pulse beat hard, at her throat, in her wrists, between her legs, an insistent rhythm, a vibrant counterpoint to good sense.

Jake shook his head. "I'm sorry, Mira. It's not you."

Had he really said that? The thing about that cliché, the thing she had always hated most, was that it worked so damn well. There was no argument against it. It was the perfect put-down, the definitive end point.

"It's me. I'm—a mess," Jake said.

Don't argue with him. Tell him he's right. Tell him you're a mess, too, and you're in no position to be involved with anyone. For, say, the next five years. Let alone someone who comes with the baggage he does. Let alone someone whose DNA is in a Gordian knot with yours.

But what came out instead was, "You're going to have to do better than that."

"What?"

God, what was she doing? She hadn't jumped out of her father's frying pan to fall into some other alpha asshole's fire.

Words were somehow still coming out of her mouth, and they had the pressure of truth, the heat of conviction behind them. "You look at you and you see a mess. I look at you and I see a good-looking guy, a guy who was badly injured but who is obviously doing a great job of rehabbing. A guy who helped me out of a fix today."

He was shaking his head again, but she kept going. "I see the stuff I read about you online yesterday, which was all about what a good soldier you were. I see the emails you sent me, which told me you're good with kids, good with your mom. So if there's something else I'm supposed to be seeing, you're going to have to spell it out for me."

"Fine," he said. He crossed his arms, his face grim. "I'll spell it out. I'm here today, but barely, because it practically killed me just to haul myself out of bed and get myself here. I haven't done anything since I left Afghanistan except eat, sleep, and learn to use this hunk of metal, because it's a full-time job figuring out how to be human."

She waited. Because she knew there was more. Because she could see it in the coiled, angry set of his shoulders, in the rage behind his eyes. Because she knew—she wasn't sure how—that he hadn't said these words to anyone before, and that his saying them to her was the beginning of something that mattered. To her. To him.

"You think you want me, but if you knew, you wouldn't."

"Try me," she said.

That only made him angrier, the words coming rapid fire.

"I don't have a job. I don't *want* a job. I've only ever wanted to be a soldier. I don't know how to want to be anything other than a soldier. I drink too much, but not *too much* too much because I don't want to be my father. And I can't get it up, except for when some psychiatrist at Walter Reed put me on antidepressants and I got hard-ons for three hours at a time and couldn't get myself off."

She winced. *Yowch.*

She hurt for him. For the boy he'd been that night at the lake, for the soldier who'd lost his leg, and something much bigger. For the man who had laid out in raw detail all the ways he believed himself not a man. She wanted to wrap him in her arms and stroke his hair and move her lips against his cheek and his ear, whispering words of comfort she couldn't even articulate yet.

He wasn't done. His breath was coming as fast as it had when she'd grabbed his waistband. "So I don't know what you think you're doing, but I am bad fucking juju. I'm not what you want in your life. And I am most definitely not what you want in Sam's life."

The echo of her father's words brought her back. To the world she was trying to build here for herself and Sam, one where bossy men didn't tell her what to do or what to feel. One where her father didn't get to decide who she should sleep with, who she should expose her son to, how she should live.

And neither did this guy, because he was too damn pathetic to get to make decisions for her. "You know, if you don't want to have sex with me, that's fine. I get it. Your life is complicated enough as it is. And yeah, I can see, getting mixed up with us would be a lot for a guy in your situation. But don't tell me what I want. And don't tell me what's good for Sam. Just man up and say you don't want this."

He raked a hand through his hair. The anger and the wild hair conspired to make him look frightening, but she wasn't scared of him.

"And for the record, you *can* get it up. I can definitely attest to that."

He was on her so fast he startled her, backing her up until her shoulder blades hit the wall, pressing himself close so she could feel the long, hard line of his erection against her hip. He kissed her, fierce, hard, and mean. It hurt her, and she pressed back, needing more.

Then it was over. He stepped away, and the loss of his body heat, the loss of that long, solid line of muscle, felt like plunging into cold water.

"I gotta go," he said.

She leaned her head against the wall and listened for the crunch of the front door easing shut, her heart beating a harsh, uneven rhythm in her ears.

9

"Y̲ou're *really* quiet."

That was Opal, Mira's new friend at work. They were eating lunch on one of the benches outside the office, their paper-wrapped sandwiches balanced on their knees. They were in the middle of an unusually long run of sunny days, and it was warm, too, near 80, Seattle bliss.

Mira had met Opal on her first day of work after Mira had been taken to task in her cube by her new boss for showing up a week late. Opal had launched a piece of crumpled paper over the wall:

"We want to be as accommodating as we can of your life. Just see that you keep your personal problems from interfering with your ability to get the job done." Does she listen to herself? —Opal, next door

Mira felt as if she were in seventh grade and a popular girl had passed her a note.

I don't think so!

She tossed the note back over the wall. She prayed she had its source correct—she thought it had come from the

cube directly to her right. She'd noticed that desk was occupied by a woman about her age.

A head peeked around the corner. "Hi," said the woman.
"I'm Opal. I'm in the marketing department, and I'm
supposed to work closely with you on the accessories
launch." Opal didn't look like an Opal. She had a lot of red
curly hair, like Little Orphan Annie, and freckles so closely
packed on her face they were almost a continuous tan. She
also had the nicest smile Mira had ever seen, big and totally
unreserved. It was like a gift after Mira's last run-in.

"I'm Mira."

"Welcome."

Opal was also, officially, the first person to make an over-
ture of friendship to Mira since she and Sam had arrived in
Seattle. Mira had met one old friend, who also had kids, at a
playground the first week after the move, but then Sam had
taken his spill, and that and unpacking had consumed most
of her resources since. Mira had nearly forgotten how much
fun it was to make a new friend.

"I can't possibly express how relieved I am to discover that
you're normal-looking," Opal said. "Do you want to have
lunch?"

Mira smiled. "Sure."

"I love your shoes. Are they ours?"

"Yeah." One of the perks of the job was 30 percent off a
new pair of shoes every month. These were Mira's first—cork-
heeled, strappy, red patent sandals.

"Do they come in any other colors?"

"Lime green, lemon yellow, orange, purple."

"Would I be treading on your toes—no pun intended—if
I bought a pair in a different color?"

Mira wanted to hug her. "No. I'll send you a link."

"Would you?" Opal grinned, a mouthful of straight white teeth. "Thanks. Hey, if you have any questions about anything, you know, how to do stuff, or just—well, you know where to find me." And she ducked back behind the wall. A moment later, a crushed wad of paper flew over. *Glad you're here.*

This was the fourth day she'd eaten on this bench with Opal, who was a relentless talker, an excellent feature at the moment since Mira hadn't felt much like talking since she'd kissed and dismissed her emergency babysitter.

She was still having hot flashes of stupid shame several days after the fact. First, because she'd let anything happen in the first place. She had seen it coming, had seen the look on his face, felt the combustion when anger turned to lust. She could have backed off. She could have made herself busy, made excuses. And when he'd said those words, "This is a bad idea," she could have said, "Damn straight," and run the other way.

Instead, she'd let him kiss her. She'd more than let him; she'd dived straight into the center of it, thrown herself whimpering at him. *Hmm, let's see . . . I'll fly across the country to get some space for myself and then serve myself on a platter to the most complicated man on earth.*

And then, when he'd given her the perfect out, *she'd* gone and taunted him into one more kiss.

Gawd.

And yet, she couldn't quite find it in herself to completely regret it.

It wasn't like he was just some guy. He was *that* guy. That guy whose mouth she absolutely 100 percent shouldn't stick her tongue into. That guy who had always had the ability to make her abandon caution. And she knew that ability, multiplied by the effect of his being Sam's dad, multiplied by his being an alpha guy who wanted to call the shots, would equal, like, 600 million.

"What's going on, girl?" Opal asked. "And don't lie to me. I know it's not nothing. I just told you I could get you a pair of Louboutins for fifty bucks if you played your cards right, and you said, 'Uh-huh.'"

"It's complicated," Mira said, and then thought, *And I could have kept it simple.*

"Maybe that works on some of your friends, but I *like* it complicated. Serve it up, hon."

Mira wanted to tell someone. Because there was a part of her that still couldn't quite believe it was real. That she'd seen him, that she'd told him, that she'd hired him, that she'd kissed him.

That it had felt so good. That she wanted more.

"I did something I really, really, really shouldn't have."

"Let me be the judge of that." Opal took a last bite of sandwich and crumpled her wax paper. She dug into the paper bag and pulled out a gigantic chocolate chip cookie. She unwrapped it and handed half to Mira.

Mira didn't know Opal super well yet, but the path to real friendship was paved with confessions, and she needed someone to either absolve or condemn her. "Long version, or short version?"

"Um, Mira, have you met me? I'm not conversant with the short version of *anything.*"

So Mira told Opal the whole story, starting with the long, long time ago part, and leading right up to the present.

Opal proved to be as good a listener as she was a talker. "You're right," she said, when Mira was done. "Complicated."

"I wish I could un-kiss him," Mira said.

Opal tilted her head and gave Mira a doubtful look.

Under her scrutiny, Mira caved and laughed. "No, you're right. You know what I really wish? I wish he weren't Sam's father. I wish he were just some guy. And I could tell him I wanted to have a nonserious, fling-y type thing with him, and it wouldn't be complicated at all. I wouldn't have to worry that he'd want to move in and start making decisions about Sam's upbringing, or that Sam would find out who Jake was and then something would go wrong and Sam would be crushed."

"And you have reason to think something would go wrong?"

"He's grumpy and messed up in the head . . ." She gave Opal a quick outline of Jake's explanation of why she shouldn't want him.

Opal smiled, all dimples and teeth. "Sounds like a real prize."

"So you see why I'm not supposed to get involved with him."

"I do." Opal's smile faded. "But despite all that, you kissed him—why?"

"He—I—" She could feel the heat rising in her face as she remembered. "God. It's, like . . ." But words seemed to have failed her completely.

"Oh, hon," Opal said, her big, freckled face as sad as Mira had seen it. "In my experience, 'not supposed to' is a *really* flimsy barrier against chemistry like that."

JAKE WAITED in a cushy chair in the new prosthetist's office, an unfamiliar sensation in his stomach. Like nerves, only not quite. Like—

Like maybe he was looking forward to this visit. To getting fitted for a new socket and a new running leg. Just a little.

He sighed. Or maybe he was just having a flashback to another recent stint in a waiting room, when the world had shifted abruptly under him, the landslide that had dumped him out of one kind of uncertainty and into another.

Jake's PT had told him it would take several months to get an appointment with Harwood, who was new to the University of Washington prosthetics and orthotics group, fresh off a stint at Brooke Army Medical Center in Texas, but the receptionist had called him this morning to tell him there'd been a cancellation.

It was Friday, two and a half weeks since he'd kissed Mira and fled. On the way home from her house that night, he'd felt his phone buzzing in his pocket. He ignored it until he jogged back to his apartment, then fished it out. *Should have known*, he thought, when he saw the screen.

The text was from Mira. *Don't worry about tomorrow—I'll go with the new sitter.*

Of course. It made sense. They'd proved beyond a shadow of a doubt that neither of them knew how to do *simple*.

But it had still made his stomach sink.

It wasn't like she was cutting him off. She wasn't telling him he couldn't see Sam.

And he didn't *need* to be a babysitter. It wasn't a good job for a twenty-eight-year-old man. For a soldier. He needed to find something real to do. But he felt ...

Fired. Dumped.

He'd spent the shittiest night ever, tossing and turning. And he'd had some shitty nights, like the one he'd spent after his rucksack didn't make a jump and he'd frozen his balls off without a sleeping bag, bundled to the gills in layers of the other guys' clothes but still too cold to fall into more than a fitful sleep.

He'd come home from Mira's house and poured out every drop of alcohol in his apartment and lain on his bed for eight straight hours, sleepless. Eyes jammed open like that godawful scene in *A Clockwork Orange*, only for him it wasn't so much images as sensations, the feel of Mira's mouth fitting into place against his, the slide of her tongue, the tingle and squeeze and draw of his body demanding what it had been missing. Her vague floral scent, a day's sweat fighting its way through some girly deodorant, the sea smell of her arousal drowning his good sense. And those fucking noises, whimpers so low and deep in her throat he could feel them in his own chest, in his thighs, his balls, his *toes.*

He should have kept her up against that wall and peeled her out of her clothes. Gotten his thigh between hers, licked her mouth, bitten her neck, breathed against the curves of her ear until she went limp against him.

He should never have kissed her.

What the *fuck* was he thinking, kissing her? This wasn't some girl he could pick up in an off-base bar, take back to her apartment, enjoy like an ice-cream cone, and forget about. This was the *mother of his fucking child*. This was disaster and mess, weeping and ranting, judges and courts.

And he couldn't even stand on two good feet and kiss her like a man.

He had almost gotten out of bed and gone out to Downtown Spirits to replace his goddamned Jack. But then he thought of Sam, of the races they'd run, of the way the boy had collapsed beside him on the front stoop afterward and then rested his head against Jake's arm.

Jake had rolled over with a groan, pulled the covers over his head, and given sleep another try.

There was another noise she'd made, when he'd first kissed her. When his lips had only grazed hers, before the full intensity of the chemistry had registered with him. Barely more than a sigh, something like relief. *Yes. This.*

He'd felt that, too. As if they'd been waiting. Years.

He was hard again.

But for the record? You can get it up.

He'd rolled onto his belly, propped himself on his arms, sandwiched his cock between his own weight and the bed, and fucked the mattress, almost idly. He hadn't jerked off—or tried to, he guessed was more accurate—since the night he'd gotten stuck with the interminable antidepressant erection. He and the guys had once laughed at that line in the Viagra and Cialis commercials: "If you have an erection that lasts for more than four hours—"

"Then you'll find me balls deep in a very happy woman," Mike had said, hooting with laughter. Back when he laughed.

It didn't work like that in real life.

In his bed that night after he'd kissed Mira, he could feel the pressure, the arousal, building, skyrocketing, so fucking fast. The way he'd felt it when Mira's hand had slid down his chest and stomach and lodged itself in the waist of his jeans.

Jesus. His mind had leapt ahead, his dick straining toward the notion of being freed from its denim bindings, and he'd thought, *God, don't let me come in my pants right now.*

In his mind, she knelt at his feet and opened his jeans, took him deep, her blond hair tickling his thighs as she worked. She hummed and moaned, and he thrust into her mouth, down into the mattress, and came so hard he strained something in his shoulder.

First time he'd been able to get off in months.

Then he'd slept.

In the morning, he'd woken hard and mad. Mad at her, sure, but maddest at himself. For kissing her. For not staying to finish what he'd started. For being a hothead and a coward.

Fueled by anger, he'd put on running clothes and taken the bus to Green Lake. The bus dropped him off and he walked down toward the path. If he thought about it too much, he wouldn't be able to do it, so he tried not to think. He let himself break into a run. One minute he was walking, the next he was skip-jogging. *Foot, foot. Foot, foot—*

And then he realized he'd stopped thinking about it. That he was doing it, reflexively. Running.

If he'd been the kind of guy who cried, he would have. It felt that good.

He made one full loop. He passed no one. He was passed by cyclists, joggers, mothers and fathers pushing baby strollers, small children dashing ahead of their parents. Hot girls stripped down to sports bras, saggy-breasted old men who shouldn't be running shirtless. He didn't give a fuck. He'd run faster the next time. He'd run farther the next time.

Once he'd done a triathlon with Mike when they were on leave. There had been a parathlete in that race. She had worn a different prosthesis for each event of the race—he'd noticed, because he'd found her attractive even as she was strapping and unstrapping her legs.

He could do that. He could get bike and swim prostheses. He could get a real running leg. He could do a triathlon.

In some ways, the seeming unreachability of the goal was exactly what he wanted from it. He wanted to slam his body against an immovable wall, part punishment and part—well, that was what he fucking did. What soldiers did. As he'd thought the other day while running with Sam, if you didn't push yourself past where you knew it was possible to go, you couldn't know who the hell you were. And of all the things that were pissing him off right now, not knowing who he was was the biggest.

If he'd known who he was—he told himself, dick in hand for the tenth or fifteenth or hundredth time—he'd never have kissed her.

Or he'd never have stopped.

After he'd assured himself there were plenty of tri's he could run in the Seattle area, he called the prosthetist who had originally fitted his leg at Walter Reed and asked for a referral.

"Come down here," Frank Morales had said. "I'll work on the socket; I'll fit you for a leg."

"Three legs. I want the best running leg, the best biking leg, and the best swimming leg I can get."

"I can give you the best leg for making fucking pancakes, if that's what you want," Morales said.

Can you give me the best leg for . . .?

For what? For one-night stands? For delving into a woman he should be giving a wide berth? For getting himself in too deep, too weird? For wanting things he didn't deserve to have?

"I'm not coming down there," Jake said.

Because he didn't need to be reminded of what he'd lost. He'd left Walter Reed in the first place to get away from those daily reminders, the men who'd be back in the fight in a week, a month, a year, even five years. Itching to be back. Thoroughly convinced they were doing what needed to be done.

That wasn't him, and he wasn't sure it would ever be him again.

So instead of heading down to Walter Reed and working with Morales, he had this unexpected appointment today with John Harwood, a former colleague of Morales's who was now practicing in Seattle. "He's the best. Better than me," Morales had told Jake.

Harwood, short and built like a tank, and oddly hyper for such a compact man, couldn't contain his excitement at hearing Jake's request for three new legs. ("And not," he told Jake, "because it's a buttload of money.") He liked to work with athletes, he said, because it gave him more range for messing around with sophisticated knees and ankles.

"It's generous to call me an athlete because I'm training for a triathlon," Jake said. They were sitting in a large room, filled with exercise equipment like parallel bars. And other things. Strange objects. Human parts crafted from an assortment of nonhuman materials. Tubs of water and strips of cloth. A 3D printer and plaster casts of people's stumps. A cross between an artist's studio and a physical therapist's office.

"I'm a generous guy," Harwood said.

Harwood was the best socket guy on the West Coast, Morales had said, and he clearly had the combination of gear lust, curiosity, and willingness to experiment that made him perfect for building legs. He asked Jake if he wanted to be cast for the socket immediately.

"Sure," Jake said. "Nowhere I need to be."

He thought of Sam, hanging with some overgrown teenager, playing video games, watching TV, and sinking back into a version of himself that had to be careful not to overexert.

Harwood examined Jake's stump with a dispassionate, scientific interest, probing the scars and bone ends. Jake winced. "It's a little sore. I just started running."

"We're going to fix that," Harwood said.

His certainty pleased Jake.

Harwood tilted his crew-cut head. "I could do it with measurements. But I think for what you're looking for, we'll do it the old-fashioned way."

Jake's current socket had been built off intricate measurements programmed into a computer, but he knew what Harwood was talking about. The "old-fashioned way" meant that Harwood was planning to make an actual cast of Jake's residual leg and fit the socket exactly to the stump's topography. Harwood laid paper and plastic strips over the stump until Jake felt like human papier-mâché. He marked bones and other details with pens that would show through the cast so he could mold the socket to take Jake's most intense pressure points into account.

"It's an art," said Harwood. "I'm like a sculptor."

Jake personally thought the guy was kind of an egotist,

but he didn't much care as long as it resulted in a leg that fit well, felt good, and stayed put.

As Harwood was seeing Jake out of his office, he said, "Are you thinking about returning to active duty soon?"

Jake turned, startled. They'd been talking a few minutes earlier about how Jake was running a ten-minute mile. Surely he couldn't be asking that question seriously.

"I assume you're on the Temporary Disability Retirement List at the moment?"

"Yeah." Jake was drawing disability pay now, but he had to be reevaluated soon and deemed either permanently retired or fit to return to active duty.

"Lotta guys are going back fast now. Did you read that book? *Back in the Fight*? The one about the Ranger?"

"Nah," Jake said. Everyone wanted him to read some inspirational book or other. One of his buddies had brought him a book called *Amped*, about a soldier who'd lost a leg in Iraq and gone on to be a Paralympian. Jake had tossed the book in the garbage—though he was pretty sure a nurse had fished it out and recycled it through some other guys who were more willing to be inspired.

"That guy went back fast. Book starts with him in the middle of battle."

"He was BK." *Below the knee.*

"Things are changing," Harwood said. "AK guys are going back fast too. Motivated guys. You could pull it off. You could be back in a combat role in a few months, if you wanted to. With your determination, and your strength. And my socket," he added.

Jake felt a prickle of anger. What the hell did this guy know about his strength or his determination? What the hell did he know about what it felt like to lose a leg, lose a friend, lose direction? Or what it felt like to be the one who lived? "Stick to leg-building and leave the headshrinking to the trained professionals, okay?"

Harwood shrugged. "Have it your way."

He cleared out of there before Harwood could give him any more life advice. But the guy's words rang in Jake's head as he headed out for his run that day. He ran harder and faster than he'd thought he could, and he pondered it. Going back. He thought about what he missed. Order. Hierarchy. The simplicity. How it was always clear what needed to happen next, or at least whose decision it should be. Not that things never degenerated into chaos—of course they did. But he'd had a clarity in those moments of chaos, a sense of certainty about what mattered, and about what he was meant to be doing, that he couldn't recapture now.

He missed working on a team. Leading a team. Knowing those guys so well, he could half the time predict what they were going to say before they said it, almost always predict what they were going to do before they did it. Knowing their strengths and their weaknesses . . .

Knowing Mike's strengths and weaknesses hadn't helped anyone.

He hadn't gone to Mike's funeral. Hadn't made the phone call to Mike's wife. Because he'd been struggling to live, then drowning in rage and regret.

Pain shot through his residual leg and he nearly fell. There was so much sweat between the silicone sheath and his own flesh that it was a miracle the prosthesis was still on.

He'd been fueled, fighting all those years, by conviction. What would it be like to fight without that certainty? What would keep you slogging up mountains, through snow, across wasted desert land?

In the beginning he'd fought because of 9/11. Although maybe he'd lied to himself about that. Maybe he'd just needed to run away from his dad's emptiness and rage, his mother's self-loathing, and his siblings' self-destruction. Either way, like most guys, in the end he'd fought for the guy next to him. Mike had been the guy next to him. And now he wasn't—because of what Jake had done, or *not* done—and when Jake looked in his heart for reasons to fight, he couldn't find them.

The explosion had blown them to hell.

Maybe going back to the war would be better than this.

At least, if he went back, he wouldn't be his father.

He was *someone's* father, though. Whether he liked it or not. What would it mean to Sam if he went back in? What would it mean to Mira?

Whatever Mira wanted from him—if she wanted anything at all, and he was decidedly not convinced she did —it shouldn't keep him from doing what he was supposed to be doing. It shouldn't keep him from finishing what he'd started. If he could go back in, he'd visit Sam on leave, do his best to be a father in the time he had with his son.

He would let a month or two go by. He'd let the urgency die out of his own feelings, and he'd let her cool off. Then he'd ask her if he could take Sam to a baseball game or something. He'd try to arrange outings where there wouldn't be a lot of opportunity for him and Mira to be alone, and over time—he was sure—they'd figure out how to ignore any lingering chemistry. They'd focus on Sam's needs. They'd get into a rhythm that would work for all of them, regardless of whether he retired or went back to serving.

It was a good plan.

If his brain kept trying to write Mira back into it, he could ignore that.

10

R unning with the new prosthesis was a whole new ball game. It had been hard to catch the rhythm—new socket, new knee, and best of all, new foot. The first time the running foot—which looked more like a curved hook than an actual foot—had bounced him off the ground at the track where he and Harwood had been playing around with it, he'd almost fallen flat on his face, but he was getting it now, and it was such a high. He was doing five miles now, no problem, and even though he didn't think he'd ever be a parathlete, he could understand the draw. Why you might come out of an accident broken, put yourself back together with spare parts, and throw yourself wholeheartedly into a new fight.

He took another lap of the Discovery Park path he liked to run on, slower now, cooling off. Not even minding the slight chafe of the socket against his thigh. Having Harwood in his court made all the difference. The guy was a perfectionist, totally obsessed. If he asked Jake, "How's it feel?" and Jake answered with anything other than "Like my own leg," he'd be in there with measurements and tools and adjustments, tweaking socks and sheaths, as if it were his own stump they were trying to baby.

Jake had started biking, too, on a special bike outfitted to work with his new cycling prosthesis, and next week he'd start swimming. In the mornings he worked out, and in the evenings he worked with a trainer, a guy named John Spiro, who specialized in men like him. Men who'd lost limbs and wanted to get back in army shape. Who wanted to convince the Medical and Physical Examination Boards to give them another shot. Every millimeter of his body, muscles he hadn't known he had, hurt like a motherfucker every hour of the day. Every night he fell into bed exhausted.

He hadn't told anyone what he was doing, not his physical therapist, not his mother, not his siblings—although it had occurred to him that maybe he'd give Pierce a call, see if he wanted to run a mile or two together. As they once had, growing up, and when Jake came home on leave.

But he hadn't yet, hadn't told anyone yet, because he didn't want to see doubt on anyone's face. *You? Fight again?* And because he didn't want to jinx it. Didn't want to tell too many people what he was trying to do, in case he couldn't pull it off. It was a long shot, after all, as strong as he felt, as quickly as he was getting mobility and nimbleness back. There was still the fact that he was an above-the-knee amputee, and trying to do anything with a manufactured knee took a lot of goddamned work.

Plus, he wasn't sure. He didn't know if he wanted to fight without Mike. He doubted his own motives—was he pursuing this route because he didn't know what else to do? Working toward *some*thing felt great, but he didn't have confidence that it was the *right* thing.

He hated not being sure.

He jogged to a halt and sat down at a picnic table. He watched kids play on the nearby playground.

"Jake!"

One of the kids was running toward him. Sam. Behind him, slower, came Mira. She wasn't quite smiling. Well, neither was he. Because this was exactly what he'd been trying to avoid. Open-ended, casual time with her.

And yet, he was ridiculously happy to see her.

"That's a cool leg!" Sam said, pointing at the curved metal foot of his running prosthesis.

"It's my running leg," Jake said.

"Watch me climb!" Sam instructed, and ran back toward the playground. Jake got up from the table and followed him.

Mira fell in beside him. "Fancy meeting you here. What are the odds? You don't have to watch him if you're busy."

"I'm not busy." It was the truth, and the run had made him feel loose and a little reckless. Plus, the sun was out, and it had gotten in her hair so it looked like something was shining out from the inside. She wore a scoop-neck tight T-shirt and jeans that hugged her ass, and as much as he wanted to run and hide, he hated that man. Soldiers engaged, and even if he wasn't one anymore, he wasn't going to be a fucking wuss.

Sam began climbing on a structure that looked like a rope spiderweb.

"It's seven-year-old boy heaven," Jake observed.

"So, this is weird."

"Small world."

"How have you been? You were running?"

"Trying."

The last time he'd been this close to her, he'd had his hands all over her. Shoved her up against a wall. It was hard to get those pictures out of his head. Even harder to get rid of the feel of her, how soft she'd felt, the cloud of hair, the curve of her breasts and ass, the way her mouth had slid and opened under his.

Jesus.

How fast could he get himself out of here, before he did something stupid again?

"I've been meaning—I should have called you," she said. "Can we talk?"

His stomach sank. Not fast enough, then. "Here?"

They stood together under one of the taller trees. The ground was smattered with round, sturdy pinecones over a thick carpet of long pine needles. Other kids played and shouted on the structure, their parents scattered around the perimeter.

"As good a place as any, right?"

"I guess."

She laughed. "You guess?"

"Look, I'm not much for talking."

"I don't want to rehash anything that happened between us. I get that it's not a good idea. I totally agree that we need to keep things as simple as possible between you and me."

Was that *disappointment* he was feeling? She'd let him off the hook. Given him permission not to do something impossibly self-destructive. And once again, his stupid dick was trying to take the reins.

She'd goaded him into kissing her again. He'd gotten hard fifty times since then, thinking about it. *You can get it up. I can definitely attest to that.*

Down, boy. She wants to talk.

"It's not about that. It's about Sam. He said something last night. And, okay, what he said was, 'Do you think my father is like Jake?'"

Once, before the accident that had taken his leg, he had been within the percussion zone of a big explosion. Not close enough to be injured, not close enough to take shrapnel, not close enough to lose an eardrum, but close enough to feel the air hit his body like a blow. Her revelation felt like that. He said, "Shit. That must've freaked you out."

"Kinda. I didn't know what to say. I said, 'Yeah, he's a lot like Jake.' But it felt like a lie. And it made me feel awful. I know, I know—" She waved his protest away. "I realize it doesn't seem like a very big lie after the whole sperm donor thing..."

Jake shook his head. "I've kind of gotten used to the sperm donor idea—I mean to the idea of it as an explanation. It's clever. And you're right, what else can you tell a little kid?"

"Right, it felt different then, but now he's old enough to understand the truth, or a version of it, and I'm lying about someone who's in his life—" She stopped, and met his eyes. "Sorry. See, that's the thing: I don't know if you are or aren't. Or if I want you to be or not. Or—I'm sorry," she said. "I'm making this really complicated.

"No, don't apologize," he said. "It *is* complicated."

"And I don't want what happened between us to affect—I mean, I want you and Sam to be able to have a relationship without it getting all mucked with—"

She gestured vaguely, but it didn't keep him from manufacturing his own vivid images. The way it had felt to pin her against the wall, how soft she was but how passionately she'd responded, how intensely she'd kissed him back and given herself over. The whole length of her pressed against him.

"This can be whatever we want it to be," he said.

"What if I want it to be you and Sam? For now?"

"It could be that." But he couldn't suppress his regret, and maybe she saw it, because for a moment, he thought he saw it echoed on her face, too. Regret and longing. That hadn't been an ordinary kiss. It had been like the kisses all those years ago, packed full of things they both needed and wanted to say but couldn't get out in words. Old mistakes and new cravings and bad ideas that didn't feel bad. Crazy shit he'd seen, stupid stuff he'd done, people he'd let down.

Situations where emotions—where love, specifically— had clouded his judgment.

He turned away from her and watched Sam climb higher on the structure.

"That's high enough, Sam," Mira called.

God, he wished she wouldn't do that. The kid was seven years old and a monkey. He could handle a child's play structure.

What did Mira want from him?

What did he want from her?

And how did Sam fit in? How could they make sure that no matter what happened between them, Sam wouldn't get hurt?

That one day when Jake had babysat Sam, when they'd finished running, Jake had plopped down on the front stoop and Sam had collapsed in his lap, a heap of sweaty little kid, warm and panting. Totally trusting. And Jake had thought:

You don't want to put your eggs in this basket, kid. I've made some really bad decisions. The kind of bad where people died.

Every once in a while, it was there. Clear as day. Irrefutable.

"I meant everything I said. I'm not good for much. I'm not good for you, and I'm not good for him."

She crossed her arms. "You're wrong. He was really down before that day you sat. And he's been—a different kid since. Cheerful and energetic and full of himself."

"That was what I was hoping. He was so proud of what he did that day we ran. I'm glad it carried over."

He eyed Sam, now descending the play structure far more cautiously than he'd scrambled up it. She'd put her own fear in him, and she didn't even realize what she was doing. That must be the toughest thing about being a single parent: having to be brave enough for two so your own fear wouldn't become infectious.

Maybe he could help. He could be a buffer. For both of them.

"We don't have to tell him the truth yet. I'm mostly saying that he has questions."

She didn't say, *I have questions*, but when he met her eyes, he could see them there. *What the hell happened that night in my kitchen?*

He nodded. "Yeah. Okay. So, don't say anything to him now. I mean, I don't intend to disappoint him. But like I told you, I'm—"

He stopped.

"What?" She said it so gently. She was watching Sam, not looking at him.

"I'm not the man I was. I'm not sure that man even exists anymore. I don't know *who* I am, really." She made a soft sound of protest, but he ignored it. "What I'm saying is, I can't

promise things, and I especially don't want to promise things that involve Sam, because I get what you're saying. He's a kid and he doesn't understand."

Now she turned to look at him, and her face was soft with gratitude. He wanted her to look away again, because her emotion was levering itself under his skin. If he were going to turn back, if he were going to stop whatever this was that felt so inevitable, now was the time to lay down the boundaries. To draw the lines.

He wasn't sure if he could.

No, he was sure he couldn't. Not standing here next to her, craving her again, wanting to grab her and do it all over again. To choose, this time, what had felt like compulsion last time. To let her know: This is what I want. Him, yes, but also *you*.

Something big and hard catapulted itself into his good leg, and he had to grab Mira to steady himself. Sam—Sam had slammed himself against Jake for a hug. Jake regained his footing and released the handful of Mira's sweatshirt he was clutching. His heart pounded, a cocktail of adrenaline and shame. He felt unmanly. Weak. The voices that had drilled into his head during training were rising from the basement of his brain to torment him again. *That the best you can do, girls? You're a worthless, pathetic bunch of losers.*

I'm not. I can run. I can bike. I ran five miles today.

Who are you arguing with, douchebag?!

"Climb that tree with me?"

"I'm not much for tree climbing these days," Jake told him.

"Please?"

"He doesn't go that high," Mira said. "Just out on that big

branch." She gestured to one that was low and nearly horizontal, thick as a man's thigh.

Jake eyed it.

"I have a better idea," he said. It would give him some space, too, put some physical distance between him and Mira.

"What?" Sam's voice was suspicious.

"We're going to play baseball."

"I didn't bring my glove or my bat or my ball."

"You don't need them to play this kind of baseball." Jake picked up a stick about as long as his forearm. "Here's your bat."

"Where's the ball?"

"Go stand over there." Jake pointed to the tree.

Sam went.

Jake bent, picked up a pinecone, and pitched it, underhand and easy, to Sam, who swung. The pinecone sailed past Jake's ear.

"Nice!" Mira called. She grinned at him. "Clever."

"Nah. Used to making do with whatever's on hand. Nimble, maybe. Not clever." He grabbed a new "ball" and pitched again.

"Well, whatever it is, it's cool."

He hazarded a glance in her direction. She was watching him with genuine admiration. It made his gut glow.

God. Simple had receded far into the background, like a dream he'd had but had almost forgotten by the time his eyes were fully open. There was nothing simple about this, not about any of it. Not about the pleasure of pitching pinecones to his *son*, not about how the glow in his gut had lit him up hard, not about the conversation they'd had before Sam had barreled into him. It was all complication, and he didn't hate it half as much as he wanted to.

He didn't hate it at all.

He liked it, too fucking much.

He hated *that*.

11

S am and Jake played pinecone baseball while she sat at a nearby picnic table and watched them. Watched the rough contours of Jake's body under the gray T-shirt he wore, watched how even when he was dispatching a pinecone, she could see muscle flirt with fabric. He had a funny half-straddle he did to pick up the pinecones, and even that was sexy, because he made it into a graceful performance. His hair was mussed, as it always was, and he needed to shave. He looked haunted, the bones in his face rough and high under the skin, darkness under his eyes that even sunlight didn't chase away, a grim set around his mouth that only occasionally gave way to something you might call a smile, when Sam did something particularly charming or funny.

This was a moment she had fantasized about when Sam was little, but it was different from the fantasy. In the fantasy, Jake had been light, joyful. He romped with Sam, his mind not on his physical limitations but on the adventures that he and his son could have together, how high they could go in the tree, how far and how fast they could run. In the fantasy, he crouched down to show Sam something at eye level. In the fantasy, he swept her off her feet and carried her, both of them laughing, while Sam demanded to be included in the embrace.

She didn't want that fantasy anymore. She didn't want to be with the Jake she had imagined, who now seemed frivolous. The Jake she'd dreamed up was a party Jake, a celebration Jake, a fair-weather Jake. Her life was hard edges: Sam's health issues, the brutish reality of working to support herself and her son, the immutable fact of waking up every day to do all of it again, dishes and dust, crumpled homework papers left too long at the bottom of a backpack, a bed that never got warm even when you curled up and wrapped the covers tight.

This Jake knew a day could be an uphill climb.

She wasn't supposed to want either Jake. Any Jake.

She closed her eyes, because when her eyes were open, she saw a new detail every minute, a connected chain of them. The way sunlight angled through pine needles to find the brightest spots in Jake's hair, the ones that were more golden than brown. The angle of Jake's eyebrows, its echo on Sam's face. The gusts of pain that moved across Jake's face and vanished again. The way he and Sam looked at each other, when they thought the other wasn't looking back, with fascination and hunger.

With her eyes closed, she could think about consequences, about potential disasters. About the person she wanted to be, who wasn't someone concerned with consequences or potential disasters. She wanted to be someone who would seize joy and hold on tight, someone who would even, occasionally, laugh at worry. But she hadn't been that person, not since she'd gotten pregnant with Sam.

"Mom? Can we ride the Ferris wheel?"

She'd been promising Sam a ride on the ten-story Seattle Ferris wheel since it was installed last summer. But so far the timing had sucked. The timing sucked now, too. She didn't think either she or Jake would benefit from being shut up in close proximity to each other.

"Please, Mom? Please?"

On the other hand, it was a beautiful afternoon. Warm, but not hot.

The sky blazed blue, as clear as it ever got. They'd be able to see for miles. Driving here, they'd seen the mountains, Cascades to the east, Olympics to the west, framing her world in a way she'd missed in Florida. It would be hard to imagine a more gorgeous day to be ten stories above Puget Sound, gazing across to Kitsap Peninsula, the city in relief behind them.

"Okay. You don't have to come with us," she told Jake hastily, and then, not wanting to sound like she was opposed to his joining them, "You're invited, though, if you want." To Sam, she said, "We're going to eat our picnic first. Then I'll take you to the Ferris wheel."

Jake shrugged. "If I don't go with you, I have to do laundry."

But his eyes caught hers, and she understood that his feelings were not unlike her own. That he was balanced at the same strange tipping point, that he also wanted to resist, that he was doing no better a job than she was.

"I'll just need a minute before we go—I've got a gym bag at the visitor center, and I can swap legs and change my T-shirt."

"Yeah, no worries."

She pulled out the lunch she'd packed for her and Sam. She'd made too many sandwiches, because that was what she did, and she offered one to Jake.

"No, thanks," he said.

"My mom makes *really* good chicken salad," Sam said.

"Just eat it," she said, pinning him with a stare.

Something opened in Jake's face, something like, but not quite, surprise. He gave her a look. There was heat behind it, heat that sank deep and rose high and filled her fast.

"Okay, then." He said it mildly, but his eyes were still locked on hers. Her heart clamored, sending blood rushing everywhere in her body.

Then as quickly as it had happened, it was over, the connection broken. She was left with the jazzed-up, buzzy feeling of what had passed between them, the swollen warmth between her legs, the anticipation he'd started like a thrum in her veins.

Sam was looking from her face to Jake's, trying, she guessed, to read a foreign expression on his mother's face. She composed herself and handed him the sandwich.

Jake swallowed hard, which made her feel better. *I'm not the only one.*

"So tell me about your work," he said. A stab at bringing this back to small talk and a picnic lunch and two people who were supposed to keep some distance between them. "What do you do?"

She explained to him about the app she'd designed and how she was adapting it to work with the new company's website.

"That sounds pretty interesting."

"It's okay. It's a job. The best part is the shoes."

"The shoes?"

"We sell shoes. I'm—well, honestly, I'm kind of obsessed with shoes."

He tipped over and peered under the table.

Today, she was wearing a pair of Converse-style high-tops with black and white, Escher-like drawings all over them. She found herself wishing they were something sexier, like her chunky-heeled sandals with a big flower on the toe.

Also, she hoped her ass looked half as good in her jeans as his looked in his.

"Those are pretty cool," he said. "I don't know anything about shoes, and I don't give a crap, personally, about my own. I guess that's a good thing."

Silence.

Oh, right. He probably didn't do a lot of shoe shopping, given that he was still relearning how to walk. She gave him a sideways, slightly sheepish smile, and he said, "Don't worry about it. If I had a quarter for every awkward moment, I'd be rich. I don't care. You can show off your shoes to me. So your company sells shoes?"

"Yeah." She thought about her boss with a pang of anxiety. There had been no further tensions, but she felt on edge. Like she was on probation. Not unlike how her father had always made her feel, like it was only a matter of time until her less positive traits burst through. *Like your mother.*

"Hey. Way back, you know, before—"

She nodded.

"You wanted to be an illustrator. Of kids' books."

"Yeah, well. That never happened. For kind of obvious reasons."

He frowned. "You ever draw and paint anymore?"

"Nah. No time."

She'd showed him her work once, watercolors she'd done for a book that seemed, nearly a decade later, to be infantile in its simplicity. She hadn't thought much about the illustrating lately, but he was right. Once upon a time, it had been all she'd wanted to do.

She remembered so clearly: He'd looked at her drawings and paintings with such seriousness. No one had ever pored over her stuff like that, like it was beautiful, like it meant something. Like he was trying to figure out everything she'd been thinking when she'd put pencil and brush to paper.

She didn't even think she'd unpacked the box with her art supplies in it. She doubted her watercolor paints were any good anymore. Maybe she'd think about picking up some new ones. Maybe she'd dabble a little.

The sun filtered down in dribs and drabs and a breeze rustled both men's hair. She had never thought of Sam as a man until she had seen him with Jake. Jake made it possible to imagine who Sam might become. He made it easier to see who Sam was, to see the balance between the lighthearted Sam, an echo of Jake at eighteen, and the serious Sam, an echo of this Jake.

Jake made Sam make sense.

"This sandwich is really good," Jake said.

"Thank you."

He'd rested both elbows on the picnic table and she admired the ridge and groove of his biceps, the way the muscles bunched and released.

"I haven't had anything home cooked for so long. I eat a ridiculous amount of Progresso soup and beans and tuna fish."

At twenty, he'd been a marvel of engineering, power, and beauty, every inch of him thick and hard. He'd given off the sense of something tightly leashed and barely restrained in coiled muscle, held back under the tautness of his skin. Delicious.

He was leaner now, but no less beautiful.

"I could teach you how to cook." *And my motives are totally pure. Nothing to do with wanting to watch you move around my kitchen.*

"I *can* cook, believe it or not," he said. "Nothing special, but I can follow a recipe. My mom was kind of a mess, so all of us cooked. I'll cook for you sometime."

"We don't always eat takeout. These last couple of days— sometimes I'm too fried to cook."

"It must be hard work, what you do," he said.

It *was* hard, tougher than she'd expected. Exhausting, working and still having something good in her left to give to Sam at the end of the day. She got up early to make Sam's lunch and stayed up late so she could clean the house and do the laundry. And there was no one to depend on but herself.

But it was good, too, the way having a newborn was hard as hell but so, so sweet.

It had been a long time since anyone had noticed or acknowledged that about her life, and it loosened something tight in her chest. There was a gentleness to him that totally went against the man she'd seen that first day in the physical therapist's office. That went against stereotype, for sure. Of course, she'd rejected her dad's stereotypes years ago. He was convinced that soldiers were poor, uneducated grunts tricked into fighting unjust wars for a hawkish government. Vulnerable clods at best, hawks themselves at worst.

Mira's parents were peaceniks, like a lot of the people she'd grown up around. They held candles during vigils to ward off U.S. intervention in other countries and slapped pithy bumper stickers on their cars. As a kid, Mira herself had held candles in the dark, flanked by her parents, in protest.

But after Jake, she hadn't been able to bring herself to protest anymore. She'd stayed home when her parents stood on street corners and held up signs, urging cars to toot their horns, and she wouldn't let Sam go with them, either, even though he wanted to hold a sign, a candle, anything. "It's complicated," she'd said, and she had thought about Jake, somewhere, risking his life for her, for Sam, for her parents, for freedom, for the world, for better or for worse.

Maybe everything worth thinking about was complicated.

Certainly, being a soldier didn't make you cold or unfeeling. He was watching her face, waiting for her to acknowledge what he'd said.

It is hard. It was so, so hard. I missed you.

But she'd shut that weakness down in herself long ago. And how could she say that, that she'd missed him, when she'd never known him? When even now she didn't, because, as he'd said, *he didn't know himself?*

"I think it's hard to be a parent, no matter what. It was lonely sometimes." She tried a joke: "I could've used some company."

Guilt chased regret across his face. "I'm sorry."

"It's not your fault. You didn't know."

"The other kind of 'I'm sorry.' I wish you hadn't had to do all that by yourself."

She looked over at Sam, but he was dismantling his sandwich, oblivious to the fact that they were discussing him and his childhood. She wanted to ask Jake, *Do you think you really would have done things differently if you'd known?* But she couldn't bring herself to do it with Sam in earshot.

She wasn't sure she wanted to know the answer, either. What if he said no?

THEY DROVE down to the wharves and stood in line for Ferris wheel tickets, then waited their turn to go up. A fresh, salty breeze blew off Puget Sound. The sky was luminous, sparkles dancing over the surface of the water.

A ferry docked. Passengers flowed out along the walkway and into the pedestrian overpass; cars and bikes and motorcycles rolled out from the ferry's cavernous belly.

She was hyperaware of Jake, of the disruption he caused as they moved through the crowd. People stared at his leg, murmured to their friends and family. They tried to be subtle about it, but they didn't do a very good job. But Jake seemed not to notice. He stood beside her, big enough to loom. To make her feel petite, and she was not a teeny person. He was close enough for her to feel that ever-present hum that came off him, the sensation of her pheromones bouncing off his in the gap, as if they were two synapses about to spark.

Not supposed to notsupposedtonotsupposedto—

She wanted to throw it all skyward and reach for him. Right now. To turn her face into his chest, to grasp his T-shirt in her fists, to breathe the scent of him deep into her lungs, to rub herself all over him and go weak against him for the sheer mindless pleasure of having him hold her.

"Tomorrow I want to go to Bainbridge Island," Sam said, startling her out of her self-destructive reverie.

Mira had read aloud to him from the *Seattle Times* last week about Bainbridge. There was a world-class playground, designed by the island's own children. There was an ice-cream shop that specialized in blackberry and lavender and other local flavors. Right now, you could comb the island for a collection of child-sized glossy frogs painted by local artists, a scavenger hunt of sorts.

She knew *exactly* what was coming.

"Jake, do you want to—"

"Sam," she said sharply, and he looked up at her, wounded.

"Excuse us a moment," she said to Jake. She took Sam aside. "There's a rule I never told you about invitations," she said. "So it's not your fault you didn't know, but I'm going to tell you, so now you'll know. The rule is, you can't invite people to things unless you ask me first in private."

"Mom? Can I invite Jake to come with us to Bainbridge Island tomorrow?"

She almost laughed, because Sam's cravings were as unrestrained, as transparent and vivid, as hers. Instead she kissed him in the middle of his forehead, a tenderness he probably wouldn't allow for much longer. "Sam, we've just gotten to know Jake. When you've just gotten to know someone, you can't see them all the time, every day." *You can't lose your sanity, you can't lose your sense of direction.*

"How long till we can see him all the time, every day?"

He was like some kind of sea creature that hadn't grown a shell yet, so soft and squishy and vulnerable. And she desperately wanted him to stay this way forever, but she knew that he needed to grow up or he'd get stepped on. "We have to wait and see."

The thing was, it didn't matter how careful you were sometimes, because while you were busy being careful, things happened, and got out of your control. Like the way that Sam was already all set to get his heart broken.

Like the way she couldn't control the way she felt, or what she wanted so much it turned her nerve endings to sparklers.

"Grown-ups have so many rules," Sam said. "I don't want to grow up, because then I have to have all those rules."

"I hear you, Sammy." She put her hands under his armpits and counted off a silent three by wiggling him slightly. On three, he jumped into her arms, the same as he had as a two-year-old. She rarely did this anymore, because he was getting so big, but right now she needed one of his hugs where he wrapped his legs around her waist and his arms around her neck and held on like she was going to save him from drowning.

When he began to squirm in her arms, she set him down, and they walked back.

For a moment, she couldn't locate Jake in line, and she panicked.

Then she spotted him, nearly at the front of the line. He was turned so she could see his profile, and with the light behind him, it was almost a silhouette. Strong, clean, sharp. As she got closer, her heart beat faster instead of slowing down. At how physically glorious he was, how broad across the shoulders and chest, how much space he took up in line. At the guarded expression on his face, and then, when he spotted them, at the sudden warmth that broke it down.

At the surge of relief and desire her own body answered with.

It had only been a few seconds that she'd sought him with her gaze and failed to find him, but in those few seconds, she saw so much truth about this situation. She didn't trust that he was here, not in a way that mattered. Not in a way that fit how much she already liked him, how much Sam already counted on him.

What if he disappeared? What if he freaked out and couldn't deal with them, with this mysterious thing that seemed to be happening too fast for anyone to process? What if she came back today, tomorrow, next week, next month, to find him gone? Because after all, that was what had happened before.

"Hey," he said. "We're next."

The operator corralled them into the glass pod, along with a crowd of people behind them. Their car was full, so she sat with Sam on one side of her, his nose pressed against the glass, and Jake on the other. They rose off the ground and the world fell away beneath them, vast and blue, the city tilting vertiginously away.

"Oh, man!" Sam said, over and over again, while an older couple beamed at him.

Jake was still beside her, the length of his thigh hard against hers. It had turned her to liquid, made her soft and stupid. The air between them, the molecules that moved in the boundary between her skin and the rest of the world, were charged up like a science experiment, so that she was almost afraid to move. To lift her eyes.

He moved his shoulder incrementally closer to hers, and

a wave of heat broke over her. His *shoulder*. She didn't even know if the movement had been deliberate.

Fool.

The wharves stretched out below like tick marks, their details fading and then coming back into view.

"That's Bainbridge," Sam said, pointing. "That's where Mom and I are going tomorrow. It's going to be super fun. I bet people who don't go with us will be sad they didn't."

She smiled behind her hand. You could teach a seven-year-old manners, but he would always wriggle his way out from under them to pursue his own agenda.

As the pod was touching back to earth on its final round, Jake leaned close, so Sam couldn't hear, and murmured, "Let me take you guys to dinner."

Say no thank you.

"Yay, Mom!" Sam had heard anyway. When it concerned him, he found a way.

Say no thank you. Say you need to get Sam home and washed up and in his PJs or he'll fall asleep in the car on the way home and—

"Mom, please, can we?"

Tell him that's sweet of him but tomorrow's a school day and it would be irresponsible of you.

She didn't want the day to end. She didn't want him to walk away, didn't want to feel their chemistry stretch and break like a child's bubble as he stepped out of the force field. She didn't want to admire his retreating back, gauge the width of his shoulders, or distantly note the aesthetics of his butt as he retreated.

She wanted him beside her, with them, for as long as she could finagle it, and she wanted a chance to measure his shoulders and drag him against her with her own itchy palms.

They were both watching her, waiting for her answer, two pairs of identical eyes.

She answered Sam, "Sure," but she was talking to Jake, and she didn't know whether to hope, or not, that she wasn't agreeing to just dinner.

12

"Sam's asleep," Jake said. Sam's head was canted at an awkward angle, his mouth open, his face slack.

She peeked in the rearview mirror. "That was fast. We wore him out."

Jake was worn out, too, from craving. From watching her smile at Sam, at the waiter, at random people passing their table, then look at him and turn serious. Dark brown eyes on him like a touch. Like she was drinking him in, memorizing him.

She had high, strong cheekbones, pink from too much sun today. Just about the fairest skin you could have. A pixie face, a pointy chin, a slightly upturned nose.

All those things were like unconnected pieces of information his brain took in, but it was her smile that put them together. Made her beautiful. Made it impossible for him to stop staring, except when she looked back and he couldn't hold the intensity of her gaze.

This was, in a word, impossible. He couldn't be around

her and not want her, couldn't be in their lives, near her, and not have her.

She'd asked him, point blank, at the playground to help her keep this simple. For Sam. But he understood better than anyone that the kinds of emotions that Mira brought to the surface would not let him be sane or rational, not let him anywhere near *simple*.

On top of that, the path he was on with his new trainer led back to the army. The last thing he wanted was a perfect repeat of eight years ago: longing, falling, and then—like hitting bottom—being right back where they started, in too deep with him headed off to the ends of the earth.

No. He had to do his level best to be what she'd asked him to be. Sam's father, her friend, a guy who could put their needs above his irrational, gut-twisting craving for her.

"Do you want me to drop you at your place?" she asked.

The car got so quiet he could hear the rough in-and-out of Sam's breath. They were both waiting. Each for the other.

"Probably for the best," he said, at the same time she said, "I should, shouldn't I?"

They both laughed. Awkwardly.

"Keeping it simple, right?" he asked.

"Yeah."

It was silent again for a moment. "Go left here. And then right at the light," he instructed her.

She maneuvered through the downtown streets toward his apartment.

"I signed on with a trainer," he said.

"Yeah?"

"A guy whose specialty is helping soldiers with amputations get back up to speed."

"Like—back in the army?"

"Yeah," he said.

"Like, you'd fight again?"

"Well, maybe. Or a noncombat role, but active duty."

"That's cool, Jake. I didn't even know—"

She broke off, and he saved her. "Yeah, it's getting more common. Anyway, something I'm exploring. But—another reason for keeping things simple, right?"

"Right," she said.

They were quiet for a bit. Then he asked, "Mira?"

"Uh-huh?"

"Who's Aaron?"

She sighed. "Did Sam mention Aaron?"

"Yeah."

"What did he say?"

"That Aaron was a friend of yours, and his. That he sometimes plays Forbidden Island with him, which I assumed was a board game."

"I dated him when I was living in Florida."

"Was it serious?"

She hesitated. "Yeah, I guess you could say that."

Something tilted and fell in his chest. Not that he was allowed to give a fuck, because they were—as they'd just established for the thousandth time—keeping things simple. But still. He'd kind of hoped she'd dismiss Aaron with a wave of her hand.

"We might have gotten married if I'd stayed in Florida. I thought I was in love with him. But it would have been a mistake for me. Sometimes I think I came here partly because my subconscious knew it wasn't—*enough*."

He found himself feeling sorry for the guy, whoever he

was. And, yeah, there was jealousy, too. Because that guy had kissed her and held her and . . .

Again and again.

Whew, that was quite a parade of visuals his brain had mustered up for him. And substituted him in Aaron's place. And hell, since this was a fantasy, he also had two good legs and the ability to hoist her up against the wall and go to town.

"Take a right up there. That's a tough way to break up with someone. Tough on you, I mean. A three-thousand-plus-mile move."

"I felt like I couldn't grow up there. My parents were taking care of me and Sam in a way that made me feel like I'd never graduated from high school. And Aaron was priming himself to take over the role. We would have moved right in with him and become his pets, effectively."

"I can't imagine you as anyone's pet. You've got too many opinions."

"But that's the thing. I didn't, there. I'd never gotten in the habit of it. My dad and my stepmom were the ones with the opinions, and I just kind of—I was like a kid. And they thought Aaron was great. Aaron was someone my dad had met through woodworking. He introduced us, and he kept on bringing him around until—until I think it was inevitable that we were together." She hesitated. "The reason I left—I found out my dad was giving Aaron money. For dates and things, and to buy me gifts."

"Jesus," he said.

"It was the last straw. When you and I were—after you left, I made a break. Figured out how to get myself to art school. But then—things got complicated with Sam, and then I needed my parents' help. Pride wasn't that important anymore, and before I knew it, there we were, living with them, and it wasn't so bad, most days. But it was the last straw, finding out my dad had been orchestrating things. Like I couldn't even run my own romantic life. I'd been seriously thinking about moving in with Aaron to get away from my father, and it felt like—it felt like there was nowhere to go, there. So I came out here. But I promised myself that I'd let some time pass before I got involved with anyone, to prove I could take care of Sam all on my own. So there you have it. That's my 'keep it simple.'"

"Last building on the right," he said, and she pulled up to the curb.

He wanted to ask her up to his cruddy little apartment with its rails and other accommodations, but Sam was sleeping in the back and they'd given each other too many good reasons why this couldn't happen.

She reached out her hand and touched his knee. The touch resonated, vibrations up his thigh, a tightening in his balls. An ache in the middle of his chest.

"I had such a good time today," she said.

"Me, too." He couldn't have lied, couldn't have held himself back, couldn't have kept the emotion and truth out of his voice, if she'd paid him. He'd had more fun today than he'd had in years. She was possibly the easiest person to talk to that he'd ever met.

And God, he wanted her.

Which meant the only good and right thing he could do was grab his gym bag, swing his door open, thank her again, and get the hell out of there.

13

M ira's phone vibrated on the wide conference table. She was in a meeting with the team that was working toward the handbags and belts launch. It felt like it had been going on for days, instead of hours. She knew she was supposed to feel grateful for this opportunity, was supposed to feel like it was the pinnacle of what she'd been working toward, but to be honest, she was having trouble concentrating at all. She reached for the phone, grateful for a diversion.

It was the babysitter, Cindy.

She got up and went into the hallway to answer it. "Hello?"

"Mira?"

The tone of the babysitter's voice made Mira's heart pound. It was whispered, faint, hysterical.

"What's wrong?" Adrenaline surged in her blood.

"I'm so, so, so sorry," the babysitter said. "I would never call you if it wasn't serious—nothing's wrong with Sam. God, I should have said that first."

Mira drew her first full breath since she'd heard Cindy's voice.

"I'm so sorry," Cindy said again.

"Is it the house?" Mira's heart pounded. She didn't like the way Cindy sounded, as if she didn't want to be heard. What if it was a home invasion? What if they were being held at gunpoint?

Calm down. She would have called the police, not you.

"It's not the house," Cindy said. "It's my stupid ex-boyfriend. He's here. And he's drunk, and I can't get him to leave. We're in the upstairs bathroom with the door locked."

Oh, *God.* Sam. "Do you think he's dangerous?"

The silence on the other end of the phone was too long.

"Cindy?"

Cindy was crying, small, almost silent sobs. "He's never hurt me, but the stuff he's saying—it's pretty crazy, and he's got a foul mouth, and—this is all my *fault.*" Her voice rose to a wail, and Mira felt herself wanting to shush the girl. *Shhh, quiet—don't let him know you're on the phone with me.*

"I'm calling the police," Mira said.

She heard sniffling on the other end. "He's got a possession record. They'll—"

"I'm putting you on hold," Mira said. She called the police and explained the situation, giving her address and her cell number.

She kept picturing some huge enraged man rampaging around her house, threatening her son, scaring the crap out of him. Police barging in, a showdown, scaring Sam even worse.

She'd never felt so helpless in her life.

She switched back over to Cindy. "I'll be right there," she

said, but as she said it, she knew it wasn't true. Even if she left now, she was on the east side and it could take her, assuming normal traffic, as much as forty-five minutes to reach them.

Haley poked her head into the hallway and gave her a meaningful look. *We need you in here.*

Her head felt like it was going to explode. Her anxiety about Sam had crowded out everything else, but she knew how much Haley wanted her to impress the other people at this meeting. For Mira's sake, and for Haley's own, because— as she'd reminded Mira many times over the last week— she'd gone to bat for her with these people, and this meeting was Mira's chance to make Haley look brilliant.

Not that that mattered when Sam's well-being was at stake, but it sucked.

"Can you put Sam on the phone?"

There was a shuffling noise and Sam's breathing.

"Hi, Sam."

"Hi, Mom. There's a weird guy here."

"Cindy's gonna take care of you," Mira told him, wishing she could hug him, wishing she could hold him.

What she wouldn't give for Jake right now. For someone familiar and competent to be Sam's advocate, to focus on Sam's needs.

Maybe . . .

Probably it was a terrible idea, but it was the best one she had right then. "Sam, put Cindy back on."

"Hello?"

"I'm going to call Sam's—"

She'd been about to say Sam's father, before she thought twice about the advisability of outing Jake to a near-stranger that way. "A friend of mine. I'm going to see if he can get there faster. I bet he can get there in fifteen minutes if he takes a cab."

She hung up with Cindy and called him. Her heart sped up while the phone rang. It had been three weeks since their Seattle outing, three weeks during which she hadn't heard a peep out of him. During which she'd kept putting Sam off, telling him they'd see Jake soon, they'd make a date to go to Bainbridge on the ferry together, she promised, soon, maybe next weekend . . .

Jake had texted her a couple of times with possible activities for him to do with Sam, but she'd made up excuses. Too many excuses—his last few replies had broadcast his irritation. *I'd grab Sam fast,* he'd texted last time. *You wouldn't even have to talk to me.*

He answered, "'lo?"

"It's Mira."

"Hey." Not unfriendly, but not brimming with joy, either. She deserved that.

"Sam's in a situation, and I think you can get to him faster than I can. I'm on the east side. If you take a cab, I think you can be there in ten or fifteen."

"What's going on?"

She explained the whole situation to him as quickly and succinctly as she could.

"I'm on my way."

"Thank you." Her voice was thick with gratitude and the need to cry. "I'm an hour behind you. Maybe less if I drive fast."

"Be careful."

She hung up the phone and took a moment to compose herself. *I'm on my way.*

What she had longed for all those years.

A knight in shining armor, galloping off to her rescue. So tempting, so much the fulfillment of her every fantasy.

He wasn't her knight, though. He was Sam's. He hadn't answered the phone all eager to do her bidding, ready to slay whatever dragon she'd presented. But he would slay dragons for Sam in a heartbeat.

Haley came into the hallway. "What's going on? They've got a question for you about whether it'll work for scarves, too."

"I just got a call from my babysitter," Mira said.

But before she could say anything else, Haley said, "Not the babysitter again."

Her heart kicked up, hard. Bad enough that Sam was in danger, bad enough she couldn't get there as fast as she wanted, but *fuck*, did this have to be yet another thing that was going to screw her at work? "There's a situation."

"There always is, isn't there?"

She should have known Haley wouldn't be sympathetic.

"I teed up this meeting for you, Mira. This is your chance to knock 'em dead."

And, Haley's expression clearly added, *your chance not to piss me off epically*.

"My son is in trouble, Haley."

Her voice was surprisingly strong and steady, and Haley's glare wavered.

"I've said it before, Mira, but I mean it this time. This is the last time this can happen. Or you're fired." Haley turned and headed back into the conference room.

Mira stood for a moment, as if caught mid-decision, but of course, there was no decision. When it came to Sam, there had never been a choice for her.

She headed out to her car, dialing Cindy as she went. "I'm on my way."

14

The twenty minutes between when he answered Mira's phone call and when the cab pulled up in front of her house were the longest of Jake's life, and that was saying something, because being a good soldier was all about waiting.

There was a cop car out front. Jake scouted around the outside of the house, trying to get the lay of the land. He couldn't see anything obviously amiss, and he couldn't hear anything from inside.

He pounded on the front door, which was opened by a uniformed officer, round-faced, middle-aged. "I'm—"

He'd been about to say, "I'm Sam's dad," but that would have been a whole long, complicated thing. Where the officer would ask Sam, "Is this guy your dad?" and Sam would say no, and then there would be suspicion and complication and explaining.

"Jake Taylor. I take care of Sam sometimes."

The police officer gave him a look, and Jake sighed. "You can call Sam's mom," he said.

The cop accepted Jake's outstretched phone, radioed to the station for the number Mira had given them, and called her. Jake couldn't hear much of the conversation, only the timbre of Mira's voice spiking out of the cell phone periodically. He itched all over to get inside to Sam, but he waited patiently. Being a hothead wasn't going to make this go any faster.

The cop nodded a few times, hung up the phone, and opened the door wide to admit Jake. "Officer Fredricksen," he said as Jake went by, and Jake acknowledged the intro with a nod.

Sam and the girl were in the living room. This time Jake knew to anticipate the impact and braced himself against the door frame, so he kept his balance when Sam hurtled himself into his arms. Sam was crying. "Where's my mom?" he asked. "Where's my mom?"

"She's on her way," Jake said.

"There was a guy—"

"Shh. I know, bud." His heart thudded in his chest, rattling his ribs like something in a cage, too big for the space. "He's gone."

"The police came and took him away and I wanted them to leave, too, but they wouldn't until you got here—"

"You're okay now. I'm here."

His chest ached. Bad. He wrapped the boy tighter and felt his sobs start to calm to hiccups. It hurt in Jake's jaw, and ears, too, as if those sobs had gotten into his head.

"Thank you," Jake said to the tear-streaked babysitter over Sam's head. "You can go home now. I'm sorry this happened to you."

She hesitated.

He pulled out his wallet and handed her two twenties. "Get some rest."

She was sniffling. "Should I come back tomorrow?"

"No," Jake said. "No, we're all set."

"Should I ask Mira?"

"I'll have her give you a call and you can talk to her about it, okay?"

She looked like she wanted to protest, but she didn't have it in her. She was too young to be in this kind of situation, too young to be in charge of a seven-year-old all day, and too young to have an ex-boyfriend who was such a jerk. He felt sorry for her. But he also wanted her out of there.

He was sure Mira would agree, but if she didn't, he'd do his level best to convince her. He wished he'd fought harder when she'd texted him to say he didn't need to finish out the week with Sam. He wished he'd talked her into letting him sit until she found someone she was crazy about to take his place. Instead, he'd let the complexity of his own feelings get in the way of his ability to take care of Sam.

He wouldn't do it again. This was no crazier than the situation of most divorced parents, and dads did a perfectly good job of sticking around and delivering childcare even when they'd been booted out of the marriage bed. There had to be a lot of bruised egos under those circumstances. A lot of guys who still wanted to be getting laid who weren't. But that didn't keep them from doing the dad thing.

"Tell Mira I'm sorry—"

"I will." Jake had tucked his head down next to Sam's. He heard her open and close the front door, heard her talking to the cop on the stoop, and put his nose against Sam's warm, wet cheek. Sam clutched him.

The cop came in. "I'm going to take her home. I'm going to need Sam's mom's statement. Have her call the station."

"Will do," Jake said. "Thanks."

"Welcome." The cop went out the front door, and Jake heard the sound of his car pulling away.

He hugged Sam tighter.

"You're okay, dude," he said.

"It was *scary*."

"You were brave. You were a soldier."

"I was?"

"Yeah. Can I tell you something?"

Sam nodded, all big wet eyes and occasional hiccupy shudders.

"Some people think being brave means not being afraid."

"It doesn't?"

"No. Being brave means being afraid and *still* doing what you want to do or have to do."

It means sending a guy home from combat if you know he's not fit, a voice in his head said. *Even if he's your friend. Even if he begs you to give him another chance.*

Shut the fuck up, he told the voice, but not before that same reptile part of his brain supplied him with the look of the platoon sergeant's face when he visited Jake in the hospital, when the cold, hard knot of knowledge that Mike was dead took permanent root somewhere between gut and heart. *Because you were too afraid to do what had to be done.*

"But I didn't want to or have to do anything," Sam said.

"Sometimes it's not a big thing that you want to do or have to do," Jake said. "Sometimes staying put when things are scary is the hardest part. You stayed in that bathroom with your babysitter and you listened to what she told you to do, and that was what you needed to do today. And you did it even though you were scared, so that makes you brave."

Sam got a faraway look on his face. "Do you think I could be a soldier someday?"

Oh, God, Mira was going to kill him.

He thought hard about his answer. "I think you would make a very good soldier if you decided that was what you wanted to do. But there are a lot of good things to do in the world, and being a soldier is definitely not the only way to be brave."

"Is it the best way?"

I used to think so. "No. There's no one best way."

"What are some other ways?"

"Cops are brave. Firefighters."

He thought of Mira. He didn't know shit about childbirth other than what he'd seen in movies, but it didn't seem like it could be any easier than combat. "Moms are brave."

"Dads, too," Sam said. "My dad is brave. If he were here, he would have done the same thing you did. He would have come and gotten me out of the bathroom."

He almost said it. He almost said, "I'm your dad, Sam."

But Sam had had enough for one day. He didn't want to break the boy's little brain. Or have Mira walk into the middle of a shitstorm.

"I'm really hungry," Sam said. "I didn't have lunch."

Oh, Jesus. It was almost three now. The kid had been locked in a bathroom for an hour, starving. "I'll make you some lunch."

Sam wrapped his arms around Jake's neck and squeezed. "Is my mom coming soon?"

"She's on her way."

"I'm glad you came. I'm less scared with you here."

The irony of this struck Jake, suddenly. Because he was ten times more scared because Sam was in the world than he'd been before he'd known. Because shit like this happened, because there were madmen and unexpected dangers, because sometimes no one got there in time. Because there were terrorists and acts of destruction, and that was before you took into account things like the Cascadia, the mammoth earthquake that would someday, without warning, split the earth nearly under Sam's house.

He'd heard guys talk about having a wife and kids at home, and he knew they were more fearful for it. It was one thing to know you might die, and another thing to know you were stranding the people you loved, the ones who counted on you. That was part of why he had never wanted a family.

He wondered how much that had entered into Mike's freak-out. Mike had a wife and kids at home, and maybe he hadn't been able to stop thinking about them when he was supposed to be fighting. Maybe that was what he'd been thinking about that day in the truck when he hadn't slammed his foot down on the gas in response to Jake's command, when he'd stared, frozen in space. When he'd delivered them all like sitting ducks into the maw of that explosion.

He led Sam downstairs to the kitchen and got out some bread and cheese to make him a grilled cheese sandwich. Sam sat at the table, swinging his legs and watching. He was hiccuping only occasionally now, and he hummed a little, something he did, Jake had noticed, when he was happy. Man, kids were resilient. He wondered how traumatized Sam would be by what had happened today. He wondered what he'd remember most vividly, whether he'd imprinted the inside of the bathroom the way Jake had imprinted the inside of that goddamned truck. The reptile brain thinking, *This is my tomb*, before the higher-order mind could even register, *Danger*.

He heard Mira's car outside, and part of him wanted to flee. Because he didn't think he could deal with how big her emotions were going to be.

Because he didn't want to see her face—the worry, the suffering. The loveliness. He didn't *want* to want to wrap her up. He didn't *want* to want to comfort, succor, soothe. He didn't want the ache in his chest or his balls.

She came into the kitchen and flung her arms around Sam. Jake personally would have played it a little lower key, given that Sam had recovered from his ordeal and was distracted. But Sam didn't seem to mind. He buried his face in Mira's chest and said, "Mom."

Just that. Like it was its own mantra.

Jake hadn't had much of that in his life as a kid. But his mom had woken up in the last five years and been there for him. Care packages in the army, letters, emails, and then— so many days, such a long vigil beside his bed in the hospital.

Stay alive. That's my request.

For the first time, Jake registered fully that for his mother, his prosthetic leg was not the end of everything. It was the visible manifestation of the greatest blessing, an amazing escape.

And sometime in the last few weeks, sometime between when he'd felt the wind rush past his face as he ran with Sam and now, it had ceased to be the end of everything for him, too.

He made himself look at Mira's face. At her relief, at her unveiled, unabashed love.

She was examining Sam now, scrutinizing his face, touching his arms and legs. "Everything okay? Sam, are you okay?"

"I'm fine." Sam had clearly decided he was going to play the tough guy now, Jake observed with some amusement. He'd done all his crying in Jake's lap, and now he was going to pretend to be all man for his mother. Jake couldn't blame him. He probably would have done the same thing as an almost-eight-year-old, not that his mom had been much for Band-Aids and wiping away tears.

In fact, that's what he'd do in a minute when Mira turned her attention to him to ask what had happened. He'd be all male nonchalance too.

"Did the police want to talk to me?" She tipped her face up to look at him. Cheeks pink, mouth red, skin porcelain. He could see down her blouse, and he made himself not look.

"Yeah," he said. "They want your statement. I told Cindy to go home. I told her you'd call her if you wanted her to come back."

She sighed. "Crap. I can't believe I have to look for yet another sitter. This is absurd."

"You don't need another sitter. You have me."

A look crossed her face that might have been relief. Then she shook her head. "I don't need you."

He felt a surge of desire for her. Because she wasn't afraid of anything. Because she gave as good as she got.

Because the curve of her breasts inside that silky shirt was like a promise and a dare.

"I can watch Sam." He crossed his arms.

"I don't think—"

"I can watch Sam," he repeated. He used the voice he'd used when his guys had tried to argue with him. The *don't bother* voice.

"Mom—"

She silenced Sam with a hard look, then turned it on him. Eyes narrowed in a way that shouldn't have made his heart rate pick up but did. "This is my decision."

He wouldn't want her to be any other way, he thought. He wouldn't want his son's mother to be meek and obedient.

"Of course it's your decision," he said quietly.

She turned away, into the corner, as if the answer were written there. Then she turned back. "Okay," she said. "But it's just for a few more weeks. The rest of the summer. After that, Sam goes back to school, and then he's in before- and after-school programs."

"Deal," he said. "Now. Sit down and put your feet up. I'm cooking you guys dinner tonight."

15

She frowned at him. "Um, what ever happened to 'Mind if I stay for dinner?' or 'Hey, Mira, how would you feel about me cooking you dinner?'"

"Not my style."

"And rolling over and showing my pale white belly isn't mine," she said, and then was sorry, because he shot her a look that made her pale white belly, and parts south, flame.

The thing was, she wanted him here. She knew Sam would want him here. And besides, the stress of the day had exhausted her, and she loved the idea of not having to cook.

"Thanks for asking, Jake. I'd love it if you cooked us some dinner."

He grinned, and she could see from his expression that he felt like he'd won a round. *Damn him.*

"My kitchen isn't exactly well-stocked. I do have some cubes of beef in the freezer. I was going to make a stew at some point, and then I didn't."

"I'll make chili."

"Where'd you learn to make chili?" She was trying to picture him cooking for other soldiers.

"My mom taught me. When I was a kid. It's been a long time, but I think I remember. We had it a lot in my house, and whenever we ate it, I made it. Besides, it's one of those things you can't ruin. You can throw in pretty much everything in the entire kitchen and it works out somehow. It has to simmer a while, though."

"We could play a board game," Sam offered.

Jake tilted his head to ask Mira, *Okay?*

"Sure," she said.

"Monopoly." Sam ran to get it.

Mira groaned. "He's going to beat us."

"I don't believe it," Jake said.

"He's gonna take us *down*."

"Nah," Jake said. "I might, though. Take you. Down."

His eyes were still on her face. Considering. His smile spreading a little.

She felt color flood her face, sudden heat, and she saw him register it, his pupils widening, one eyebrow diving.

She wasn't sure whether or not they were still talking about a Monopoly game. She only knew she wanted him to keep looking at her that way, as if he had a specific, dirty plan for her.

Uh-oh.

Sam came back with Monopoly.

"I'll get the chili going; then we can play," Jake told him.

"Go read in the living room for a bit," Mira said, and Sam went.

Mira watched Jake as he browned beef and cut up onions, admiring his ropy forearms, his strong, serviceable hands.

She watched the bunch and movement of muscle under his T-shirt as he opened cans of tomato products and beans, the way he strode from corner to corner in search of ingredients and tools as if he owned the place. It was the same way he'd kissed her, with mastery. Without hesitation.

She wondered if that was how she was when she painted. She'd taken out her watercolors and paper the day after he kissed her, as if being with him had reminded her of her long-ago lost self. She'd covered the kitchen table with paper and spread out the tubes, setting Sam up across from her with his own kiddie row of paints.

"What are you drawing, Mommy?" he'd asked.

"I'm not sure."

She'd made some sketches, but none of them satisfied her.

She had put the paints away without using them. But she'd taken them out every night since, after Sam had gone to bed.

While the chili cooked, they played Monopoly—which Sam indeed won—and then Munchkin, an absurd card game that made Sam belly laugh and Jake smile a near-full smile that twisted her heart.

The chili was amazing—rich, thick, and tomatoey. Not too spicy, the meat falling-apart tender. She eyed Jake covetously as he spooned chili into his mouth. Hunched over slightly, as if he'd had one too many army meals he'd had to eat quickly, ravenously, shoulders working, forearms lean and twice as edible as the dinner. The way he ate was not so different from the way he'd kissed her, like she was something he had to get enough of before she got snatched away from him.

Jake had made cornbread, too, which they slathered with butter and honey, and she ate so much of it there was an ache high up in her stomach. She'd read once somewhere that if your body wanted something it couldn't have, it would compensate with excessive hunger in other areas, which was why it was important to get plenty of sleep and drink plenty of water and have plenty of sex if you wanted to lose weight.

Or conversely, important to get lots of sleep and eat well if you wanted to resist sexual temptation.

She ate another piece of cornbread, but it didn't fill the hollow spots.

Because he'd cooked dinner, she made him chocolate chip cookies. When she took them out of the oven, he ate them straight off the cookie sheet, the soft cookies sagging over his fingers, chocolate everywhere. He licked his fingers clean and it was too much, the juxtaposition of her two hungers. She had to not look or she'd be sucking chocolate off him before she got Sam into bed.

She had to get rid of him before that. That was going to be the key, if he was going to babysit and she was going to keep things platonic between them. No inviting him to stay for takeout, no sending Sam upstairs to brush his teeth. No dangerous moments together like the one that had led to that ill-advised, wonderful kiss.

"Well," she said, pushing her chair back, rising from the table. "Thank you. Thank you for everything today. For coming to our rescue and making us dinner, and—"

"Sam," Jake interrupted.

"Yeah?"

"Go brush your teeth and get ready for bed, please."

She glared at Jake, but he gave her a smug smile and waved Sam off.

"That wasn't your place," she said, when Sam had gone.

"You were trying to get rid of me," he said. And he gave her the same look he'd given her when she'd accidentally mentioned rolling onto her back and showing him her vulnerable parts. Said vulnerable parts tingled, hot and fierce, like the traitors to the cause they were. "Do you want to get rid of me?"

"Yes," she said.

"Really?" He pushed his chair back and stood, and she had to retreat.

"Yes. We talked about why this can't happen. You've got places to go and enemies to shoot. I've got a life to make for myself and Sam."

"This doesn't have to disrupt any of that. This can be Sam, and sex. It doesn't have to be more complicated than that."

The way he was looking at her was melting her resolve. Quickly.

"I don't think it works that way," she said. "I think we tried that once. I don't think we do simple. We do complicated."

"We're older now. Smarter."

"No," she said. "I don't think so. I think we make each other stupid."

He was in her space now, backing her up. She could feel the heat of his body. Smell soap and musk, which called to the most primitive part of her brain: *You want this.*

"Fine," he said. "Let's be stupid."

16

H e took her hand. Threaded his fingers through hers. She made a noise. "It's just holding hands," she said. "But it's totally messing with me."

"Yeah." He moved his fingers between hers, and that, too, he felt everywhere—all over the surface of his skin.

"What is it?"

"I don't know."

"I've had sex that isn't this good."

She startled a laugh out of him, and she turned her head to look at him. "Did you just laugh?"

"I did. Isn't that allowed?"

"You don't do it much."

"I haven't felt like laughing in a long time."

"Well, then, I'm flattered. But I'm still going to kick you out."

"No, you're not," he said.

"Jake—"

"Come here," he said, and pulled her in.

He kissed her.

Friction. Heat. Pressure. And the sweet, silky feel of her mouth opening under his, of her tongue teasing his. A slick back and forth, a satisfying slide, a request, a demand, an ode to whatever current ran between them and always had. A heated rush for union, a dive into the deep, dark heart of stupid. He was bent on showing her exactly how stupid he was. How stupid they were going to be.

And how fucking great it was going to feel.

He was like some kind of short-fused missile right now, his control a rope slipping out, scraping his hands as it played. Or maybe it was just the alchemy of Mira. The flowery scent of her hair, and the softness of it against his face. The curves of her body, pressing his in all the right places, activating some primal *grab* impulse that made his hands range over the surface of her clothing, finding secret passages under hems.

She lifted her face, exposing the pale line of her throat, and he kissed her there, kissed down her throat and the bare expanse of her chest, journeyed back up to kiss her mouth again because he craved it, craved the heat, the avidness of her response, the way her breath quickened and her hands sought him, the way his sought her. It was impossible to deny. He wanted to lift her up so he could notch himself there, but he was afraid of losing his balance and dropping her.

He hated the sensation of being afraid. He always had, but he'd tolerated it when the thing he feared was death. Fearing himself was intolerable.

"Jake?"

Now it was a question. *Where'd you go?*

He'd gone back into his head. Just for a second.

And she knew somehow. She knew well enough that she

said, "Come back." And put both her hands behind his skull, her fingers weaving into his hair, and pulled him into the currents where the chatter faded into the dull roar of *want*. Kiss after kiss, quick ones now so they could breathe and moan and touch each other's faces with a dreamy, early wonder.

Then:

"Mommy!"

A small but demanding voice from upstairs.

She pulled away. Breathless, flushed. Gorgeous. All wrong. All right.

"Mommy, did you *forget*? I need you to snuggle me."

She laughed. He couldn't. He was wound too tight around what they'd been doing. He craved more. More of her.

"I'd better go tuck him in," she said, still breathing hard, smiling at him.

"I'll leave," he said.

She scrutinized him. He wanted to look away. He wanted to hide under something so she couldn't look into his eyes with that peculiar penetration.

"No. Please don't. Unless you want to."

He did and he didn't.

He wanted to stay, to find out what happened next. Where else she was as soft and yielding as her mouth. How else she could use those hands. Who would direct their bodies, how they'd cling, where they'd move. The first removal of an article of clothing.

How far this could, and would, go.

And he wanted to leave. To slip out from under the layers of complication already piling up. *Sam, and sex,* he'd said. But really? Could it happen that way?

And if it could, if he could make this only the scratching of an itch, would he?

He wasn't sure.

As usual, since the blast had rearranged his world, he had no idea what he wanted.

"I don't know," he confessed.

"Then stay, okay? Just sit there a minute. I'll put him to bed, and we'll—we'll figure it out."

He knew his eyes were giving him away, showing her all his doubts, his confusion. "Will we?"

"Maybe it's simpler than you think."

"Maybe it's more complicated than you think."

She smiled. "Maybe the truth's somewhere in the middle."

"Go," he said. "Put Sam to bed."

"Will you be here when I come back downstairs?"

He regarded her for a moment. Her gaze was steady on his. She was a brave woman. None of what she'd done to raise a child alone could have been easy. None of what she was doing now, flirting with his broken spirit, testing the boundary line where complicated bled into disastrous, was easy. But she was doing it.

He wanted to know her better. He wanted to know what she'd be like under fire.

He wanted to know what she'd be like under *him*.

Most of all, he wanted to be honest with her.

"What if 'probably' is the best I can do right now?"

She smiled, such a full, generous smile that it cracked a sheet of ice right behind his ribs. "I can handle that."

She went upstairs, feeling tugged in two. One part of her needed to be there for Sam, craved the nightly ritual, sitting at the side of his bed, running her fingers through his too-long bangs, soothing her fingers over his forehead until his blinks got longer and longer, as they had when he was a newborn.

The other part worried that Jake would disappear again. All day she'd waited for him to retreat into the foxhole like he had after their kitchen kiss. She wasn't at all sure he'd be there when she went back downstairs.

She wasn't sure if she wanted him to be.

She knew it was crazy to imagine he could somehow fill the hole he'd left. That he could come home to a family he'd never claimed. Never, for that matter, been offered.

The question was, could she take what she wanted from him without getting hurt?

Her brain whispered caution, but her body bellowed, *You need this.* Her longing for him drowned out common sense.

"Mommy, is Jake still here?"

Sam lay in bed with his covers pulled up to his nose, only those blue-gray eyes—Jake's eyes—peeking out.

She sat on the edge of his bed and smoothed his hair back. "I think so."

"Is he going to sleep over?"

She hesitated.

"Probably not," she hazarded. "I don't know him very well. You have to be good friends with someone to have a sleepover."

Sex ed for seven-year-olds.

"But you were good friends with Aaron and Aaron never slept over."

She touched his cheek, smooth and soft. "Oh, Sam." She kissed his nose, then his forehead. Both cheeks. The feel of his cheek on her lips still had the power to make her teary. She wondered if that would ever change. Someday that cheek would be rough and stubbled. Would she still be able to recapture the feeling of kissing her baby? Would she still remember the satiny sensation of his face under the pad of her thumb?

Time went fast. Eight years ago she'd been a teenager, choked with the feeling of the world wanting to get inside her. Determined to shake off parental control. Eight years from now, Sam would be a teenager, bent on making the same kind of trouble.

"Just because a thing is true in one direction doesn't mean it's true in the other. You should always be good friends with someone before you have a sleepover, but that doesn't mean that because you're good friends with them you have to have a sleepover."

"But you didn't answer why Aaron didn't."

Smart boy. Damn.

"Grammy and Grampy weren't the biggest fans of sleepover parties," she told him. Even though toward the end there, her father probably would have begged for her to have Aaron sleep over if it would make her stay. If it would somehow convince her to marry him and settle permanently in Fort Myers.

Sam wrinkled his nose, as if piecing together the adult lessons he'd learned. "Could *I* have Jake for a sleepover? Because he's my good friend. He came and helped me out today."

She laughed, but this line of conversation made her nervous. The excitement, the sizzle, of being with Jake had worn off, leaving her with damp, cooling panties and a mother's anxiety. This situation was a dangling piano, waiting to fall. Jake had been totally up front with her from the beginning. He'd told her he was damaged, fearful. He had told her he was bad for her. Bad for Sam. He'd told her he wanted to go back to the fight if he could, told her flat out that he might not stick around. What kind of idiot wouldn't listen to those warning signs?

What kind of mother wouldn't listen to them?

"Sam, Jake is just a babysitter right now. Okay? Babysitters come and go. Like do you remember Maura, who watched you a couple of times? It was fun playing with her, but then she had to stop coming. It might be like that with Jake. He might come a few times, then we might get a different babysitter."

She tried to think about how that would translate for her. *He might get laid and move on.*

She didn't like that. Not at all.

Maybe it would be better if he was gone when she went downstairs.

She kissed Sam again, naming the body parts as she went. "Forehead. Cheek, cheek. Nose. Chin. I love you, buddy."

"G'night, Mommy."

"G'night, Sammy."

She pushed the edge of his comforter more securely between the bed and wall, then turned and went out, shutting off his light. At the top of the stairs, she hesitated.

Do I hope he's down there, or that he's not?

Her mind had no answer for her.

She went downstairs. She could hear him pacing. There was only the slightest unevenness to his tread—as if his weight didn't come down as heavily on the artificial leg as the natural one. Her heart contracted, not quite a leap, not quite a palpitation. Something wedged halfway between anticipation and fear.

He was in the kitchen, wiping the table clean with a sponge. He set the sponge down. "I'm still here," he said. There was a question in his tone and on his face.

Something unfurled in her chest, like the release right before tears.

17

She looked different. Relaxed. A little rumpled, as if from the mere proximity to a bed. He wanted to rumple her more.

"Yeah. You're still here."

They stood facing each other. He wasn't sure where things went now. It had seemed more possible, before she went upstairs, to pick up again where they'd left off. Now complications loomed again.

"Let me get you another beer."

He nodded, and she went to the fridge, pulled out two beers, and poured them. He could get used to the frosted stein thing. Maybe he should buy himself a set. Or just spend more time at her place.

It was disturbingly easy to contemplate.

"Couch?"

They took their beers into the living room and sat at either end of the couch. She tucked herself into the corner in a way that was so wholly feminine, it made him want to smile.

"Your kid's cute," he said, to give himself a little space.

She shook her head and smiled. "He's your kid, too."

"You did all the hard work."

The whole childbirth thing was an act of heroism, women humping thirty pounds on their fronts, down low where it had to beat the shit out of your lower back. Passing a bowling ball between their legs. And then, in Mira's case, being a single mom. As for his own mom . . .

She'd let him down. Sometimes. Often. Drunk when he'd needed her, cringing when he desperately wanted her to stand up for herself. But other times she'd hung in and shielded him as best she could and she'd given some normalcy to his childhood, cooking dinners and tucking him into bed and—when sober—helping him get his homework done, which was way more than he could say for his dad. And after his dad died, she'd gotten it together. Quit drinking, started managing one of the shops in the Oregon beach town where she lived. She'd rebuilt herself quite handily.

Not a saint, but there was some heroism to her, too.

She had a grandson she'd never met.

"I'd love to take Sam down to the Oregon coast sometime, to meet my mom. Once we tell him. If we decide to tell him, that is."

"God," she said. "I sort of forgot. I forgot this means Sam has a whole other family. You have siblings, too, right?"

"Yeah. He should meet his aunt and uncle, too. I've got a sister in Vancouver, Washington, and a brother in Portland, who has two kids. So, a boy and a girl cousin."

"I don't have brothers or sisters," Mira said. "Sam doesn't have cousins. Until now, I mean. Except, I guess, he's had them all along, right? Only not known it. How weird is that?"

"I'm going down tomorrow, and my brother and sister are coming to the beach house, but that's pretty short notice. Maybe in a couple of weeks. You could come with us. It's beautiful down there."

He imagined building a sand castle with Sam, with buckets and an army-issue shovel and a small U.S. flag to fly from the ramparts the way they had when they'd visited the Oregon coast as kids. He imagined walking on the beach with Mira at night while his mother kept watch over a sleeping Sam. Tending a bonfire on the beach, his arm tight around her, her face lit by the flickering flames, eyes aglow.

"We'd have to tell him the truth, though, right?" Her expression was deeply wary.

"Yeah. When we're ready."

Mira pulled the beer mug up to her breasts, where he wanted to bury his face, and regarded him for a moment. He felt the question before it came, a rush of dread in his stomach.

"I don't know if it's a really bad question, and you don't have to answer it, but will you tell me what happened to your leg?"

He wanted not to answer at all. He wanted to shake his head, reject the question like a pitcher brushing off a catcher's signals. *Damn straight it's a really bad question.*

"I don't tell this story much."

"You don't have to," she said again.

But they both knew he'd tell it. She was leading him along, tugging him deeper. One bargain with the devil after another, each feeling negotiable because it was only a baby step, until he would realize that the hillside had slid out from under him, that there was no terra firma left.

Of course there had never been terra firma. Not *since*. There were only these baby steps—somewhere. Into the dark.

"We were on our way to a training exercise. We were supposed to teach some Afghan soldiers how to storm an empty building. That's mostly what we were doing there, trying to train the Afghans to fight their own war. We were heading north toward Kandahar. A bunch of kids blocked our progress. Blocked the road."

He couldn't tell the story without seeing it. The rough surface you could barely call a road, the skinny kids in their motley mix of traditional and Western clothes, the movie advancing, herky-jerky, slow mo, then in a vivid forward rush, the mind's collection of images before trauma. Dust on everything, in everything, all the time, the scent of that dust, like ash and metal, mingling with diesel exhaust. The silence that fell in the truck, five men collectively registering danger.

"My gut was screaming at me that it was an ambush, that something was wrong. I wasn't driving. One of my guys was driving."

Mike had been driving. Mike, who should have been on a plane home. Who would have been on a plane home if Jake had been able to do what needed to be done, if he'd been able to man up.

Mike's home was barely an hour from here, in DuPont. Mike's wife lived there, still.

"You talk to any guy who's fought in Afghanistan or Iraq, he's learned to *read* kids. Kids are a barometer in unconventional warfare. Like if you're in a village, and it's totally deserted of all kid life, you know something's wrong. Probably an attack coming. The villagers know, because they've heard it through the grapevine, because someone's got ties to the Taliban, so they make all the kids come inside, out of danger. The kids vanish, and it's like when the birds stop singing before a storm. Too quiet."

Like the inside of the truck. The only sound Mike's breathing, too fast. Jake had willed it to slow down. *You're okay, dude. You told me you were okay.*

Even now he was doing it. Willing Mike to calm down, to focus, to hang in. As if he could change the past.

He was getting too far inside his head. He was supposed to be telling Mira his story. He made himself come back out again, made himself see her, the beer mug snuggled to her chest, her eyes big, hair a little wild, something he could smooth down. Something he could make wilder.

The thought was steadying. An anchor to the here and now.

"Plus you have to be careful not to get suckered by kids. Because the other side will use them as bait, use them to trigger IEDs.

"These kids, they blocked the road. I told my guys it felt wrong. They agreed. I told one of my guys to get out of the truck and get them out of the way, that we needed to move and we needed to move fast. He started to scatter the kids. I saw one had a cell phone, which is how they detonate IEDs usually. I screamed at Mike, who was driving, to go, go, go—and that was the last thing I remember."

Her eyes were big. The softness in them was killing him, splitting his tough skin like gutting a fish. "Other guys were injured?"

"Some. Percussion injuries—busted eardrums, a lot of shrapnel. The driver was killed."

The driver, he'd said. Michael J. Watson. He'd given his full name, like that, before he'd shaken Jake's hand on the first day of Ranger training.

"God."

That was all. Just "God." If he were the kind of guy to see stuff this way, he'd have said it was almost like a single-word prayer. And she was clutching that beer so hard that her fingers were white against the glass.

It hadn't been as hard to tell her as he'd expected it to be. Of course, he hadn't told her the whole story. But he couldn't go any further. Down this path were the mistakes that had gotten Mike killed and cost Jake a leg, a calling, a life. Down this path was self-flagellation and a dark night, and he was pretty sure that wasn't where either of them wanted this to go. He was pretty sure both of them had better ideas for how to spend this evening.

He sure as hell did. He wanted to kiss her stupid again. He wanted to find out if all her skin tasted the same as her throat and her cleavage. He wanted to find out if her noises would get deeper and more guttural when she was splayed out under him on a couch, on a bed. What she would cry out when she came.

"Put the beer down," he said.

18

S he did him one better. She set her beer on a coaster on
  the coffee table and crawled across the couch to kiss
him. He put his arms around her and groaned into her
mouth, and his hands were grabby, picking at her clothes as if
he couldn't wait to get them off her. She had seen in his face
that he couldn't talk about what had happened any more,
and she understood that now he needed a way to lose
himself. She wanted to be that way for him. She wouldn't
have thought she had any kind of savior complex, any need to
drown someone's pain, but the thought of him unburdening
himself in that particular, visceral way, inside her, lit her up.
She could feel lines of heat moving through her limbs, radi-
ating from her core.

He stretched out under her and she luxuriated over him,
settling herself into the warmth of his body, finding that place
where she could grind against him. Aaron had been a good
size but she'd remembered Jake being bigger, and he was.
There was enough of him that she figured that had probably

been a factor in why they hadn't been able to go through with it at the lake. Even now, well past virginity, she'd have a tough time handling him. She'd be at that thin line between full and too much, and she knew—*knew*—it would take her someplace she'd never been.

She concentrated on his erection for a moment, rubbing, and he made a harsh, desperate sound that kicked her own arousal up a notch.

His body under hers was lean and hard. Something about the way they moved against each other, something straining and ample, had gotten deep into her brain, deep into that well of mind-body where sex happened, where emotion met sensation, where the glow of physical arousal met longing, and she was tumbling down into it, faster than she'd intended.

She lost the sense of where she left off and he began, a losing of boundaries that began at her mouth but spread all over her body, got in her arms and legs and her teeth. In her toes. She wanted even less definition, wanted the sense of her excitement building to get mixed up in the feeling of melting into him. There was all this *body* between them, all this technical stuff, the way he rubbed his erection against her, the building heat between her legs, the way their mouths fit— and sometimes didn't fit—perfectly, the way their teeth clicked, the way their tongues battled over who was the boss. She liked the battle; it matched the way the rest of her body felt against his, one of them and then the other taking control of the encounter, trading off.

Things were familiar and unfamiliar. No smell of the lake —algae, clean mountain water, whatever that strange recipe had been. But the smell of his sweat, distinctly male, salt and effort and drive, was so like that night. And the skin beyond the sweat, something human, vulnerable, superheated, and so personal, the scent of every pheromone, every strand of DNA that made him who he was. She wondered if the message of him was hidden, somehow, in Sam. As if she were reclaiming something she knew belonged to her because the fresh sunshine-on-warm-kiddo scent of Sam had been preparing her for this moment for years.

Jake wove his fingers through hers the way he had in the kitchen, but more explicitly now, slipping them in and out, a parody, a tease, a delight. A small echo of their legs inter-twined, the warm, real feel of him between her thighs, the prosthesis cool but its own kind of intimacy, part of who he was, part of where he'd been, part of what she'd missed knowing about him. If he had asked her right then if she wanted him to take it off, she would have said no. And not because of some nonsense fetish-y thing. Because it was *him*.

Him. Rough. Not as polished as Aaron, not as nice. She'd been pleased by Aaron, by the fit of their bodies together, by his attentiveness. But this was different and better, partly because it had a messier feel, sandpaper edges, not only the scrape of his stubble against her face but the rough way he was kissing her now, like there was anger under his desire. He wasn't hurting her, but he wasn't treating her like she was delicate, either.

She had a feeling he would not always wait for her to come first. But by the same token, that he would be right there with her. Not hovering some distance above, wondering if he'd gotten it all right, analyzing and calculating. He'd be down in his body, in her body, in the moment.

"Can I get you out of some of these?" He had a fistful of her silk top. Against her bare arms, the couch had a velvety softness. Sex made your brain wake up and take notice of things. At the same time it made you forget things that should have been important, like the fact that you were taking off your clothes in the living room while your seven-year-old drowsed upstairs.

"I'm going to run upstairs. Make sure—"

"Go," he agreed.

On wobbly legs, she climbed the stairs to where Sam slumbered. "Good night, buddy," she said, and kissed him on the forehead. He sighed and settled deeper into sleep.

She stopped in her bedroom and grabbed a chain of condom packets, sticking them in her pocket. This time, she knew Jake would be on the sofa when she went downstairs. And she knew how she'd feel . . .

Though not, she realized, when she stepped back into the living room and saw him sitting on the couch, staring into a middle distance, seeing God knows what, how deep in her gut she'd feel it.

"He's asleep."

She said it like a challenge, hands on hip, eyes full of suggestion. The provocation went straight to his dick, riling up some part of him that desperately wanted to run this show. That had been cowering under her because he didn't know how to use his new body to flip her over, the way he would have before. The littlest things tripped him up, literally and figuratively. Sex was all new, complex and so different from the regular motion of foot against the ground, different even from the various complicated things he'd learned to do in the meantime: go up and down stairs, lunge for something that was falling, catch his balance when he was the thing falling. But now he had a fresh chance, and he would get her under him on this sofa so he could pin her there with the weight of his body and pantomime the way he'd thrust when he was inside her.

First, he wanted her naked.

"Take your clothes off."

He'd been trying for suggestion, but his brain knew what it wanted, and the words came out a command. He had a split second to wonder how she'd feel about that before she crossed her arms and pulled her blouse over her head. Underneath, she was softer and rounder than she'd been at eighteen. Her bra was all lace, and through it, he could see her nipples clearly, the areolae larger and darker than he remembered. His brain was shorting out, seeing all the curves, the softness he wanted under his palms—he hoped his hands weren't offensively rough, and then he realized he hoped they were, hoped she'd feel calluses against her skin, hoped it would turn her on the way it was turning him on right now thinking about it, the contrasts he craved.

"Unzip your pants."

She made a small sound in the back of her throat, and her hand went to her fly.

"You like it when I tell you what to do?"

"Yeah."

"Take them off."

She pushed them down, a slow tease of revealed flesh.

Her legs were pale and smooth, and he wanted to pinch the soft skin on her vulnerable inner thighs. Better yet, bite it.

"Step out of them."

She did. Her panties matched the nude lace of her bra, and through them, he could see the dark triangle of her curls. He wanted her to stand there and let him look. Let the pressure build in his groin, at the base of his spine, the demand expanding and unfolding in him, ancient and familiar, but brand new, too, as much a relief as a torment. *Hello, old friend.* He'd had no idea how much he'd missed the garden-variety experience of wanting to bang a woman into next week until he'd gone months without it.

She took a step toward him.

"Stand there a minute. Let me look at you."

"I'm self-conscious."

"There is not a fucking thing for you to be self-conscious about."

"You're staring."

"I've had sex that isn't as good as staring at you."

She laughed. "You're full of shit."

"No." He said it quietly. Because it didn't need emphasis, it was so simply true. "Best sex I've had in over a year, for sure."

Her face stilled. She understood what this meant to him, or at least she was trying to.

"You haven't had sex since you lost your leg."

He shook his head. "No. I haven't."

She didn't say anything. He hoped she wouldn't make too big a deal out of it. At the same time, he was glad that she knew.

He'd been there the first time she'd had sex. It made cosmic sense she'd be here now, while his leg lost its virginity.

He felt the smile under the surface, not quite making the connection all the way up to his mouth, trying to remember its old pathway.

When she finally spoke, she said, "I want to know what it feels like."

"What what feels like?"

"This purely visual sexual experience you're having."

"You want me to talk dirty?"

"Yeah," she admitted.

"I'm not a poet."

"I don't like poetry."

"I'm like a locker room."

"Just talk."

"I'm supposed to be giving the commands around here." Bantering with her this way was making him even harder.

"Command away," she said with a wave of her hand. "But if I'm going to stand here while you sit over there, you're going to have to tell me what's going on in your head. Big and little. Not that there's anything little about you," she amended quickly, and made him laugh. Again.

"It feels fucking good," he said. "My dick is harder than it's been possibly ever, and you haven't even touched it. This is like blow-job hard."

"Is blow-job hard the gold standard?"

"You set a new gold standard, baby. Lie down." He stood up.

She stretched that gorgeous body of hers out along the length of the couch. He wanted to look some more, but he made himself pull his T-shirt over his head instead.

The look on her face.

He'd forgotten.

"God, Jake."

"Shrapnel."

In his sleep, he could catalog them, the scars, every one. The ones like polka dots dug into the cap of his shoulder, the ones like claw marks a little lower than his kidney. The single, deep, puckered red gouge on his thigh. When he couldn't sleep, he fingered them one by one, counting them, ticking them off in his mind, taking a strange comfort from them.

She got up and came toward him.

He couldn't have said why, but he didn't want her to touch the scars. "Don't."

She looked startled. His voice had been much harsher than he'd intended, a voice you'd use to call off a focused soldier, not a woman who only wanted to be gentle with you.

"Lie down." His voice still rough.

She did it, and he saw something on her face that wasn't fear and wasn't surprise. She liked the harshness.

Everything that had happened up to this point had been playing. He could see that now. He could see it on her face; he could feel it in the surge of blood that rocked his erection. He got his clothes off fast. He got himself on the couch over her, wearing only his briefs, a thin layer of cotton and a thinner layer of lace between them. She moaned and clutched at him, and he clutched back, kissing her face, kissing her mouth, biting her, licking her, rubbing himself all over her, and she was struggling with his briefs, trying to get him free, and he helped her shove them down. "Condom," she whimpered. "They're in the pocket of my pants."

He levered himself down and grabbed them, but he

couldn't brace himself properly over her so he could get the condom on. He had to stand up. *Fucking prosthetic leg.* He should take it off. He knew most guys did, when they had sex, so the socket wouldn't get in the way. But he should have done it sooner. Now it would be a thing. An awkward, weird, moment-killing thing. Better to do the best he could. He rolled the condom down, watching her eyes on his hands.

He wanted to redeem what had happened between them at the lake. He wanted to prove to himself that he could still do what men did.

It was too much pressure to put on anything. A smarter man would have stopped. Would have put some space between his own expectations and what he was about to do. But he wouldn't. Maybe because she was lying there and looking at him like he was a fucking god, and no one had looked at him like he was anything other than a peculiarity in so long he'd forgotten what it felt like. Or maybe because he liked her so goddamned much. Or because the demand in his body, the tightness of his balls, the roar from his chest down to his knees, was too much to ignore.

He wouldn't stop. He *couldn't* stop.

Getting himself back on the couch was awkward. He knelt with his good leg beside her hip and swung his prosthesis over her. He had to brace himself, hard, on his hands, but his body, even broken, remembered the routine. There was still the same magnetic pull, the way her desire tugged on his, the deep need to bury himself in her. She licked her lips and he took the bait, falling into a long, sweet tangle of tongues that wrenched him outside his head, brought him without conscious thought to the brink of her, the tip of his dick pressed to her wetness, as she thrust her hips up at him. The heat between her legs, her curves and swells and generosity all around him, wrapping him, inviting him. The scent of her —rich, salty, primordial—boring down right to the center of his reptile brain. He knew exactly what came next, and he did it, pressing up into her with a long, thick slide that drew a harsh groan of pleasure from her.

She was tight. Hot. Her eyes were closed, her head thrown back, her lips parted. She was panting and begging, still, his name, over and over, and *please*, and his body responded. The urge to thrust boiled up in him, deeper than brain, deeper than balls, deeper than heart. He withdrew, got ready to plunge again, all the way this time. He wanted to drive into her with all the force he was capable of. He wanted to press her so deep into the couch cushions that they would hold an imprint of her body for days. He wanted every stroke into her to shove her toward the head of the couch—hell, he wanted to inch her up the cushions until she had to brace herself so he didn't drive her head into the arm of the couch. So she'd be pushing back against his thrusts with equal and opposite force, a primitive balance. He wanted to rut, to rub, to fuck the hell out of her.

His prosthesis slipped between the couch cushions and the back of the couch and wedged there.

He didn't have enough control or enough mobility to unstick himself. He still had enough leverage to fuck her, but not as deeply, not as *thoroughly*, as he wanted to.

Instead, he was stuck with the narrow range of motion allowed to him by his wedged knee. And the reality of the knee had also tethered his brain. His mind was stuck in that broken, aching, fucked-up part of him instead of in his dick where it was supposed to be, or inhabiting his body fully as she arched under him and her skin slid, slick with sweat, across the roughness of his chest hair.

He was a piece of silicone and metal and wire buried between two couch cushions.

And he was losing his erection.

19

"Don't run away."

Jake was struggling back into his clothes. He wouldn't look at her.

She pulled a fleece throw off the back of the couch and covered herself, sitting up. "I'm serious, Jake. I'm not upset. You warned me. You said yourself, this is how it's been. And there's obviously nothing wrong with you physically, so—just —don't run away. Please."

"You don't understand."

His face was hard, expressionless, as he zipped and buttoned and dragged his T-shirt over his head. When his head reappeared she saw it—the humiliation in his eyes.

"Maybe I don't. But I want to."

It had been good, so good. She didn't have words for how full of him she had felt even when they were just kissing, for how the reality of his cock inside her had pushed that fullness over some edge she'd never even imagined existed. She didn't have words for the silky slip, the glossy slide of him against her sensitive opening, the heaviness of his weight, the look on his face when he'd finally gotten all the way inside her, prayer and curse, blessing and blasphemy. She didn't have words for how she'd wanted to receive everything about him, the anger she could see on his face, his need begging in his eyes, the way he braced himself as if he were going to deliver something that was part gift, part mean withholding. She wanted it as rough as he wanted to give it; she wanted it for as long as he could hold out; she wanted it now and then again after the first time. She feared she would never be done wanting it.

"I don't want to talk. This isn't some talk-show therapy session about erectile dysfunction. This is my fucking life, okay?"

He said it over his shoulder. He was walking toward the door. He was going to run away and she couldn't let him. Not again.

He was so angry. All the lust and the desperation that he'd needed to pour into her had nowhere to go now. Everything about him—the stiffness in his shoulders, the tightness of his jaw, the way he'd half turned away from her—kept her at bay. Until the moment when he lifted his chin and turned to her, and she saw his eyes. They were dark and naked and needy and she was willing to be slapped down by him if that was what was going to happen, because he was Jake and he'd taken care of her, of Sam, today, and if he needed her, needed something, needed *anything*, she would not run away from him, no matter how scary he looked.

"So don't talk. Just sit here. I won't ask you questions. Just don't run away. I don't care if you talk. You can sit there and stare into space and say nothing. But stay. Stay with me."

For a moment, she thought he would ignore her. Then he

turned and came back to her. Sat heavily on the couch. "Don't try to psychoanalyze me."

"I don't want to."

They were quiet, so quiet she could hear the ice moving in the fridge ice-maker in the next room. The low hum of her next-door neighbor's heat pump kicking on. But it was not a bad silence. It was a silence in which she could feel him doing what she'd asked. Staying.

"Don't move," she said. She got up and went to the bookshelf, pulling several thick volumes off the bottom shelf. She came back and sat beside him, not close enough to touch, but close enough that she could feel the warmth of his body. She set the volumes next to her and pulled one onto her lap. Opened it.

"Is that him?"

She nodded. The first page was all Sam, on the warming table, swaddled in the bassinet, held in various people's arms. She'd bled, badly, so they'd been busy stabilizing her and she wasn't in any of the pictures, not those early ones.

He examined them closely, one by one.

She felt a wave of regret and remorse. It was partially the memories the photos brought on, the terror of being alone with such a vulnerable little creature, the desperate wish for someone who would take half the responsibility for keeping him alive. But it was also the awe on Jake's face, the realization that when she'd made the decision to stop searching for him, she'd also made a decision about what moments in Sam's life to deprive him of.

She led him through the moments, through the photos. Sam sitting up for the first time, canted forward, in imminent danger of a face plant that came the moment after she took the picture. Sam crawling for the first time, chasing one of her shoes across the room. Sam's first step, Sam's first restaurant, Sam's first insipid, folksy kid-music concert.

Jake got stuck on Disney World, his hand suspended with the page half-turned as he pored over the shots of Sam—in mouse ears, sandwiched between his grandparents, high above in the people mover.

"Did you ever go?" she asked.

"Yeah." There was a look on his face.

"Good?"

"It was one of our better family trips," he said. "It was not too long after my dad stopped being able to work, before he was drinking so much."

Their ride on the Ferris wheel seemed like a paltry substitute for five days of watching Sam gleefully shoot neon aliens and communicate directly with characters from *Monsters, Inc.* Although on the plus side, Jake had escaped Sam's pink cotton-candy vomit and his epic meltdown at the hotel pool.

She wanted to apologize to Jake for what he'd missed.

Instead, she reached out and took his hand. At first there was only passive resistance, his fingers lumps of unwilling flesh. Then, as if making a decision, his hand grabbed hers, hard. A lifeline.

"You know it's not you." He said it fiercely. "Why I—why I couldn't—"

She did. "I know. And it wasn't you. At the lake. I was a virgin."

"I know."

"I was scared. I was really young."

"I shouldn't have pressured you," he said.

"You didn't pressure me," she said. "I was the one who

rushed everything that night. I didn't want to go off to college still a virgin. And—I wanted you."

"I had more experience. I was older. I should've known better."

"You were two years older," she said. "That hardly makes you a real grown-up. It's not like you were thirty-five, and had all this romantic past to draw on."

He shook his head, refusing to let himself off the hook, and his eyes scanned the far corners of the room as if there were an answer hidden there.

"I was—confused."

"Me too," she said.

"I'd thought of it as a fling and then there we were and it felt like more. I was scared. And angry. At myself. For letting myself feel as much as I did."

She felt a rush of warmth at his words. *How much did you feel?* she wanted to demand. *As much as I did?*

But she couldn't, not without forcing *this* moment in the here and now. "We were really young," she said instead.

He nodded. His gaze was faraway. Remembering that night? Did it have as much clarity for him as it did for her? Like something carved out of marble and animated, glossy, perfectly sharp and defined?

"Jake, there's something I should tell you."

His eyes found her face, startled and wary.

"I tried to find you. But only at first. Then—then I didn't. I stopped trying."

When the phone calls to bases had dead-ended, she'd sent printed letters to every army base in the United States, addressed to "Jake Taylor." She'd Googled him. She'd had every intention of posting to Facebook to ask if anyone knew him, but at the last minute, something had stayed her hand. Once she posted his name there, even if she didn't explicitly identify him as Sam's father, a handful of people, maybe as many as a hundred, would know. They would link his name in their minds with Sam, and there would be no turning back.

Still, she'd made one more round of phone calls before Sam was six months old. She remembered the last with perfect clarity. It was one of the more frustrating, the JAG on the other end of the line impatient and scornful. She put her iPhone down too hard on the table and turned to see Sam rocking back and forth on his hands and knees, his round belly hanging down, his bare arms and legs dimpled. She got down on the floor with him, sticking her face close to his so he chortled and collapsed on his belly and chortled some more. She blew raspberries on his face, and then she turned him on his back and blew raspberries in his belly, and he grabbed her hair and pulled it and shrieked at the top of his lungs. It hurt her scalp and it hurt her ears, but her tears had nothing to do with the pain. The tears were because she knew—*knew in her gut*—that she and Sam had everything they needed.

She wasn't going to look for Jake anymore. Because, for better or for worse, she was giving him up—shutting down the possibility that he would be part of their lives.

"You couldn't chase after me forever," he said. "As much as I wish I'd had that time with him, we both had things we needed to do. I needed to fight and you needed time with Sam. You can't beat yourself up."

Even after she'd made the decision not to search for him any longer, she'd kept having the fantasies and the cravings.

At odd, vulnerable moments, she wished that he'd arrive and rescue her. That he'd vanquish the allergies, the asthma, the first-day-of-school fears, that he knew the secret formula for comforting a child heartbroken about moving across the country from his beloved grandparents.

He stared down at where her hand covered his, opened his mouth as if to say something, and closed it again. Then he said, "I should go." He set Sam's photo albums to the side.

She turned away, hurt. For a moment there, she'd thought things were going to be okay between them. That they'd connected some piece of the past to the present, that—

But he was going to run away. Still.

"Mira."

"Don't say, 'It's not you.' That's the stupidest line in all of stupid linedom. Just—if you have to go, go."

She wasn't looking in his direction but she could tell he hadn't moved. He sighed. Took an audible, deep breath.

"My knee got stuck, okay? My knee got stuck between the couch cushions, and I couldn't stop thinking about it. One minute I was so into it, so into you, and the next—I don't know. I couldn't get back to where my head had been a minute ago. I kept thinking about how I couldn't do what you needed me to do."

His voice was tense, rich, almost pleading.

"You should have told me that."

"I don't know who you think I am, Mira. Maybe some guys can do that, say whatever's in their heads, but I'm not that guy."

"Well, that's abundantly clear."

He sighed again, but he was still there. Still sitting beside her, with her, listening, talking, despite what he'd said about himself. Maybe he was a man's man, maybe he didn't want to be psychoanalyzed, but everything about him right now told her he wanted to be there. Right now, despite all the times he'd walked away from the possibility of her—the notion of Sam—right now, he wanted to stay. And even though she was terrified it wouldn't last, she wanted to do whatever she could to keep him there.

"So you lost your erection because you started thinking about your knee, and how you couldn't do what you thought I needed you to do. You know you were doing exactly what I needed you to do, right? God," she said, and let it all into her voice—all the heat, all the lust, all the built-up longing he'd infused her with—"exactly. What. I. Needed. You. To. Do."

"I wanted to . . ."

"You wanted to what?"

"I wanted to fuck you into next week."

She felt the words, hot and explicit, as laden with desire as hers had been, a surge to her core. She felt the expression on his face, raw and real and male.

"I could see that on your face," he said, with awe evident in his voice. "I just watched you get turned on."

"Yeah," she said, because it was all the language she could manage, and because she knew what he meant, had felt the flush come into her face, had felt her lids grow heavy and her jaw go slack.

"I'm really fucking hard right now."

"I can help you with that."

She watched the color rise in *his* face now. She leaned in and kissed his lower lip, suckled it, and the growl that came out of him felt as direct and explicit as if he'd set his hand between her legs.

"Can I make a suggestion?" she asked him.

He was breathing heavily, his chest rising and falling, the rhythm calling her. "Yeah."

"Let's go upstairs. I have a queen-size bed. Your knee won't get stuck."

He hesitated.

"What?"

She could tell he didn't want to answer her.

"Are you worried about Sam? Don't. He's sound asleep and there's a lock on the door."

"No."

"Just. Tell. Me."

"I don't want to screw it up again."

She put her hand out, ran her thumb over the stubble on his jaw, touched the pad to the softness of his mouth. His mouth opened, involuntarily, and she watched his eyes darken.

"Dude," she said. "I already think you suck at sex. What's the worst that could happen—you can't get it up?"

She got to see him laugh this time, got to see how it softened him and made him bright.

20

H e followed her up the stairs. She'd wrapped the little throw from the sofa around herself. It covered her, but only barely, and he wanted to flip it up and investigate the shadowy space where her thighs met. Or tug it off entirely. He was not, however, confident of his ability to take her on the stairs. That would have to wait until he'd mastered the simpler things.

She'd been . . .

She'd been perfect. There weren't a lot of women who could have carried off what had gone down between them without making him feel either like a failure or a eunuch. She'd managed it, though. She hadn't tried to strip him bare and read his thoughts. She hadn't reassured and she hadn't panicked. She'd been herself, the girl he'd let himself feel too much for all those years ago, the woman he could find himself caring too much for now. The sort of person it was worth doing something crazy for, worth taking risks for.

She dropped her clothes by the side of the bed, let the blanket fall. He wondered if the impact of her naked body would fade with familiarity. He wasn't used to it yet. Her voluptuousness, emerging from under the fleece, hit him like a ton of bricks, as it had downstairs when she pulled off her T-shirt.

He reached for her, his mouth finding one breast, his fingers the other, one nipple between his fingers, the other hard against his tongue. *Hell, yeah.* She whimpered, and he felt her knees buckle. "Too much?"

She shook her head.

"Do you want more?"

She nodded.

His palm slid down her belly, warm and soft, and he parted her curls and cupped her. Her clit was swollen, and his finger slipped easily over it. He paused there, watching a flush mottle her chest and face.

"Mmmph," she said, or something like that, and she pushed her face into his chest and rocked against his hand.

"Lie down," he said, and followed her down. He loved the slick feel of her clit, the reckless expression on her face, the red of her lips and cheeks.

"Unh."

"What? Tell me."

"If you keep doing that, I'm gonna come."

"Is that supposed to be a threat?"

She came then, her body tightening all over, her head thrown back, making small, helpless noises that made him have to wrap a hand around the base of his cock to keep from coming too.

"God," she said, when she could talk.

"Condoms?"

She pointed to where she'd dropped them on the bed,

then said, "You're probably too stubborn to let me help with that, right?"

"Oh, hell no. Whenever any woman asks if she can touch my dick in any capacity, I always say yes."

She made a face at him. "Way to make me feel special."

He tilted his head to one side. "If you're not convinced yet that you're special, I'm not sure what I can say to convince you."

Her expression softened. "You could show me."

"Happily."

She tore the packet, then bent her head and licked a drop of pre-cum from the tip of his dick. "Holy—" Whatever he'd been about to say—and he had no idea what it was—got strangled off. He was going to be having blow-job fantasies about her round-the-clock until they got around to her using that talented tongue in other ways. If they did. This was assuming the sex actually happened and wasn't yet another laughable disaster.

She rolled the condom down.

"Feels so much fucking better when you do it," he said.

She wrapped her hand around him and squeezed.

"Don't add premature ejaculation to our list of sex disasters," he said.

"But you're big. And hard. And you feel really good." She jerked her hand up and down his length a few times and he groaned.

She lay down on the bed. "Can we try that again?"

He eased himself down and braced himself beside her.

"What if I just do it?" he said. "No frills."

"You mean, wham bam thank you ma'am?"

"I meant—yes, I guess that's sort of what I meant. I guess

more that it might not be such a bad thing if I did it instead of—"

"Instead of thinking about it and talking about it so much?"

"Yeah."

"Go for it."

He rolled his weight onto her and did exactly that, a rough thrust, a slow satin slide, his groan, her whimper. He kept his focus on her, on the way his thrusts made her breasts bounce, on the way each withdrawal and surge rolled her eyes back in her head. On the wet heat enveloping him, her tightness, her little squeezes, the fact that she seemed to know at least ten different angles at which to hold her hips, each of which contacted some brand-new part of him.

His dick felt bigger and harder and more capable of delivering pleasure straight to his brain than he remembered. Maybe it was lack of use. Heightened sensitivity. Or maybe the difference was her, either the series of throaty little noises she was making or the soft, slick sounds coming from where her body clasped his, or—

"If you do that, you're going to make me come in about thirty seconds," he warned.

She'd tipped her hips and squeezed her inner muscles at the same time. Grinned at him. Stared right into his eyes.

He tried to thrust forward but the goddamned socket of his prosthetic leg hit her thigh and stopped him.

No. No, no, no.

I can't.

It made his head hurt to think it. "Can't" wasn't a word he wanted in his vocabulary. It wasn't a word he'd ever *had* in his vocabulary.

Fuck the socket, fuck the leg. He'd made it this far, had come up the stairs to do this thing, and he wasn't going to fail her again.

"Don't stop. Please don't stop."

That turned off his brain in a hurry. Got all the blood back where it was supposed to go.

"Jake, you're killing me. Come on. More. Please."

He wanted to. He needed to. Somehow. Some way.

He pulled out

She groaned. "Why'd you do that?"

"Turn over."

"Like this?"

She lay on her stomach on the bed, her knees slightly bent, ass tipped a little so he could see the wetness glistening on her swollen lips.

"Fuck," he said. He knelt behind her, palmed her ass with both hands, squeezing, then spread her and slid into her folds. The heat alone almost made him lose it.

It wasn't perfect. The socket still got in his way, but the heat and tightness around his dick was blotting out thought. He pivoted his hips so he could thrust deeper without the prosthesis impeding him. It was awkward, but she couldn't see him, and that made it tolerable.

He thought of the night he'd done this solo, and how much better this felt, and how much worse. That night there hadn't been anything but him and his body, however damaged, however unfamiliar. Tonight, there was silicone and titanium and the distance between what he wanted and what he could have. He wanted the curve of her ass slapping against his abs, the give of her flesh as he pressed her hard into the mattress.

Instead he was getting this. This halfway thing. And it sucked, but, *fuck*, it was working for him anyway. The jiggle of her ass as he thrust, the way her hands gripped the fitted sheet, her fingers white where they dug into the bed. The noises she was making, a cry for each stroke, before he withdrew and stroked again. The way she tilted her hips higher and higher, reaching back for him, ratcheting him up faster than he wanted. Unless he stopped, he was going to come.

He didn't want it to be over. He wanted to be in her, forgetting himself, forgetting the part of him that wasn't him, feeling the familiar and unfamiliar sensation of being heated and surrounded and gripped.

But this thing was far beyond his control. The way he felt around her, in her, was way beyond his control. The way he'd felt when he looked up to see her at Discovery Park, the way he'd felt beside her in the Ferris wheel car, the way he'd felt sitting on her couch while she was upstairs tucking Sam in. And then—without meaning to, because he knew that she didn't do it on purpose, it was just the person she was—she had dismantled him. She had made him talk without trying, the way she used to, the stories pouring out of him, a perfect flow, all those words, all the things he didn't mean to reveal about himself, the leg, Mike, the wedged knee. And somehow this, this sex with her, was part of what she could make him reveal, part of what she could draw out of him, part of what she could take from him against his will. Only afterward he would find that it hadn't been against his will at all, that it had been what he needed to give and give up, that it had been everything that was missing.

The feeling that gathered in his chest, in his gut, in his throat, was too much—it couldn't be held back. Her wet heat,

the rub of her mons against his balls each time he entered
her, each time he pulled back, a vague but insistent friction.
God, he wanted that last inch or two, wanted it like nothing
fucking else, but it wasn't his, not tonight, and instead of
taking it and shoving the edge of the socket deep into her
flesh, he used his hip to press her down as hard as he could
into the mattress, pushed her tight against the resistance, and
she arched under him, cried and shook, involuntary squeezes
tight around his base until he couldn't hold out any longer
and gave himself up to the sensation, coming in long,
draining pulses that were a stew of frustration and triumph.

He became slowly aware of how slick they were with
sweat, how hard she was breathing. He extricated himself
and rolled off her, staring at the ceiling, trying to catch his
breath, trying to get his bearing. Trying to understand the
sensation he had that his world had shifted around him, as
profoundly and as seismically as it had in the wake of the
literal explosion.

"Wow," she said.

He was drowning in something—gratitude, he thought.
As if he'd been waiting all this time, his libido held in
suspense, and only now finished what they'd started all those
years ago.

He made it into a joke, because that was the only way he
could get his head around it. "Whew," he said. "That was
some serious foreplay. Eight years."

They both laughed.

"It kind of feels like that, right?"

He reached for her hand.

His body was heavy as lead, that post-sex torpor he'd
missed like a mo-fo sneaking over him. In a minute or two

he'd be asleep, and he didn't want to be that guy. So he made himself lie on one side, facing her. It was a little awkward, but all the endorphins made everything easier. Maybe next time he'd take the leg off. Get that last inch or two, that sensation of burying himself as deep as it was possible to go into her.

What would she think about that? How would she react to his residual leg, to the scars and lumpiness and just plain not-thereness of it? Not everyone wanted to make love to a one-legged man. Although if anyone would take it in stride, it would be Mira. Nothing got her.

"That was good," he said. "No, fucking great. That was fucking great. Thank you."

"So you got to be my first, and I got to be your first."

"Do you think of me as your first?"

"Yeah," she said. Quietly. All the kidding around gone out of her voice. "I do. Maybe I wouldn't have if it hadn't been for Sam, but no matter what happened after, no matter how weird it was, you can't deny we had sex."

"I shouldn't have denied it. In the PT's office."

"You were—"

"A grumpy asshole," he finished with her.

"You're not as grumpy now."

"A lot has changed," he said. And thought about it. Everything that had come to pass since he'd met her. The new legs, training for the triathlon, working toward going back into the army. How much of that would have happened if it hadn't been for her and Sam? He'd been so stuck, so stuck in his vision of himself as broken. "You and Sam got me back on track. I'm grateful to you in so many ways."

There was a strange expression on her face.

"What?" he asked.

"I'm grateful, too," she said.

"What's changed for you?"

"Wait here a sec," she said.

She got out of bed and wrapped herself in her robe. She thumped down the stairs—he took advantage of the moment to get up and throw away the condom—and came back up with a stack of drawings in her hands. She laid the pages in his lap.

They were colored pencil and watercolor, that strange mixture of pale and vivid. Although they were soft and vague, he recognized immediately who she'd painted.

Jake and Sam. Running races, playing pinecone baseball, sitting together on the Ferris wheel, suspended above a city of murky color.

He grazed a finger across Sam's hair. She'd painted it with so much love, each brushstroke, almost each hair, distinct. And they looked alike, man and boy.

Father and son.

"These are *amazing*," he said. "You're amazing."

"I don't know about that, but you got me thinking. And if I turn out not to have a job after Monday, maybe I'll try to find something a little more about design and a little less about programming. Another way to shake off my dad's influence."

"I don't think you have to worry about that," Jake said.

"About what?"

"About shaking off your dad's influence. You're on the other side of the country."

"Yeah, well, it's not far enough," she said. "Anyway, the point is, I'm grateful to you, too. Thank you."

There was something in her voice now that he recognized. He became aware that she was still standing up.

Wrapped tightly in her robe. "You're trying to get rid of me again!"

"Sam asked me about sleepovers, earlier. I just—I don't want to build expectations for him that we can't live up to."

"You're kicking me out."

"Are you mad?"

He thought about that. He'd have no right to be mad, would he? She'd been honest with him, every step of the way. As he had with her. And tonight, when he'd convinced her to let him stay, he'd known he was using sex to muscle his way in.

Even if there had been times tonight he'd forgotten that this was supposed to be simple. Even if he'd talked to her about things he'd never discussed with anyone else. Even if he'd lost himself so completely in sex with her that afterward had felt like waking out of a dream—or from unconsciousness.

Eight years ago, he'd had trouble with this boundary, too, but he was eight years older and a soldier, and he could hold the line now like a grown man.

Sam, and sex. Those were the rules. Those were what the rules had to be.

"What are the parameters here? Do I have to leave right this second? Or just before Sam wakes up tomorrow morning."

He'd surprised her. "Um, before Sam? I guess?"

"Okay, that's good. I need to get an early start to Oregon tomorrow, anyway. But not right this second. Because I have some other plans," he explained.

"Other plans?"

"That sex was great, but—"

She made a face of mock outrage. "But? But what? I ended a year-plus-long drought for you. I didn't hear you complaining."

"Oh, I wasn't complaining. But it wasn't enough."

She made a small, strangled sound.

He lay down beside her and kissed her all over her throat, all over her chest, circling in until he kissed her nipples, then licked and sucked them, one after the other. His other hand played in her curls, found her clit. She closed her eyes. "Mmm," she said.

"Faster? Slower? Harder? Softer?"

"Yeah," she said, and he laughed and eased a finger inside her, loving the soft feel of her, curling his fingertip into her G-spot and making her moan. He could feel it, that moan, in the pit of his belly, at the bottom of his spine, where his own body was drawing up tight. He slid a second finger inside her and she made a fractured sound, which he swallowed with a kiss that turned into a leisurely exploration of her mouth, until she was humming.

He kept his hand where it was, not wanting to rush things. He wanted this to last a long time, long enough to watch her face, to watch the pleasure mount behind her eyes, to watch her mouth fall open.

When her hips rose off the bed so she could get a better purchase on his hand, he teased, "Want something more?"

She answered him with a noise that definitely wasn't any word he'd ever heard. He got a condom from the nightstand, and he rolled it down and slid the head of his cock, so hard the condom felt too small, into her folds. She gasped and pressed up to him, and he was halfway in her without trying, she was that wet, she was that open. And tight, too—how was it possible she could be so wet and so tight at the same time? She was gripping him, and he was never going to last, except that just then, the socket of his prosthesis bumped her thigh and stopped his progress.

He hesitated, and she felt it.

Their eyes met.

He rolled off her.

"Don't you *dare*," she said.

"Wait," he said.

"If you lose your erection . . ." She made it sound like a threat. Which made him smile.

"If I lose my erection I'm going to make you suck me until I get it back," he said. He made it sound like a threat, too, and her eyes narrowed and she emitted a sound that roughly translated might have been, "Nngha."

He sat on the edge of the bed and reached down and pulled the prosthesis off. He didn't turn to see how she was reacting. It was Mira, after all. She would react however she did, and it would somehow be okay.

He began rolling back the layers of socks that compressed his residual leg, peeling himself like an onion back to his skin.

The silicone sheath came off second-to-last with a sucking sound he hated, but in the scheme of what they were doing, it was just one of those things, like the wet sound of his body in hers. And then he pulled off the liner and saw the thing that looked like a thigh only all wrong, and he had a millisecond of panic. That he'd done the wrong thing, that she'd scream and run away, or worse, stay, and be secretly disgusted.

But then he remembered.

It was Mira.

His heart slowed down.

He knew her, knew her well enough to know that she wasn't going to make a big fuss over his stump, kissing it and petting it and pretending like it was something special. Nor would she make a fuss of him, as if he'd done something brave instead of what had to be done. And she didn't—she put her hand on his arm, handed him a new condom, and waited for him.

She didn't have to do anything to make him hard again except lie back on the bed and smile and beckon. He rolled to her, braced himself on his arms. With effort, he found a balance point, a strange, awkward triangulation that let him be on one knee and his shorter residual leg.

She let him find his way, then guided him back to her. Her heat and wetness waited for him, like a reward, like a blessing.

He buried himself to the hilt and he couldn't help himself —the groan ripped out of him, loud and desperate, as he got that last inch he'd been craving, as he got the full effect of driving his body into and against hers, as he watched her eyes roll back in her head with pleasure.

It was awkward fucking her like this, more awkward with only one leg to brace him, but it felt more like him. With the prosthetic it had felt all wrong, like there was something between them. Like the fucking condom, which—well, if he had his way, he'd have peeled that back, too, and thrust straight into her wet heat without it.

Fucking her—oh, fucking hell, making love to her—like this was *off*, but in all the right ways. He could have everything, all of her, could brace himself and give himself completely into her, like a crazy backwards gift, because of course, she was the gift.

His balance was off, his thrusts ungainly and uneven, but he didn't give a shit, because she'd grabbed his ass in both her hands and was tugging him into her with so much force. Anyway, all the thrust was coming from his ass cheeks, and the tension there was becoming part of the tension in his lower belly and dick, part of the tension on her face, and it was all one big giant gathering storm of fucking awesomeness. The first time, the glory had gotten lost in frustration and triumph, in proving something and quenching thirst and scratching an itch. This time it was all glory, all bliss, the look on Mira's face, all wrecked and open, a silent scream and her eyes squeezed shut and her hands coming off his ass and flopping back on the pillow behind her head as she arched up into him and he started to come.

"Fuck, *fuck!*"

Probably he yelled it, because he was beyond caring. He was beyond anything except the sensation of her clenching around him, the look of total abandon on her face, the fresh salt smell of her rising up from where their bodies met, and the wide, ripped-apart sense of falling and rising and turning inside out, the sense of being wrung, of having the resistance purged from him, of being remade, recast, and finally, finally, of crashing back down, spent, wherever and however she wanted him.

21

"Jake. Jake. Wake up."

It was too late. The sound that had roused Mira from sleep was the sound of her door opening, the herald of Sam's morning entrance. She'd somehow forgotten to lock the door, and apparently, they'd accidentally fallen asleep after—after that—

—that epic, totally amazing, good-sense-melting sex. That colossal error in her personal judgment, that slow, should-have-been-able-to-stop-but-could-only-hang-on-for-the-ride slide down a slippery slope into *really, really complicated.*

Oh, God. Opal had been so right. "Not supposed to" was a flimsy barrier to the chemistry between her and Jake.

Jake scrambled to sitting and yanked the covers up. "Whoops. Sorry!" He looked as dazed as she felt. Maybe more so. His hair was mussed, his were eyes sleepy, and a pattern of pillow creases crisscrossed his cheek.

She had woken to discover her face snug up against his chest, her hand on his morning erection, but luckily he would not need to know that, since she'd disentangled herself before calling him awake.

Sam came over to Jake's side of the bed. He regarded Jake thoughtfully. "You slept over."

"I did," Jake said.

"C'mere, Sam," Mira said, but her son stayed where he was, scrutinizing Jake. She started to feel the beginning edge of worry about how thoughtful he looked.

"Does that mean you're a good friend?"

Jake gave her an uncertain look, then dove in. "Yes. It does."

The kind of good friend who could make you come several times in one night, harder than you'd ever come before, and who could leave you wanting more. The kind of friend who was commanding. Needy. Masterful. Desperate. Rough. Grateful. *And funny. Don't forget funny.*

He'd felt so good inside her. Not only the sensation of being stretched and filled, but the connection it forged between her body and her emotions. Her heart. As if she'd let him in *every way*, not just the obvious one.

And it wasn't only the sex. It was everything that had led up to it. His rescuing them, his cooking for them, his almost running away and then not. It was all the secrets laid bare—the story of what had happened to his leg, their mutual confessions about how they'd avoided each other with the truth about Sam, and the biggest truth he'd told her, the truth about how humiliating it had been for him when his knee got caught in the sofa.

I kept thinking about how I couldn't do what you needed me to do.

She hadn't been bullshitting him when she'd answered him. When she'd told him he'd been everything she needed.

So ... maybe ...?

Maybe she could stop fighting him off? Stop keeping him at bay? Let what was going to happen happen, and ...

And have her heart broken twice in exactly the same way?

Only this time, of course, her heart was not the only one on the line.

Now there was a seven-year-old tilting his head to one side, exactly the way he did when he was trying to figure out a difficult riddle. Oh, *hell.*

"You slept in my mom's bed," Sam said. "She doesn't even let me do that."

"Because you squirm and snore and you put your head on *top* of my head, and because sometimes you turn all the way around and stick your feet up my nose."

"My feet wouldn't fit up your nose," Sam said.

"It was late and cold and it didn't make sense for Jake to go back to his house last night," Mira said.

Also, we were both limp, boneless, ecstatic pools of human being, and there was no way either of us was moving. The last thing she remembered thinking was, *I should make him leave before we fall asleep.* And then she'd heard her door creak.

She needed to get Sam off whatever puzzle was running in his brain. She needed to not let him think too hard about the situation. Because even though he was a little kid, he had a fatherless little kid's obsession with the missing piece in his life. Too much more time to think about it and he'd have slotted Jake right into the Jake-sized hole he'd left in their lives.

Not so different from what she'd been doing herself.

A change of subject was in order.

Mira said, brightly, "Let's go downstairs and make some pancakes."

"Ooh, pancakes!" Sam said, because luckily, even smart seven-year-olds had the attention span of hamsters.

"I could use a shower first," Jake said. "Then I could make pancakes. I know how to do that."

Shower. Jake in the shower.

"Maybe I need a shower, too," she said.

"We could, you know, conserve water," he said, his eyes hot on hers.

Yes, yes, they could.

But she'd let herself get distracted at a fatal moment, and Sam hadn't.

"You slept over. And you're a soldier," he said, and she could see it coming with all the force of a slow-motion impending disaster.

"My real dad's a soldier."

"Sam, do you want to watch Saturday morning cartoons?"

But *Ninjago* had nothing on the need for a small boy to understand his paternity.

"Are you my real dad?"

HE'D SEEN IT COMING, but that didn't keep it from bowling him over. He'd stupidly thought he could only be surprised by bomb blasts and unexpected appearances, but it turned out that a simple line of questioning could carve its way through his defenses. Then, when the inevitable words wound their way into his heart, they pierced like a single, perfectly aimed bullet. *Are you my real dad?*

The last twenty-four hours had led to this moment, the fear he'd felt as he'd hurried to rescue Sam, the sense of peace it had given him to hold and comfort his scared child. The relief and freedom he'd experienced last night with Mira, the hurt he'd tried to tamp down when she'd told him she wanted him to leave, mixed with the relief he'd felt that she was holding him at exactly the distance at which he wanted to be held. Approach, avoid. Have sex, but don't stay the night. Friends with benefits, a father pretending to be a babysitter. It was the perfect, safe distance.

This, however, was not.

This was a seven-year-old staring at him as if he could see straight into Jake's head, which for all Jake knew, he could. Maybe sharing genes with someone gave him a more than usual ability to read your thoughts. It wouldn't surprise him. Sometimes he felt like he and Sam shared more than eye color, an affection for pinecone baseball and lipstick bowling, and a love of running.

Lie? Tell the truth?

Before he could decide, Mira stepped in. "Why would you think that, Sam?"

Excellent dodge, Mom.

It was a good idea, but she was messing with the wrong seven-year-old. Sam had apparently done a lot of thinking on this subject.

"My dad is a soldier, and you're a soldier."

"*Was* a soldier," Jake said.

"*Are* a soldier," Mira said. "You *are* a soldier."

She meant it as an expression of faith in him: *You're afraid you can't do it, but you can.* But it felt like a warning: *Be careful what you promise him, because there will come a time when you have to go.*

"You took care of me yesterday like a dad," Sam said. "I just thought..."

There was defeat in Sam's voice. Mira's ploy was working. Sam had backed down, realized that he'd made a colossal leap, and was preparing to retrench.

His words fully penetrated Jake's brain.

You took care of me yesterday like a dad.

He remembered how hard his heart had beat in the cab on the way over. The way it did when he was infiltrating a theoretically empty building at night, men ahead of him waving him on, men behind him covering his ass. Because some loser had showed up to harass his son's babysitter, and he was going to cut off that loser's balls and shove them down his throat.

He remembered the feel of Sam, curled in his lap, crying. Not because he was weak but because he was a seven-year-old boy and the world was still unpredictable and incomprehensible and he depended on adults to make sense out of it. To fight for him and tell him the truth and take care of him.

He remembered the way he'd set his nose against Sam's tear-stained cheek, the snuffles and sighs and hiccups Sam emitted as he'd realized he was safe and begun to relax in Jake's arms.

He remembered how easily the words had come.

Being brave means being afraid and still doing what you want to do or have to do.

A father's words.

"Can I help make pancakes?"

Sam had given up. Decided, under his own steam, that he'd been an idiot to draw the conclusions he had. He'd probably never ask the question again, or not for years.

Jake could be "the babysitter" for as long as he wanted.

He thought of the paternity test Mira had offered him, weeks ago. The time when it might have mattered seemed so long ago. When loving Sam might have been a matter of a technicality and not an inevitability.

He turned to Mira, and she must have somehow seen the question in his eyes, because her face softened, as sweet and vulnerable as it had been that night by the lake, before life had toughened her up. But he mouthed it anyway, because he wanted to be sure, because he didn't want to take anything from her, because she deserved this decision after she'd made so many on her own, feeling her way in the dark, alone. *Can I tell him the truth?*

She nodded. Just that, a barely-there gesture that had the power to change three lives.

"Yeah," he said, and he reached out and touched Sam's cheek, still warm from sleep. "I'm your real dad."

They made and ate an obscene number of pancakes and way too much bacon, and they answered Sam's questions and absorbed his small-person recriminations. Sam was very, very angry with both of them. He accused Mira of telling lies.

She had, of course, lied to him. There was no getting around that. But she calmly—as calmly as she could with her heart thudding in her chest, with her mind racing to try to figure out what the hell *this* meant—explained to him that she'd tried to find Jake but that she hadn't known his full name or that he'd been a Ranger, and rather than telling Sam that his dad was out there in the world but couldn't be found, which might make him upset, she had told him the sperm donor story.

"I *am* upset," Sam said, with unusual acuity for a seven-year-old.

"I'm really sorry, buddy," Jake had said, and served him three more pancakes polka-dotted with chocolate chips, which calmed him down a bit.

There would probably be years and years of therapy to sort that one out, but for now, things were peaceful.

Mira did the dishes while Sam and Jake played chess.

"How would you feel—?"

Jake had startled her, coming up behind her while she was doing the dishes and whispering in her ear. Not sweet nothings, though. A real question. "How would you feel if I took Sam to Oregon to meet his grandmother and aunt and uncle and cousins?"

"Now? Today?"

"You can come, too, if you want."

"It feels—too soon."

"Too soon for what?" he asked.

Too soon for another family to get involved in her son's life, and maybe have opinions about how he should be raised. Her own family was bad enough, and she had years of experience dealing with them.

"They don't know, right? About Sam? About me?"

He shook his head. "I didn't want to tell them before Sam knew, in case . . ."

He didn't have to finish. They both knew all the reasons for caution.

"What if they don't react well?"

"They probably won't," he said. "Because of the weird musty smell that follows you everywhere."

She couldn't help it; she giggled.

"They're going to love Sam, and they're going to be thrilled to have new family. Take my word for it."

He made it seem so simple.

She packed her things, and Sam's. The plan was to pick

Jake's stuff up on the way. "I can pack in five minutes," he said.

"I'm envious."

"It didn't take you so long."

"Longer than five minutes."

"Did you pack—?"

She reached down and pulled out the box of condoms, and he grinned.

Her phone vibrated in her pocket.

"My dad," she said. "I usually call him early Saturday mornings, so he's probably just calling to make sure I'm still alive. He worries." She swiped to answer it. "Hey."

"Hi, sweetheart. Just calling to check in on my two favorite people."

"Can Sam and I maybe give you a call tomorrow? We're about to head out."

"Out where?"

That was not a question she could answer.

"Mom!" said Sam, bounding into the bedroom. "Who's that—is that Grampy?"

She nodded.

"Can I just talk to him for a second?" her father asked. "I want to tell him what I did yesterday."

She handed the phone to Sam.

"Grampy! We're going to Oregon."

It was one of those slow-unfolding-disaster moments. She reached for the phone and put her finger to her lips to shush Sam, but there was no averting this one.

"With Jake! To meet my aunt and uncle and other grandmother!"

She could hear her father's voice, but not what he was saying, and then Sam said, "He's here. He slept—"

She snatched the phone back, Sam protesting.

"Dad—"

"Was he about to tell me Jake slept over?"

She sucked her breath in sharply. Jake was watching the whole thing, creases deepening between his brows. She grimaced. *I know.*

"Mommy? Can I have the phone back? Why'd you grab it?"

"Don't lie to me, Mira."

"Dad, calm down."

"I will *not* calm down. We had a conversation about this. I told you what a bad idea I thought this was. I told you all the ways I thought this could end badly for you and Sam. Are you *sleeping* with him?"

"That's none of your business."

"Mommy?"

"Mira, what are you *thinking*? I was there last time. I watched it all play out. You got your heart broken. You got left holding the bag in the most serious of ways. You can't trust him not to hurt you again like that."

"Dad, *stop*. I'm a grown woman. I can run my own life."

"Mira, this isn't just your life. This is Sam's life, too, and I can't just stand by and let you—"

"Hey, Dad? We have to hit the road. I'll talk to you tomorrow," she told her father, and hit "End."

"Mommy, I wanted to talk to Grampy!"

"We'll call him back tomorrow." She wracked her brain for a distraction. "Sam, did you want to bring some of your cars with you? There are Legos at the beach house. You can get a big Ziploc out of the kitchen drawer and fill it up."

When Sam had raced downstairs, Jake said, "That didn't look like fun."

"Not fun."

"He's not my biggest fan." It was a statement, not a question.

"No."

"You okay?"

"I just wish—I wish he'd give me some credit for knowing my own mind and being able to take care of myself."

He reached out and put his arms around her. She leaned against him and let the heat and comfort of his body soak into hers. He bent his head and touched his lips to her hair, his breath warm against her scalp. She loved that he didn't try to argue with her or say that her dad probably gave her more credit than she knew. He just let her have the moment. Once, a long time ago, he had been the easiest person in the world to talk to, and all the things that had bothered her had come unknotted. He could still do it, could still work her emotions loose.

"Hey," he asked. "Can I ask you a favor? Can I drive down to the beach?"

"Why?"

"I feel more comfortable when I'm driving."

All the ease that had just flowed into her leached out again. What was it with men who thought they could handle things better than she could? "I'm a really good driver."

"I know you are," he said. "It's just—I hate being driven by anyone else. Because of—"

"Oh," she said.

He sighed deeply, and the tension dissipated from his shoulders. "Yeah," he said.

"Oh, Jake," she said. "I'm sorry. I'm an idiot."

"No. You're fine. You would have no way of knowing."

"Why don't you have a car?"

He sighed. "It's part of my not getting my life together yet. I felt like there was no point if I was going to go back to active duty."

"Buses aren't a problem?"

"No, for whatever reason. If there are enough people, it's distracting. But cabs are."

"Oh, God, and you took a cab to come help Sam yesterday."

He waved it off. "It's crazy. I should get over it. Probably if I were still in therapy, the therapist would tell me that I have to do exposure therapy until it doesn't freak me out to be driven by other people anymore."

She tilted her head. "You want me to drive? You can expose yourself." She gave him a dirty wink.

He laughed, and then the laugh twisted off.

"You okay?" she asked.

"You make me laugh. And you make things okay that I didn't think would ever be okay again. You know?"

She nodded. Yeah, she knew.

He came close and kissed her, his mouth hard on hers, tongue possessive. "If Sam weren't down the hall . . ."

"Yeah?"

"I'd bend you over the bed," he said.

An arrow of pleasure diffused in her pelvis like bright light. "Wow," she said. "Um, hold that thought?"

"Held. Make you a deal," he said.

"Uh-huh?"

"I'll let you drive part of the time, but I drive in bed tonight."

Oh, God, that turned her on, too. What was *wrong* with her? She liked the whole big male dominant gorilla act *way too much*. "I can live with that." She could better than live with it; she'd be fantasizing about it all the way to the Oregon coast.

"Where are we staying at your mom's house?"

"Sadly, probably with Sam," he said. "But I will find a way. Trust me?"

"Completely," she said. And meant it.

Oh, God, what am I doing?

"Okay if I drive first?"

She touched his hair, put her lips to his clean-shaven cheek, and breathed the soap scent of him in. "Yeah."

23

J ake drove the whole way. Instead of taking I-5 south, he took the route that brought them closer to the Pacific, so he could wind down through the bays and inlets of Raymond and the other oystering towns of the southern Washington coast. The sun was out, and the broad, flat expanses of water sparkled and shone. Sam fell asleep first, his breathing buzzy from the backseat. Ten minutes later, Jake looked over to see Mira's head lolling back against her seat. It was peaceful, driving the two of them as they slept, the car like a bubble, warm and quiet.

He had called his mother early this morning to tell her he was bringing "someone who was very important to him." He'd been scheduled to spend this weekend with her anyway, and his sister, brother, niece, and nephew were all supposed to head out to join them. He didn't tell her who Sam was. Too weird to do that over the phone. Better to show up and shock the hell out of her.

Over pancakes, Sam had issued an endless series of questions.

"Can I tell the kids at school? That I got a dad?"

"Huh," Mira said. "Let me give that some thought, okay, Sam?"

"What do I *call* you?"

Jake had given Mira a stricken look. Because he suddenly couldn't find his voice. It was choked back beneath layers of grief, and he was afraid that if he spoke, he'd break down, and he didn't want to scare the hell out of Sam.

"What do you *want* to call him?"

"Can I call him Dad?"

Mira looked to him for approval. For a moment he was too staggered to move. He hadn't thought it would matter to him what Sam called him, but it mattered. God, it mattered. He nodded.

Sam mulled it over carefully. "I might forget sometimes and still call him Jake."

"That's okay, too," Mira said.

Jake had looked at Mira over the top of Sam's head, and she'd smiled at him, and he'd thought, *This.*

And then, *I'm in so deep.*

Mira woke up when they pulled onto the bumpy access road to his mom's beach house. "Are we here?"

"Uh-huh."

He parked in the driveway, and Sam whimpered in the backseat and woke up.

"Is this my other grandma's house?"

"Yup."

And there, in the doorway, was Sam's other grandma. She looked good, a little heavier than Jake remembered, which wasn't a bad thing, because she tended not to eat when she was stressed out. She'd been barely more than a frame to hang clothes off by the time he'd left Walter Reed. Her hair was all puffed out like she'd been walking on the beach, a mass of silver that was sometimes tight curls but right now was a cloud. She came down the steps to the car and hugged Jake. "Look at you!" she said. "Look at you driving and walking and—you look great! You look—happy. Healthy. Oh, so good to see you looking so good. Oh, Jake." She reached up and patted his face.

"Mom. I have some people I need you to meet."

Mira got out of the car. She was pale; he could see it from here.

"Mom, this is Mira."

"Hello, Mira." His mother extended her hand, polite. Her face was quizzical, but she was willing to be patient, he could see, to find out what all this meant. Who Mira was to him.

I'd explain it if I understood it, Mom.

"And this guy—" Jake put his arm around Sam's shoulders. "This is Sam. Mom. You might want to sit down."

He tried to warn her with his voice. To give her a moment, a little space to process what was sure to be a large shock.

His mom took a step back. Then another. Then she took his advice and sat down on the steps leading up to the house. Her eyes were huge and fixed on Sam's face.

"He's mine," Jake said.

"Oh, my God," she said. "Oh, my God. Jake. I would have known. Just look at him. Why—why didn't you—" Her hands came up, open, pleading.

"I didn't know. Until I came home."

His mother's eyes flicked to Mira's face, but he shook his head. "It's not her fault. She tried to get in touch with me. She tried for a long time. She thought my name was Jake and that

I was a grunt, and it didn't occur to her to look for a Ranger named Jackson. And then I was so off the grid for so long— she would never have been able to track me down, even if she'd had the right name."

"I should have called you Jack," his mother said, irrelevantly, staring at Sam without taking her eyes off him. "My God. Sam, you said? Sam, how old are you?"

"Seven. Almost eight."

"God. Jake."

There were tears in Jake's mother's eyes. He'd given her so goddamned much to cry about this year. He hated that more than anything. If he never put tears in her eyes again, it would be too soon.

I'm sorry, Mom. So sorry for everything. For scaring you half to death. For coming home broken.

When he'd been a boy, she'd sometimes said—like when she had to pour isopropyl alcohol on an open cut—"This hurts me more than it hurts you."

This hurts me more than it hurts you, Mom.

"I've made you cry. Again."

She looked up at him. Saw the look on his face, the apology, the pain. "Don't be ridiculous," she said, over Sam's head. "Don't be ridiculous."

"*Are* you crying, New Grandma?" Sam asked.

Mira made a small sound behind him.

"I am," New Grandma said. "And do you know why?"

"Why?" Sam asked.

"Because I have had a very lucky year. God has seen fit not only to send me back my son, alive and whole, but also to send me a grandson."

"I'm lucky, too," Sam said. "I have a new grandma and a new aunt and uncle and cousins."

There were tight bands wrapped around Jake's chest.

"And how would you feel about giving your new grandma a hug?"

"I could do that," Sam said, and came forward into Jake's mother's arms.

Over Sam's shoulder, Jake watched his mother's face crumble.

"Hello, Sam," Jake's mother said, through her tears. "Welcome to the family."

THEY WERE POLITE TO HER, but cool. And that was okay. She didn't need them to fall all over her and welcome her with open arms. It was enough that they did that for Sam. Jake's sister, Susannah, hugged and kissed Sam, and Jake's brother, Pierce, shook his hand earnestly and told him they were very, very glad to have a new nephew. Then Sam's cousins surrounded him like there were more than two of them and herded him to the guest room where, they said, there were so many Legos he wouldn't believe it wouldn't believe it wouldn't *believe* it! The cousins were Abigail, who was nine, and Dylan, who was six and had eyes like Sam's, although his face shape was different.

Then it was just the adults, and Jake's mom, Janet, set out sandwich makings. For a few minutes, Mira didn't need to make any conversation because everyone was engaged in construction and assembly.

The house was small, but it wasn't a shack. It was a well-loved cottage, with a sliding glass door out to a deck that overlooked the Pacific, and a great room with a high ceiling, a galley kitchen, a long dining table, and a living area. They sat on the couches and chairs—which occupied some charming realm between beach chic and shabby—and began to eat their sandwiches. Then the grace period was over, and Susannah asked, "So, forgive my abruptness, but I think we've all got a few questions here."

Well, yes, they would.

"How is it we have a nephew—grandson—whatever—we didn't know existed for *seven years?*"

The question was aimed at Jake, but Mira knew that ultimately, it was a question for her. That all the questions were for her.

We have a nephew. Strange how despite Susannah's hard tone, Mira could feel so grateful for those words. And so joyful, too, because this was a room full of people that belonged to Sam. His *family*.

"We met when Jake was home on leave. We fought, and we broke up."

"It was my fault," said Jake.

She shot him a look, surprised and grateful, and he gave her a lopsided smile.

"I probably should have called him right away, but I didn't, because everyone said I shouldn't tell him, that it would be unfair because he was deployed and he'd get himself killed worrying over it instead of having his head where it should be. They said I should tell him in person when he came home."

Susannah narrowed her eyes, but she nodded. "I can see that," she said.

"So I left messages, but they didn't explain."

"And I didn't get them. And I didn't come home for almost fifteen months."

"God. I remember," said Janet, exchanging glances with Susannah.

"Okay, but at some point, right?"

Mira nodded. "I tried. I was looking for 'Jake' and he was Jackson, and I—I wasn't thinking he'd be a Ranger, so there was nothing to help me narrow down 'Jake Taylor.'"

"Taylor's a common name," Susannah said gently.

It was grace, Mira understood, and she bit her lip, holding back tears.

"And we're unlisted," Susannah added, her gaze moving from Mira's face to her mother's, then pausing and softening still more on Jake's. "So you couldn't find him that way. Even if you'd had anything to go on other than 'Taylor.'"

"I wish I had," Mira said. Her heart twisted. It was their loss, too, all those years of Sam they hadn't had. She had never let herself really imagine that they existed, this other family, these people who belonged to Sam. Who could have belonged to her.

"Well," Susannah said. "We're all here now, right? That's the important thing."

Mira had to close her eyes, then, and they gave her a minute to put herself back together. When she looked up again, Susannah was smiling at her. Not an all-out, full-on smile, but one Mira recognized. Sam's tentative smile. Jake's.

"How did you guys find each other again?" Susannah asked.

Jake spoke before she could. "I ran into them in the physical therapist's office. And she told me."

"That must have taken a lot of courage," Susannah said. Not warmly, not exactly, but with admiration.

Mira shook her head. "I'd always promised myself if I ever saw him again, I'd tell him the truth."

"So just like that? Right in the physical therapist's office?"

"Right in the physical therapist's office," Jake confirmed.

Put like that, so baldly, it was a little terrifying. The way she'd cracked their lives wide open on the strength of a promise she'd made to herself years before. He could have been an awful man. Deeply broken, unhealable. Years of physical violence could have made him angry, bitter—even violent himself. But something about him must have seemed essentially unchanged to her. She must have seen, felt, some core *Jake* reaching out to her, through the grumpiness, the unwillingness. And that Jake had become more and more present every day, until now he felt like the embodiment of everything she'd let herself love about him beside the lake.

She reached out and took his hand, and he squeezed hers, hard.

Susannah and her mother exchanged glances.

"Are you two—together?"

That was Jake's brother, Pierce.

She felt panicky. She didn't know the answer, and how could she not know the answer to such an important question? Why hadn't she used the car ride down here to talk to him about where things stood? She could have brought it up tentatively, said something like, *Hey. So, I know we said we'd keep things simple, but I think we can both agree they're not anymore. Where do we go from here?*

But she hadn't. And if the same question had been on his mind, he hadn't said so.

She realized she was holding her breath. Waiting for his answer.

"We've been spending a lot of time together," Jake said cautiously.

It wasn't until her heart sank that she realized that she'd wanted more from him. That she'd wanted an emphatic *yes*. Even though she wasn't sure she would have given an emphatic yes if their situations had been reversed. Even though she had more questions than answers in her own mind.

"But—"

She wanted him to stop. She wanted him to look at her and hesitate and invite her to help him answer this question. She didn't want him to dive ahead and say,

"But Mira just came off a serious relationship and she's still trying to get her feet back under her. And I'm thinking about trying to get myself returned to active duty."

"No!"

That was Jake's mom. And Mira knew how she felt, though she'd vowed years and years ago that she'd never again say or do anything with the intention of holding him back.

"It's a long shot, Mom. Some AK guys, it's just over, and that's it. But I think I need to try. It's just, you know, this is who I am."

Jake's mother turned away, looking into a far corner. She blinked back tears. "When?" she asked.

"Not sure," he said. "I haven't decided for sure."

Susannah went to her mother and put an arm around her, and the two women clung to each other.

I want to be Susannah's friend, Mira thought.

As if Susannah had heard her thoughts, she released her mom and turned back to Mira. "So—who *are* you, instant sister-in-law?"

"I'm not—"

"Mother of our instant nephew and grandchild, then? Tell us about yourself."

No punches pulled in this family, for better or for worse.

"Mira paints these gorgeous watercolors. She's interested in becoming a children's book illustrator."

She gave Jake a look.

"It's true," he said mildly.

"It was true," she said. "Before Sam."

There was a moment of silence, during which she imagined they were all individually dying to know the story of *that*. Well, they'd have to wait. "I do user-interface design for a website that sells shoes. I figure out how users want to use the site and I design it to make it easiest for them."

"Is that more like graphic design? Or more like computer programming?"

"It's a little of both," she said. "It's actually more of a business role, in some ways. I'm trying to understand customers, understand how to make them more likely to buy, more likely to finish transactions successfully, more likely to come back. It's an interesting mix of skills."

"Sounds like it," Susannah said. "And you've been—raising Sam on your own?"

She nodded.

"That must have been hard."

"Sometimes very hard. But rewarding, too. I had help. From my parents. I was living with them in Florida until recently."

"Was it a permanent move? Out here?" Janet asked.

Mira couldn't help smiling at the transparency of that question, and at the way all those sets of eyes anxiously pinned her. "Yes. I'm planning to stay."

There was something like a collective sigh of relief in the room.

"Well," Janet said. "We're so glad you're here. You and Sam. Welcome."

It made Mira's tears flow again. She swiped them away with the back of her hand. "Thank you."

"What does it feel like? To have an instant family?"

Mira was about to respond. To say that it was a good thing. She was surprisingly comfortable here with them, despite the inquisition. The way they'd welcomed Sam. The way they regarded her warily but without judgment.

But before she could open her mouth, Jake spoke, and she realized the question had never been intended for her.

"Like Christmas in July."

24

"Did you mean that? What you said to your sister? About Christmas in July?"

"Of course I meant it."

She felt stripped bare, by all the anger and suspicion, all the love and grief, that had been in the room earlier.

Holding him at bay hadn't kept her from falling. Again. She'd told herself, told him, that she wanted things simple. That she needed space, and time, when all she needed was him.

Him.

Are you guys together?

If it had been her question to answer, she would have said: *Yes.* And shocked the hell out of herself in the process.

That afternoon, they'd watched the cousins play on the beach, then shared a jovial family dinner where everyone had talked up and over each other, voices weaving and mounting into a cacophony—as an only child of only children, Mira had never experienced anything like it, and it thrilled her that this was Sam's legacy, his destiny. And all of that, the sweetness, the joy, only amped up the emotions that threatened to boil over.

And then they'd come down here, to the brink of the Pacific, and he'd built them a beach bonfire. First he'd made a circular fire pit from the smooth round rocks that covered the upper half of the beach, then he'd refused her help at gathering driftwood from up and down the beach, even though she could see that he had trouble with his footing on those stones. But she hadn't tried to convince him. She understood him well enough now to know that it wasn't important to him to do things the most efficient possible way, but it was incredibly important to him to do them his way, himself.

Now they sat under a blanket on a huge driftwood log in the glow of the fire, and the flickering flames cast his face into beautiful relief. Shadows under his brow, his cheekbones, the hard, hard line of his jaw. There had never been any man she could stare at so happily. No man whose simple physical presence started such a thrum in her body, whose gaze on her face could make her want to give herself over, throw herself open. Body and soul.

Below them, somewhere in the dark, moonless night, the ocean gave off a steady roar that drowned the rest of the world and left them here, alone, in this circle of light.

He tucked his fingertips into her hair and turned her head so he could capture her mouth.

The first kiss was a tease. A nip, a slick, quick entry and retreat.

"You're delicious," he said.

She made a sound of protest.

"More?"

She nodded.

"Come here."

He pulled her down, hitched her legs up so she was straddling him across the log. She fitted herself to him, his erection pressing hard up between her legs, hot against her lips and her clit. She rearranged the blanket around them, and he kissed her again. More a long, slow press and glide. *This is what I'm going to do to you later.* His hands roaming, finding all the tender, striving parts of her, waking her up, making her moan.

She was dissolving, a peculiar trick of the heat of his body, the heat of the fire, and the flickering light that made everything not quite real. She melted, her whole groin and belly, her thighs, her breasts. Lost definition until he was the only thing holding her on the log.

"Take your pants off," he said.

"Anyone could see us."

"We'll be under the blanket. I want to be inside you."

She obeyed, shucking her pants, swinging her leg back over him. He'd unbuttoned and unzipped, and he extracted a condom from a pocket and did something swift and efficient under the blanket, between their bodies.

It was absurd. Driftwood splintery under them, the socket of his artificial leg rubbing uncomfortably against her thigh, a reminder each and every time he thrust up into her. His jeans in the way, getting sticky and damp as she got wetter and wetter around him, as he pushed up unevenly and without any smoothness into her. It shouldn't have been sexy at all. It should have been all the myths of sex on the beach busted wide open—sand and saltwater in tender places, the realization that you don't like this near-stranger enough to be letting him screw you in an almost public place.

Instead it was something else. The firelight slipping and sliding into her vision as her eyelids drooped closed, as they opened again in surprise at something unexpected he'd touched, some spot he'd awoken when she didn't even know it was there. The orange and yellow flames a strange and perfect alchemy with her emotions, stirring them up, heating them up. Making it so the stray bits and pieces of things weren't obstacles, they were amplifiers. The friction, the not-quite-all-the-way, uneven thrust of him, *him*, because no one else fucked like that, the wool blanket getting in the way, his hands moving unexpectedly, reaching to push a cold, hard button out of the way— "No," she said. "Leave it there, I can feel it against my clit"—and he groaned, and bit her neck, so hard she knew he'd leave a mark she'd have to explain to her son and her new family, but she didn't give a crap, because who knew that denim scraping against the damp crack of your ass could feel so good. She couldn't move in all the ways at once that she needed to feel everything he was offering her —the hard grip of his arms around her, keeping her balanced so there was this crazy pressure in all the right places she never could have achieved if they'd planned the most perfect sex in bed ever; the sound of his breath, harsh and splintered with growls and groans, so close it hurt her ear. He was holding her too tight, and she was too hot, sweating, sweating in the wool blanket and the heat they made, the heat from the fire, and her orgasm, when it came, came from nowhere, boiled up out of the mess and the chaos, all disordered and pulled together out of threads of need into this one big thorough letting go, and she gasped his name and felt him surge up into her, rigid under her, as surprised as she was, and saying her name in a broken, hungry way that hurt her chest.

I love you.

It beat in her ears and her head like a drum, demanding. It wanted to be freed. It wanted to be spoken out loud like a chant.

Loveyouloveyouloveyouloveyouloveyou.

What would happen if she said it?

What if, for him, it wasn't like that? What if it was uncomfortable buttons sticking into his squishy parts and too much damp and sweat and clothes and blankets and his artificial leg getting between him and some smooth, easy version of the world? What if the words beating in his head were *Wow, that hurt*?

What if by instant family, and Christmas in July, he'd only meant Sam? What if she said *I love you* and he didn't say it back? What if he said, *Mira, hey, I'm flattered, but we've talked about this*?

She might die.

And conversely, what if she said *I love you* and he *did* say it back? What if they *were* an instant family?

Naive, her father's voice said in her head. *No such thing as an instant family. You want family? You come home to Florida.*

No fucking way, she told him.

What if they went home and Jake moved in and set up shop and started taking care of them, the way she craved and dreaded?

Self-indulgent.

She'd have moved all the way across the country—

Impetuous.

—and proved exactly nothing about her ability to survive the world on her own.

Flaky. Foolish.

If she said *I love you*, and Jake said it back, if those words rearranged her world so that she was no longer in charge of it, then her father would have been proved right about her.

No fucking way.

At least her father's words had drowned out the chant in her head. It had gone silent, the insistent words, the throbbing emotion, underground again.

The edge of his jeans button was painful against her now oversensitive clit. The damp clothes under her felt awful and sordid. And that was a relief.

It felt safer this way.

He made a rough sound in his throat. "How?"

That seemed to be the only word he could speak. He tried it again a few more times, and then finally managed, "How was that so hot?"

"I don't know," she whispered back.

His heart was thudding away, a thousand miles per hour. An artifact of the sex, which had stolen his breath and his thoughts, which had made him come harder than he'd ever come in his life, which had squeezed to the surface every emotion he'd thought he'd be able to hold at bay this time.

But he couldn't, could he? He'd never been able to.

All those years ago, beside the lake, it had been like this. Emotion bigger than him, bigger than his capacity to see or understand, bigger than his capacity to make the right decision. All those years ago, she'd asked him to claim her, and he'd failed her, like he'd failed her earlier in the beach house with his family when they'd asked him if he and Mira were together.

We've been spending a lot of time together.

A non-answer. As telling as his silence had been that night at the lake.

He made the same mistakes over and over, hurt the people he loved most, because love made him stupid, because caring this much about someone was a recipe for the worst possible judgment.

Get up. Go inside. Don't—

Don't what?

Don't tell her.

But the pressure of the words, of the memories, in his head was too much. This raw, uncomfortable, weird, messed-up sex, the sense of turning himself inside out into her, it made it impossible to hold anything back from her. All of him wanted out. All of him craved the freedom of her. Even if he regretted it. Even if it laid him bare and tore him apart.

"My best friend died in Afghanistan," he said.

White words, bolts of lightning, stark against the blackness of the sky, under which the foamy surface of the Pacific was only barely visible.

Her breath whistled inward. Then, "Jake."

"Don't."

"Jake."

And just like in the car all those years ago, the words spilled out of him, confessional shards. "The story I told you. He was the driver. When I told him to go, go, go, and he froze up? I knew that was going to happen. I'd seen him do it twice before in pressure situations. I'd taken him aside. I was the team sergeant. I took him aside and told him I was sending him home. He *begged* me not to. Begged. And I caved. If I'd manned up, if I'd done what I needed to do, he'd be alive."

The Pacific roared steadily on, wave after wave washing up on this shore, on every shore in western North America, in eastern Asia. Touching so many sands, connecting parts of the world that were far away. Echoing the rush of his blood through his heart, the pounding of that stupid, hopeful muscle in his chest.

He waited. He didn't know for what.

She took a breath.

"Why?"

"Why didn't I send him home?"

She nodded.

In the dark, she was perfect, as she'd been that first night, her hair glowing like pale gold, slivers of moonlight describing the contours of her face, shining in her eyes.

"I told myself I was afraid he'd kill himself. That if I shamed him and sent him away, he'd put a pistol in his mouth and pull the trigger."

"Because that's what you believed you'd do. If it were you."

Something rose up in him, in his chest, and he was drowning, couldn't catch his breath, couldn't breathe at all. It felt like a ton of ocean water was crashing down on him, a wave curling up and over his head, like he was being being tossed around in the curl and churn and whitewash under the water until he didn't know which way was up, and he had to hold his breath and pray.

"Does it make it worse? That you didn't? That you came home and managed to stay alive?"

He hadn't put a pistol in his mouth or drunk himself to death, and he'd risen to the surface after every wave that had threatened to crush and drown him, and when he'd broken back into the gaseous universe, there had been Mira and Sam and this idea of *family*. There had been something that mattered beyond what he'd imagined could.

"Because now you have to think about the fact that Mike might have, too?"

She was supposed to say, *It's not your fault.* She was supposed to absolve him and forgive him, because that was what kind and good people had done over and over again, uselessly, since the day he'd found out Mike was dead. *You shouldn't blame yourself. Don't punish yourself; you've already been punished enough. No one could have done any better.*

He hated her. For being right, for saying what no one else would ever say because no one else would ever see him that clearly. For dragging him down into this muck, this churning sand that was flaying him raw.

He loved her.

"Jake."

"Don't. *Don't.*"

She touched his face. Stroked her thumbs over his eyebrows, then his cheekbones. Leaned close. Her breath moved across his face like a benediction. Like an invitation. *Here is where you can breathe again.*

"Mira. Mira."

She held him tight while the sobs worked their way through him, and when the first wave had broken and he surfaced into the world, she kissed him and he breathed her, and then her hands were on him, sheathing him with another condom, her body over his, and he was sinking, sinking into grief and warmth and comfort. She said his name over and over again, and he clung to it and let himself be washed away, washed clean.

25

When they pulled up outside Mira's house late the next afternoon, there was a car parked outside, a white midsized Chevy that screamed rental. A dark-haired man—around Jake's age—sat behind the wheel, iPhone in hand, and as they cruised past the car to turn into Mira's stubby little driveway, he looked up from the phone and waved hello.

"Oh, *shit*," Mira said.

"*Mommy!*"

"Oh, *shoot*," she amended.

"Who is it?" Jake asked, just as Sam demanded, "Is that *Aaron*?"

The look on Mira's face said Sam was right. Jake's gut gave a sick squeeze. "What's he doing here?"

"I have no idea," Mira said.

"It's Aaron!" Sam said, bouncing in the backseat. "I wonder if he brought me Legos! Aaron always brings me Legos," he explained to Jake. "And he helps me put them together."

So that was where Sam's twenty-gallon tote of Lego pieces had come from. It figured. Jake had sat on the floor with Sam the day he'd babysat, assembling complicated visions from his son's imagination, according to Sam's detailed directions. *No, the* blue *one. No, not there,* there.

Aaron had done the same, apparently. Probably many more times. Over many more weeks, months, years, even. And how many times had Mira spent the night in Aaron's arms?

A lot more than twice.

Jealousy burned in his chest, sending a bile taste to the back of his throat, a testosterone shot to the groin.

As dismissive as she'd been when she'd told him about Aaron, he knew there was history there. Maybe *because* of how dismissive she'd been. And he knew she'd left Aaron in anger, after he'd hurt and betrayed her, which meant that there was still strong feeling. Which meant that she might be only a sincere apology away from regretting ever leaving.

Was that what this was? Had Aaron come to deliver an apology? To reclaim what was his?

She's mine now, thought Jake, but then another deeper and older part of his brain said, *You didn't say she was yours when you had the chance, did you?*

The driver's side door opened and a tall man emerged. The sort of guy who would wear a suit and work on Wall Street or as a lawyer. The sort of guy who could play the leading man in a romantic comedy, opposite Mira, who would be played by Drew Barrymore, maybe, or, in a pinch, Kirsten Dunst.

This was a guy who was committed. Who was in the world. Who had made a decision—*I'm going to get her back—*

and a plan, who had flown across the country to claim what was his. He had a job, light behind his eyes. A little swagger, but not so much Jake hated him on sight. This guy had made mistakes in the past, but now here he was, making things right.

And who was Jake? What had he done to rejoin the world? He still had no job. Still hadn't committed himself one way or the other to returning to active duty, still hadn't actually signed up for the triathlon he was theoretically planning to do. A guy in limbo. A guy who'd latched onto Mira and Sam because he needed a sense of purpose but hadn't yet been able to find one of his own. A parasite on their lives, a lurker, a hanger-on.

Aaron had something to give Mira and Sam, and all *he'd* done, all he *could* do, was take.

On top of the rest of it, on top of the grief and the longing, on top of that emotion he was too fucking scared to name, the one that had reached out to her last night through the discomfort and the awkwardness, that had connected straight to the center of her through all the messy, uncomfortable meaty bits of being human, on top of all that, he was dying of jealousy. And it was too much. Too much feeling. If there was one thing he knew about himself, it was that he made the worst decisions when he felt the most.

"I'm sorry," Mira told Jake. "I have no idea what he's doing here. I'll get rid of him."

For a moment, the part of his brain that had cried out *She's mine, now* gained the upper hand, and he almost said, *Yes—get rid of him. Get him the fuck out of here.* But he looked at Sam and he looked at Mira—so beautiful, so smart, so gutsy —and he thought, *Do the right thing. For once.*

"Maybe you should find out what he came all this way to say."

She gave him a confused look. "I guess."

She got out of the car. Jake got out, too, and stood beside Sam. It was still warm and light out, although it was probably close to nine now, and Sam had to be exhausted, ready to drop. Although he'd slept some in the car.

"Hi, Mira," Aaron said.

He had a low, steady voice, perfect for the romantic part Jake had cast him in.

Mira's face was all wide-eyed emotion. Confusion, yes, and something else, something open and vulnerable and needy.

She'd downplayed it, but she'd loved this guy once. Maybe still loved this guy.

God *damn* it.

"Hi, Aaron."

"Aaron!" Sam said, and catapulted himself into Aaron. And of course, Aaron, being Aaron and having two sound legs, did not totter or topple or have to catch himself by reaching out for Mira's arm, but instead snatched Sam up with both arms and spun him around and hugged him.

Double God *damn* it.

"I'm sorry it's taken me this long," Aaron said. "I should have come after you right away. But I was—I was doing some serious thinking about my life. I wanted, when I came, to be able to tell you this . . ."

Jake could step in now. He could say, *You're too late, man.*

He could say, *Mira, wait. I should have told you I loved you. On the beach. After we made love. Which, by the way, undid me. Turned me inside out. I was too busy spilling my guts, losing my shit, to say what needed to be said. To do what needed to be done.*

Why hadn't he said it after he'd made his confession, when they were making love to each other again and she was wiping the tears from his face; when she was telling him over and over again that it was okay; when she was absorbing his grief and his fear and making it, temporarily, really, truly okay?

Because I suck at this. I suck at feeling too much and wanting too much, and I've screwed up so many things that matter . . .

"I'm interviewing for a job in Seattle this week, and I'm up here to look for a place to live. For both of us, all of us, to live. I came up here—Mira, I came to ask if you'd—"

Aaron reached into his blazer pocket and pulled out a little navy velvet box, because somehow Jake had accidentally stumbled into this movie starring Ryan Reynolds and Katherine Hegel. Jake, it turned out, had a cameo as the rebound guy.

Aaron held out the ring box, open, and something—Jake knew what—winked and flashed. "Mira, will you marry me? I promise, I'll prove to you that your dad had *nothing* to do with my feelings for you. Just give me a little time—I'll prove it."

The turmoil in Jake's head and stomach was such that it took him a moment to realize that Mira wasn't reaching for the box in Aaron's hand. She had turned, and she was looking at him.

He needed to throw down a gauntlet, fight for her, but he couldn't fight for her because he wasn't prepared to hold the territory. He'd be some occupying army that would rape and pillage, and when he was done, he'd have nothing to offer. Not security, not safety, not peace. Aaron—Aaron had come three thousand miles, had planned and executed this, flown across the country with a ring box in his hand, a diamond glittering in the waning sunlight, a man so right for Mira that Mira's own father had hand-picked him for her.

Jake would make the right decision this time.

"He's just asking for you to give him a chance," Jake heard his own voice saying.

"Jake—"

He started to back away. Toward the street, retreating to the bus stop.

She followed him. She stepped away from Aaron, away from the tall, dark, good-looking family guy with the velvet box in his outstretched hand, and followed Jake into the street, taking a step toward him for every shaky, asymmetrical step of his retreat.

"Jake?"

They were far enough away now that their lowered voices were probably inaudible to Aaron, but he watched them from a distance, and Jake could see he was trying to figure things out. Trying to understand what had happened in his absence, trying to grasp what he was up against.

Nothing, dude—I'm no obstacle to your happily ever after. This time, I'm not going to let my emotions get in the way of making the right decision.

Because last time, he hadn't. Because he'd let his feelings get between him and what he'd known was best for Mike. For the team. Because he'd let *love* cloud his judgment.

"I'm trying to keep you from making a mistake," Jake told Mira.

"I don't understand," she said. "Really? That's all you're going to say? You're going to say, 'He's just asking you to give him a chance,' and you're going to walk away? *I don't understand.*"

"Maybe you walked away too quickly from him," Jake said.

"Jesus, Jake, *stop.* Stop with Aaron. We're not talking about Aaron. We're talking about you. You and me."

"We're talking about you and Sam."

"And *you.*"

"No," he said. "We're not talking about me. I'm not on the table here."

She was crying now.

"I can't give you what he's offering."

"I don't need you to give me what he's offering," she said. "I want what *you're* offering."

Her voice, her face, her raised hands *pleaded* with him, and something cracked behind his ribs, and he wanted to put his hands over his chest to hold the pieces together.

"I told you from the beginning. I can't give you—" Damn it, his voice was *not* going to fucking break on him right now. "We talked about this. We said it was about sex and Sam. We've known each other, what, a few weeks? The fact that my genes happen to be in Sam—"

Her face shifted, fault lines showing, but he kept talking. "That's not as important as all the time you and Sam spent with Aaron."

"You're talking me into staying with him."

"I guess I am."

"You're telling me what I want."

"Yeah, I guess I am."

"God damn it, Jake, I told you not to fucking do that."

He was startled by her vehemence. Her anger.

Her voice was low, hard. Her jaw set. "Don't you tell me what I want and what I deserve. Don't make this about me."

And he heard it now, the echo of the first night he'd kissed her. *Just man up and say you don't want this.*

Just man up.

Just man up.

If he'd done what he should have done, Mike would be alive. He'd have two whole legs.

If he had done what he should have done that night at the lake, or afterward, when he'd dropped her off, how would things be different now?

He couldn't know that. He could only start from here and make the best decision he could, do the best that he knew how by the people he loved.

He steadied his voice and made it hard as iron. "You know what? You're right. I'm being a wimp about this. I should just be honest with you. This is getting too complicated. We said we'd keep it simple, but we both know it's not."

She'd stopped crying. She was pissed.

"That's right," she said. "You've been honest with me all along. And that's all that matters, right? You never lied to me *in words.*"

And her anger was clarifying, like a cool drink of water, like Mike's anger would have been if Jake had sent him home. He'd been afraid of Mike's anger but he wasn't afraid of hers, because it was the price he had to pay for setting her free, for doing what was right for her and for Sam.

He could pay this price.

"Okay," he said.

He raised his hand and called out to Sam, "I'm going to

take off now, Sam—see you around, bud? We'll do something special soon."

He felt her there, watching him, but she didn't move, didn't say a word, as he started up the street.

"I thought he was going to stay with us?" he heard Sam say behind him, and it felt like someone was ripping his heart clear out of his chest. And he was pissed, so pissed at Mira, so pissed at himself all of a sudden, shocked by the depth of his rage, because no one had ever managed to tell Sam that family *hurt* you, that *family* sucked.

SHE WATCHED HIM GO, watched him trot up the street. The hitch in his step, the slight unevenness, was barely noticeable. So that if you didn't know how broken he was inside, the way he moved through the world would never clue you in.

Thank God she hadn't said *I love you,* hadn't left her pride scattered all over that beach, although damn, it didn't matter now, because her pride was scattered all over her street, and Aaron had seen it, too, seen her chase after him. She hoped she hadn't looked as pathetic as she'd felt, following him up the street, thinking, *What the* hell *just happened here?* Because it was one thing for her to hold him at arm's length, to keep some space between them, to keep things simple, and another thing entirely for him to hand her to Aaron on a silver platter.

As if none of it had happened. Not the wild sex on the log, not the long moment when she'd held him, both of them suspended in the weird magic they'd created, when she'd understood that loving Jake was a lose-lose proposition and that her only hope lay in not letting him know exactly how much she did love him. And not the moments that had come afterward when he'd laid himself bare to her, when he'd cried in her arms and she'd understood that it was as impossible for him to truly hold himself back as it was for her.

Yet he'd somehow held enough of himself back that he could walk away from her. Just walk away, as if he were the— the fucking babysitter.

And she had let him, because if her life had proved anything to her so far, it was that Jake was only her fantasy. And the realer he became, the faster and farther he slipped away.

He was not for her.

She turned and saw Aaron still standing beside his car, but the hand that held the velvet box had dropped to his side in defeat.

Huh. What had he seen? Whatever it was, it had told him that Mira's *yes* was far from assured.

She walked back toward him. Maybe that was the end of it. Maybe she wouldn't have to say the hard word, *No.* Maybe he would surrender and walk away, and she could take Sam inside and nurse his hurt feelings and cry herself to sleep.

But no, things weren't going to be that easy for her. The world wasn't that kind.

"Think about it," Aaron said. His handsome forehead was lined with confusion and concern. "I don't want you to give me an answer right now. Take your time."

"Aaron," she said. "I'm not going to marry you."

Because for all the things she didn't know, there were some she did know.

"Please," he said. "Don't be hasty. I'm here. I have interviews on Wednesday. I have appointments set up with Realtors for Thursday and Friday. I should at least go through with all that. And give me this week. Give me a little time to convince you I'm for real."

She shook her head. "I'm not going to change my mind."

"Mommy."

Sam was shaking her arm. He looked an awful lot like he was about to cry, and she prayed, for his sake and her own, that he would hold it together until she could get rid of Aaron. "Is Jake still going to babysit this week?"

"Oh, *fuck,*" she said aloud, and then clamped her hand to her mouth.

"Mommy, that's the worst bad word," Sam pointed out.

"Do you need someone to watch him?" Aaron asked. "Tomorrow, Tuesday, Wednesday? I was going to play tourist while you were at work—I can just as easily play tourist with Sam in tow."

"No," she said, at the same time Sam said, "Yes!" and then, with a little more caution, "Did you bring me Legos?"

"Yes, I did, buddy!"

Aaron always spoke to Sam in that slightly simpering, exclamation-mark-ridden voice, and Mira for the first time registered how much she *hated* it.

"Can we play with them?"

"We'll see," Aaron said, which Mira knew was code for *We'll see if your mother can be reasonable and let me babysit you when she knows she needs me to.*

"Let me know," Aaron said. "I'm here, I'm willing—it's gotta be easier than finding another sitter."

Yes. So much easier. And that was the goddamned thing,

her undoing. This was exactly who she had meant to avoid becoming, a woman who once again had proved that she was incapable of taking care of herself. Who let men weasel their way into her life, one act of salvation at a time.

You'll need my help paying for college, one way or another.

I don't see how you can afford to support yourself and this baby without my help, Mira.

I knew Aaron would be good for you, Mira. He's a steady guy. He'll be there for you when you need him.

She let them in at moments of weakness. When she was tired, so tired, and defeated. When she was back at square one, when she had no choices, when she had to do whatever was most expedient.

"Sam," Mira said, "go inside and get into your pajamas and brush your teeth."

"You *always* say that when things are getting interesting," Sam said.

"Oh, Sam," Mira said, and felt a rush of pure love for him. "Come here." And she threw both her arms around him and hugged him, hard, breathing in the seaweed-and-salt scent of his hair, the little-boy-in-the-sun smell of his skin. "You are such a good boy. Now. Go."

Sam went.

"He's gotten taller in the last two months. He looks great. I heard he had a spill."

"He healed fast. A few physical therapy visits and good as new."

"I miss him. I miss you."

"Aaron, don't."

"Just—don't say no. Not yet. Just—let me watch Sam for

you for a few days, okay? Give it a few days; think about it a little bit."

She couldn't help herself; she looked up the street in the direction Jake had gone.

"Were things serious with him?"

He'd used the past tense, and she hated that. But it was the dirty rotten truth of it, wasn't it? It was over, and more to the point, it had never begun.

"No," she said. And it didn't, mostly, feel like a lie. "Okay. I do need a sitter for tomorrow." *Assuming I still have a job.* She hadn't gotten an email from her boss or anything, despite Haley's threats.

"And you'll think about it?"

"I won't say *no* right this second."

"That's all I can ask."

But she couldn't help herself; she looked up the street one more time. Then she shook her head. He'd never claimed her, never promised her anything. As he'd said, he'd never lied to her.

If there had been any lying, she'd done it to herself.

26

The first few days after he walked away from her, he ran every day. He ran until it hurt, until the pain jamming up into his residual thigh, his hip, and his spine was like a column of fire that went almost all the way into his brain. He ran because the effort and the physical pain blotted out all the memories. Of the panic on Mike's face when he'd thought Jake was going to rat him out, and the relief on it when Jake had told him he'd keep his secret. And the blank, bowel-loosening paralysis as Mike had clutched the steering wheel and failed to put the pedal to the metal, the thing that would have saved his life and Jake's leg.

Of the look on Mira's face when she'd recognized him in the physical therapist's office: *No!* And *Yes!* As if she could speak the words that were in his heart, too.

Of the feel of Mira under him, on the ill-fated couch, on the firm surface of her mattress, her eyes rolling back in her head in a kind of mindless pleasure he didn't think he'd ever delivered to anyone else in his life. Of her soft welcome on the beach, a contrast to the way his jeans bound his legs, the way the log scraped his ass, a thousand discomforts rendered nonexistent by the sheer, unmuted thrill of the clutch and caress of her.

Of Sam's delight at having two parents play Monopoly with him. Of Jake's mother's joy at seeing Sam's face. At his siblings' anger turning to bemusement turning to revelatory love, because it was impossible to know Sam and not love him.

That must have been Mira's genes in him.

He ran until the pain had shape and rhythm and even a sound in his head, like a throaty hiss.

Three nights ago, after he'd gotten back downtown from Mira's house after walking out on Aaron's proposal, he'd bought a fifth of Gentleman Jack at Downtown Spirits and sat it in front of him on the table. He'd taken out all three of his intact highball glasses—he'd broken one the first week after he'd bought them, tripping over his prosthetic self. He'd arrayed the three glasses in front of him and poured two fingers of whiskey into each. Measuring out the hours.

He'd taken a slug from the first glass. It burned going down like he was a high school girl who'd never drunk the stuff before, and it tasted like failure in his mouth.

Goddamn her; she'd taken everything away, even his old refuges in self-pity and self-annihilation.

In his mind's eye, he could see them, standing together, Aaron and Mira, Sam at Mira's elbow. *Family*.

He threw the glass. It struck the far wall of his kitchen and shattered. The sharp smell of whiskey saturated the air.

Run.

It was something in the back of his reptilian brain, something older than the voice that had claimed Mira or the voice that had renounced her. It was the oldest voice back there, down there, the most primitive, the most fundamental.

If you can't fight, run.

He poured out the whiskey and went into his bedroom. He sat on the bed and strapped on his running prosthesis.

He ran along the waterfront to Myrtle Edwards Park, passing the cruise ships, as intricate and populous as small cities and drawn up into the curve of the bay like baby whales nursing, into the Sculpture Park. His back, his arms, his good leg, his residual leg—as well as his chest and his heart—loosened as he ran, as if air was flowing into all of them, breath, the breath of the world. By the big red sculpture that looked to him like a giraffe crossed with an elephant, by the giant typewriter eraser with its waving fronds, past the Eye Benches with their black obsidian folds, scrutinizing him. Seeing into the heart of his pain and loss. He wanted to call out to them, to the black eyes themselves, to the people seated on the benches, smiling, holding hands, gazing at the stretch of green grass, the sculptures jutting up, whimsical, toward the perfectly blue sky, *What do you see?*

What had she seen, what exactly, when he'd told her the truth about what he'd done? What he hadn't done? She had looked at him with sympathy, as if she saw into the center of him, and she had guessed, correctly, at some of what had passed through his mind, for better or for worse, during the moments when he'd tried to decide what the hell to do about his best friend, who was struggling with demons that might overtake him without a mission to drown them in . . .

He ran.

It hurt.

When it was hurting, he did not think about Mira.

MONDAY. Tuesday. Wednesday.

She went to work. She still had a job, though her boss had warned her that she was now in *last last-chance* mode. She did what had to be done, a foggy, dutiful slog. She ate lunch with Opal, giving her a quick-and-dirty version of what had transpired. "You were right. 'Not supposed to' is a flimsy barrier against that kind of chemistry. But it's over now."

Opal had questions in her eyes but didn't voice them aloud. She kept Mira entertained with funny stories about rejected marketing campaigns and her own recent bout of awful blind dates.

Monday. Tuesday. Wednesday. A procession of days accomplished. Marked off. Mira came home from work. She thanked Aaron for his help. She did not invite him to stay, not even when he lingered, awkwardly. Not even when he offered to pick up takeout. Not even when he asked, "Hey, what if I invited myself to dinner?"

"I'd politely decline," she said.

"We need to talk."

"I can't."

His eyes were hurt, but he didn't push it, and she was grateful. Not grateful enough to invite him to stay, but grateful.

Each night she tucked Sam into bed and answered questions to which she didn't know the answers. *Why hasn't Aaron been sleeping over? When will we see Jake again? Why hasn't Jake been sleeping over? I can still call him Dad even though he's not sleeping over, right? Does this mean you're not going to live together? Does that mean it's a divorce?*

She did her best. She felt dry and brittle, like old paper. She felt hurt and angry and weirdly relieved, because here they were, on their own, and she could still do it, could still tuck Sam into bed each night, go to work each morning. They were surviving, and one day she'd be less hurt and angry and they'd begin thriving, she and Sam, taking care of themselves. And it wouldn't matter that after only two nights of occupation, one of which had been down at the beach, Jake's side of the bed felt empty, a dark, expansive canyon of absence.

On Thursday, Mira left Sam with his former physical therapist, who had the day off. Because Aaron had things to do. Jobs to get and houses to hunt, and . . .

He'd flown across the country, apologized, proposed, and now he was arranging his life to make room for her as his wife. And she hadn't heard a word from Jake.

She acknowledged to herself that she had reached the end of some road. That she could not avoid answering Aaron's proposal forever. She owed him a decision. She owed him a conversation. She owed him serious consideration.

On Friday, when she came home from work, tired, so tired, her whole body aching like she had the flu, and he offered to pick up takeout for the three of them, she let him.

When Sam was in bed, she sat with him at the kitchen table. Not so long ago, she'd sat with Jake at this same table, and the air in the room had hummed and crackled and made every hair on her body stand on end, every last cell and fiber straining toward him.

Now the air in the room was dead. Heavy, as if with grief.

She knew. She knew from the fact that she'd chosen to talk with Aaron at the kitchen table, with a flat expanse of oak between them, and hadn't handed him a drink or invited him into the living room. She knew that no matter what he said to her, he wasn't going to change her mind, because it wasn't her mind's decision to make, anyway. It was her heart's, and her heart was aligned, like the rest of her, with Jake's magnetic north. No matter how badly he'd rejected her, no matter how well she understood that this was probably the best thing for her, no matter how sweetly simple had unfolded into complicated and no matter how violently it had collapsed back in on itself, like some kind of star with too much gravity to endure, no amount of talk, no amount of convincing, could talk her into believing that marrying Aaron would make her happy.

He knew, too. He sat heavily in the seat across from hers and said, "You're not going to say yes, are you?"

He was a good-looking man, with a strong, straight nose and dark hair. Dark brown, almost black, eyes. She'd once felt grateful to be courted by someone as attractive as him.

"No," she said.

"I shouldn't have taken his money. I get that."

"It isn't that."

"What is it, then?"

"You're a nice guy, Aaron. The best. You've been so good to me and Sam. And to my dad. You deserve someone who—"

She couldn't quite finish the sentence.

"Someone who loves me?" he asked wearily.

She nodded.

"You did, didn't you?"

"I thought I did," she said.

His face sagged a little, and she had to look away.

"That guy—the one who was here. That's Sam's father, isn't it?"

"Jake," she said.

He put his fingertips to his forehead, rubbed them back and forth over his temples, and said, "You love *him*."

She nodded. And thought, *I've always loved him.*

"But you let him walk away."

Defensiveness rose up in her like a tide. "I didn't *let* him."

"You didn't stop him."

"I tried," she said. "He told me I'd be better off with you."

He laughed, a hard, ugly sound. "How do you know he's not right?"

"Because . . ." She hesitated. "Look. I know you and my father are friends—"

"I know he hasn't always been fair, or kind, to you," Aaron said. "Even though he's my friend, I see how he underestimates you. And I told you the money had nothing to do with you, but the truth is, I think you're right that your father thinks it does, and that means it does. And I think you were right to run away from Florida. I just hoped—I hoped you'd be able to separate me from your father, to see us as two different men—"

"I do," she said. "And it means a lot to me that you would say that, but it doesn't change my mind. Not because you're somehow inextricably tied to my father in my mind, but because . . ."

"Because of *him*."

"He's one of the few things I've ever chosen in my life. I chose to move here, and I chose to be with him, and maybe my reasons are confused and screwed up, but there's this deep, strong, inside part of me that feels like those choices are the only things I know for sure about myself."

"Even if he doesn't choose you back?"

She nodded. And her heart broke a little, because she knew that was exactly what had happened the other day, when she'd walked away from Aaron and toward Jake. She'd chosen him, and he hadn't chosen her back. But that didn't make what she'd said to Aaron any less true.

"Even then."

27

Y ou could turn two weeks into a blur, Jake had discovered, if you were willing to keep moving. You could drown memory, you could drown pain, you could drown the sense of loss that woke you from the deepest sleep with the sensation of falling, as if you'd reached for her and she'd slipped from your grasp.

You could turn running and swimming and biking into a fight, a fight to hold onto purpose, a fight to hold onto sanity. And once they became a fight, you could cling to them doggedly, the way you could cling to the idea that your life would mean something if you could only avenge those tiny human figures falling like rain from the two towers.

Run.

Fight.

You want to text her? Call her? You want to know if she said yes, when the wedding date is, whether Sam will be the ring bearer?

You want to look at Facebook to see if she's posted any photos of

Sam she took, or crooked, ill-framed photos of Mira that Sam had taken?

Run, instead. Run. Fight the weakness.

His times had gotten better and better. They were at the low end, now, of what non-amputee triathletes could hope to achieve. And still rising, albeit slower and slower. Inching up.

He'd run with Pierce a few times, too. Pierce had been the only one who'd seen through the nonchalance of Jake's answer about Mira at the beach. *We've been spending a lot of time together.*

Pierce had shot him a look of clean, wry disbelief. And later that afternoon, making a before-dinner beer run with his brother, basking for the first time in almost a year in the old ease, Pierce had said, "You guys have been spending a lot of time together, huh? Can't blame you. She's hot."

"Step off."

"With both my fucking legs, man," Pierce said, and Jake knew the worst was past, the pity and the awkwardness over.

Because of that, Pierce had been the only one he'd told about breaking up with Mira, about Aaron's proposal.

He'd told the whole story on a long run, his chest and throat aching, as they had most of the last two weeks— whether from exertion or emotion, he wasn't sure.

And Pierce had said only, "You won't convince me he's the better man." And sped ahead, forcing Jake to push himself harder to catch up.

That was a brother for you.

When Jake wasn't running, he swam or biked. He biked the Burke-Gilman Trail from Fremont to Kenmore and back again. He took his bike on the ferry to Bainbridge and mapped out a trail for himself. Not a kindly trail that would

lead him around the edges of the island, not a tour of the
island's vistas—the Seattle skyline and Rich Passage—but a
harsh circuit of its ridges. A glacier had clawed six grooves in
the island's terrain, and you could ride up and down them in
succession, catching your breath before you forced yourself
over another one.

The harder it was, the more it drowned out the memories
—the scent and feel of her hair, the sound of her laughter, the
feeling that had no name, that in her presence he'd been safe
and, miraculously, whole. Those moments, with her, he'd
been happy, and he'd been able to believe, even if briefly, that
he deserved that happiness.

And then one day he ran home and found Sam sitting on
the front steps of his apartment building.

"What the hell are you doing here, Sam?" he said, before
he could think better of it or watch his language.

"That offends some people," Sam said tolerantly. "It
doesn't offend me because I think God probably has other
things to worry about besides whether we say 'hell' and
'damn' and stuff."

"Did your mother tell you that?" Jake asked, and he was
surprised by how much it hurt to invoke her, even at a slight
remove, even as "your mother" and not by name.

Sam nodded.

"Does your mother know where you are?"

Sam shook his head.

Jake pulled out his phone and texted Mira, "I've got Sam
here." No point in making her worry more than was
necessary.

"Did you text her?"

"Yeah."

"She's going to be really, really mad. The new babysitter was watching me, but she fell asleep on the couch."

"Where's Aaron?" Jake asked. He couldn't help it. It was petty and low and not a fair thing to demand of a seven-year-old boy, but it was the only question he wanted to know the answer to right then.

"He's in Florida," Sam said. "Mom told him she didn't want to marry him and he went back to Florida."

This gave Jake immense amounts of pointless pleasure, a rush of release that was almost sexual in its satisfaction. He'd meant what he said to her. He'd believed Aaron would take care of her. Take care of Sam. But when it came down to this —fuck all that. He was still glad the guy wasn't screwing Mira. He was so damn glad his throat was choked with it.

He sat down on the step next to Sam, and Sam pointed at his running prosthesis, at the curved metal "foot," and said, "That thing is kind of like Wolverine's claws. You look like a superhero."

"I know," Jake said. "And it's fast."

"Were you running?"

"I was."

"Are you still going to do a triathlon?"

"Yup."

Sam leaned over and gave the running prosthesis a thorough examination.

"Sam, maybe you should tell me why you're here so I can try to explain it to your mom and she won't be so mad. First of all, how did you get here?"

"On the bus," Sam said. "Mom always says that the bus drivers are nice and don't want you to be lost, so you can always ask them questions. So I waited for the bus near our house and asked how to get to your house. I remembered it was near Samami Restaurant, so I said that."

"You're very smart," Jake said, thinking, *I wonder how much credit I get for that genetically?*

"I came because I kept telling Mom I wanted to hang out with you and she kept saying, 'Tomorrow. I'll text him tomorrow.' And then I'd say, 'Mom, you said you'd text Jake today,' and she'd say, 'It's late' or 'I'm tired' or 'I can't think about that right now' or 'He's probably busy.' And finally I decided I needed to come find you."

"And so you did." It made him feel rotten to think of all those times Mira had decided *not* to reach out to him, even though of course he probably would have found ways to ignore her texts. Even though he had pushed her away. Handed her to Aaron on a silver platter.

She told him she didn't want to marry him.

Fuck it, that felt good, which made him an asshole.

"I wanted to tell you that I think you should ask Mom to marry you."

He turned, startled.

"You're my dad already, so it makes sense."

Sometimes Sam blew him away. "Not every two people who have a kid together are meant to be married."

"Do you love her?"

Jake nodded, as if he were a puppet driven by some other set of strings. As if it were impossible for him to lie. And maybe it *was* impossible for him to lie to Sam.

"So you should marry her."

Even when he was Sam's age, he was pretty sure he hadn't held such a romantic view of love and marriage. Even then, he was pretty sure he'd already believed that marriage, at best, was a complicated alchemy of necessity and forbearance that love had little to do with. That it was terribly easy to make the kind of mistake that would corrupt not only your own happiness, and your partner's, but the next generation's, too. How had Sam held onto this pretty, rose-colored version of the world, despite the fact that he'd believed his own origins story featured a plastic cup and a turkey baster?

"She loves you. I can tell."

Jake felt a surge of unruly, unwanted, unadmirable victory, followed by the sharp recollection of why such a victory wasn't a win for anyone.

"I wouldn't make her happy."

"Huh," Sam said thoughtfully, tilting his head to one side. "But you make really good pancakes."

Jake laughed, against his will. Sam had such a broad streak of wisdom in him, so often seemed so old for his age, that Jake had seriously expected him to say something revelatory. "Pancakes are good," he agreed. "But I don't think I could make her happy by just making really good pancakes."

"You like to go places we like to go, like Discovery Park and the Ferris wheel and the Oregon coast."

"True," Jake said.

"She smiles a lot more when you're around than when you're not," Sam said. "I don't think she's smiled since Aaron showed up, and she was really smiley before that."

Jake's stomach clenched at that. A memory resurfaced, sharp and dismal, of Sam saying that he hadn't told Mira about his lack of friends in Florida because he'd been worried about her happiness. This boy worried a lot about his mother's happiness. This boy knew the subtle degrees of Mira's emotions.

She smiles a lot more when you're around than when you're not.

And if that were true? What would it mean, anyway?

"I bet Aaron used to make her smile a lot, too," Jake said.

"Not as much," Sam said.

He should not have felt a wave of relief at that. He should not have.

He struggled to find the words to explain to Sam what he'd known with so much conviction the night he walked away from him and Mira. Because it was important to explain. It was important for Sam to understand. That he hadn't walked away to be cruel. He'd done it . . .

He'd done it to be fair.

"When you're a dad, or a husband, you take care of the people in your family. It's a big job, and to do a good job at it, you have to have your own life in order. Aaron has his life in order. He has a job and he knows what he wants, enough to fly out here and ask you guys to be in his family. I'm not like that."

"You have a job. You're a soldier."

"I *used* to be a soldier."

"Did you stop being a soldier when you lost your leg?"

"No," Jake said. And suddenly he understood the truth. "I stopped being a soldier when I lost my friend."

"You lost your friend?"

"He died in the war. And I didn't—I don't want to keep fighting. I'm done."

He expected to feel a sense of loss at the finality of his own words, but instead, he felt a rush of relief. *Done.*

"So now you could get a different job."

"I could."

"Why don't you?"

"I don't—I don't know."

Sam seemed to think about this for a long time. He actually rested his head on his palm like *The Thinker*.

"Are you afraid?"

28

S am was still waiting for his answer. *Are you afraid?*

He'd asked the question as if the thought was absurd. And all at once, Jake saw that it was. He thought of Sam's resilience, in the face of everything he'd experienced in the last several months. A move across the country, a fall, the acquisition and loss of several babysitters. The realization that he had a father he hadn't known he had. A grandmother, two aunts, an uncle, and two cousins. A whole fucking family.

The reappearance of a father figure.

The disappearance of a father figure.

And here Sam was, sitting beside him, having plotted an escape, a downtown bus trip, and—unless Jake was reading this whole thing wrong—essentially, an intervention.

Why had Jake ever thought, even for a moment, that he had *anything* to teach this kid about being brave?

As if Sam could read his mind, he said, "You told me that being brave was doing what you wanted or needed to do even if you were afraid."

Jake's throat was tight, his heart wide open with love for Sam. "Yes. I did."

But the thing was, aside from that single pithy reduction, which only put into words what Sam already embodied in the world, everything Sam knew about resilience, about being brave, he'd learned at his mother's knee.

She'd carried him and given birth to him, she'd raised him into the man he was becoming, the man he already *was*, and she'd done it without Jake. She'd made a decision relatively early on—she'd told him so herself—that she didn't need or want his help. And then, when it turned out that Aaron's partnership came at too high a price, she'd walked away from that, too. She'd driven three thousand miles, unloaded her possessions into a new house, started a new job, and then, when she stumbled straight into what had to be the most terrifying thing of all, confessing to *him* what he'd missed, she hadn't hesitated for one single second. Right there and then in the physical therapist's office, knowing almost nothing about who he was or how thoroughly he could upend her life, she'd done the right thing.

And then she'd slid down this slope with him, even though she'd been down it once before. Even though she knew where it had ended last time. Even though she knew the exact and particular ways he was driven and broken, the exact ways he could leave and break her.

That was brave.

"Yes," he said.

"It's okay to be scared," Sam said. "What are you scared of?"

A list was forming in Jake's mind. Of the things he needed to do. The people he needed to see—the ones he owed something to that he might finally deliver on, the ones he owed nothing to but might still disappoint. The ones he still hadn't met that he might have something real, something big, to give something of himself to.

"I have some things I have to do," Jake said.

"What things?" Sam asked.

"Grown-up things," Jake said.

"Scary things?"

"I thought they were. But now I think I can handle them."

In his pocket, his phone buzzed. He pulled it from his pocket. Mira, calling.

"Hey."

"What the *hell*?"

"He's totally fine. He ran away from his sitter and took the bus here." He decided not to tell her the sitter had been sleeping. Mira could figure it out. Handle it. God, she could handle anything. She could take life by the balls ten times over, and she pretty much had. Pregnant at eighteen, raising a kid on her own, fleeing her father to make something of herself. And meanwhile he was . . . Jesus, what?

Running away.

Mira was shrieking her outrage at the other end of the phone, and he handed the phone to Sam, because, after all, it was Sam's outrage to absorb. He watched Sam's face go through the same stages his would have gone through—guilt, contrition, apology, and then, when the diatribe went on several beats longer than was strictly necessary to make its point, irritation. He took the phone back. "Mira?"

"I'm going to send the sitter to pick him up," she said.

"You don't have to," Jake said. "He can hang out here for a while. We can go get cupcakes."

"Make sure—"

"I'll make sure they're allergen-free."

"I'll tell the sitter to get him around three. Does that work?"

"Yeah," Jake said. There was so much more he wanted to say to her, so much more he wanted to ask. *Sam says you're not going to marry Aaron—is that true? I know you've already given me a second chance, but how about one more?*

I love you.

But he'd told Sam he had things to do, and he'd meant it. Before he could ask for another chance, he had to deserve it.

He remembered how Mira had put it, on the beach, after he'd told her the truth about how his leg had been lost, how Mike had died. *You came home and managed to stay alive.*

He had, but he understood now that that wasn't enough. It wasn't enough that he hadn't put a gun to his head, that he hadn't drunk himself to death. It wasn't enough to sketch the outlines of living, to rise in the morning, eat three meals, and go to sleep at night. It wasn't enough to find purpose in the things that merely happened to fall in your lap, to take on responsibilities because they were handed to you and made you temporarily forget that you had no idea what came next.

Mira and Sam deserved a hell of a lot more than that.

When Sam had asked him what he was scared of, he hadn't had to think more than a second before he'd known the answer. The real answer.

Deciding to live.

29

"Mira, please talk to me."

It would have been better if it were Jake at the other end of the phone begging, if only so she could hang up on him, but it was her father.

Three weeks had passed. Three weeks since the beach, since Aaron had shown up with the ring, since Jake had walked away. Two and a half weeks since she'd sent Aaron packing. Ten days since the *first* new babysitter had fallen asleep on the couch and Sam had taken a bus downtown. The second new babysitter—Opal's second cousin's teenage daughter from Everett—was so far competent, if uninspired.

Mira went through the motions, heading to work, eating lunch with Opal on the bench, coming home, taking care of Sam. Missing Jake every minute of every day. When it came time to pick up takeout. When she cleared the table. When she sat on the couch, when she tucked Sam in, when she got into bed. When she trailed her fingers over her belly and thighs and remembered not just the sensation of him on her and in her, but all that had surrounded it—his roughness, his bossiness, the awkward *real*ness of it. That sense of connection, of dissolved boundaries, of emotion running through her like her own blood.

She hadn't spoken to her parents since Jake had walked away, because she couldn't face them. Because she couldn't bear their sympathy, couldn't bear to have her father know, even if he didn't say so, that he'd been right.

But now he was on the other end of the line, and as much as she wanted to hang up on him, she couldn't quite bring herself to do it.

Her father cleared his throat. "Lani says I haven't been fair to you."

As an apology, that didn't go far, but she waited.

"I didn't even give you a chance to explain yourself. I just waded in, guns blazing."

"Yeah, you did," she said. Not that if she'd had a chance to explain it, things would have gone much differently.

What the hell is Jake doing there?

Exactly what you think. Getting some, as long as things don't get too complicated.

He sighed. "And she's right. I know she's right. If you trust Jake with Sam, we need to trust him too. I owe both of you an apology."

A few weeks ago, she would have been ecstatic to hear those words come out of her father's mouth. Now . . .

Well, now it hardly mattered.

Still, it was nice, and it was rare for her father to admit he'd been wrong, even under pressure from Lani, so she said, "Thanks, Dad."

"So—do you want to tell me about it?"

"There's not much to tell."

There was a long silence. Then he said, "I know Aaron proposed."

Damn it, three thousand miles couldn't keep her father out of her business, and she thanked the gods and the stars and the rest of the powers out there that she'd broken up with Aaron in Florida and refused to let him back in. "What —did he ask your permission first?"

She'd been aiming for teasing, but her voice came out harsher than she'd intended, and her father was quiet for a moment before he spoke. "No. He told us he was going to fly out to see you. That was all we knew. But when he got back— it was obvious things hadn't gone well for him. He said you'd —turned him down. Mira, why?"

"Because . . ." She hesitated, too long. "Because I don't love him."

"Is this about Jake?"

"No. Saying no to Aaron had *nothing* to do with Jake."

"But—you—*care* for Jake?"

It was a funny, old-fashioned turn of phrase, but something about it snuck past her vigilance and made tears come to the surface. Because—exactly. She cared, so much, for Jake. About what he'd suffered, about who he was. About the fun she and Sam had had with him in Seattle, the burn of his kisses, the sweetness of being awake with him after Sam went to bed. And she cared, so much, *too* much, that he'd walked away. She couldn't stop caring, even though she wanted to switch it off. "It doesn't matter how I feel. Jake and I aren't going to be a couple."

This time the silence dragged out so long, she thought their connection had broken, and she said, "Hello? You there?"

"You have to remember," he said, very quietly, "that I know what it feels like. To love someone who can't love you back."

In all these years, somehow, she'd never once thought of it that way. Her father, her mother. A man who loved a woman who could walk away from her family. A man who'd been left behind, who'd seen his daughter left behind.

A man who would do anything to keep his daughter from suffering that same pain. To keep her from making the same mistakes.

So much made sense about her father right then. How much he worried, how angry he'd been at Jake eight years ago, how hard he'd been on her about making good decisions and not leaving herself vulnerable—to heartbreak, to other people's poor judgment, to *anything*. He'd wanted to armor her so she could never be hurt the way he'd been hurt.

"I never knew—I didn't know—" *that you loved her that much.* "—that she hurt you so badly."

For a long moment, she thought he was going to clam up. Then he said, softly, "I think I always knew deep down she wasn't the kind of woman who loved back. There was something missing in her that way. That's what I worry about for you. That Jake's like that. That he can't—he can't give you what you deserve."

"What do I deserve?"

"To be loved. Also, the world, handed to you on a silver platter. That's—that's all I ever wanted to give you."

There was so much pressure in her throat, her chest, behind her eyes, that she almost couldn't speak. "I know, Dad. But I never wanted the world on a silver platter."

Her father laughed. "I know," he said. "If anyone knows

that, it's me. All those times I tried to make things easier for you and you fought me tooth and nail . . ."

She started to get angry with him, old habits dying hard, but then she stopped. Because she'd just realized something important about the nature of their battles. That they weren't about her—not at all, not in the ways that mattered most.

The thing was, her father was never going to change, not much. He'd never stop worrying about her. He'd never stop worrying that she would make mistakes in who she loved, that she would love too much or not enough, that she would get left again the way she'd been left by her mother. By Jake at the lake. The way *her father* had been left.

Her father was never going to be less opinionated, less controlling, less—well, *difficult*. He was always going to think what he thought about the way she ran her life.

Her father wouldn't change. But *she* could change. She could see his overbearing love for what it was—*his* fear. The consequence of the losses he carried with him, to this day.

She didn't have to make him stop. She didn't have to get away from him. She only had to stop reacting as if it mattered, and it would stop mattering.

Because she had nothing to prove. She'd had a baby at eighteen and raised him to be possibly the best seven-year-old boy on the face of the earth. She'd stayed when she needed to stay and left when she needed to leave. She'd moved them across the country without anyone's help, gotten herself a job, and held it even when events had conspired against her. She'd run smack into the thing she feared and longed for most—Jake's reentry into their lives—and faced it down, and here they were, she and Sam, still lurching along and figuring things out like everyone else on earth.

She looked around the living room, at the fleece throw nestled in the corner of the couch, at Sam's games spread out on the floor, at the thick stripes on the curtains she'd bought for the big front window. It felt cozy, like home. Her and Sam's place. She'd done a good job.

She'd done a damn good job, and that—*that* was what mattered.

"I've so got this," she said, to no one in particular.

"What?"

"Nothing," she said. And then, "I love you, Daddy."

She hadn't called him that since the night she told him she was pregnant. Because it had felt like too much, being someone's mother and someone's baby. But now it felt just right, like scales in perfect balance.

"I love you, too, sweetheart."

"Do you want to come visit me and Sam sometime soon?"

His voice, when it came over the line, was thick with emotion. "I would love that."

30

S am was acting weird. Squirrelly. He was making her nervous.

Maybe she'd broken him. Maybe all the change and the uncertainty, losing two father figures in Florida and one here, had finally undone him. Maybe he was about to have some little-kid nervous breakdown, and it would be all her fault.

On the other hand, maybe he just had to pee and wasn't telling her. You couldn't tell with a seven-year-old.

They'd parked at the Discovery Park lot and strolled past the visitor center, where she had, in fact, pointedly asked if he needed to use the restroom before they walked out of range. He'd denied any need, and they'd ambled along the path toward the playground he liked, the one where they'd picnicked with Jake and played pinecone baseball. That seemed like an eternity ago now.

After the conversation with her father a few days ago, she'd texted Jake to try to set up a time for him to take Sam on an outing. She couldn't change her father and she couldn't make Jake love her, but she could doggedly go after what she needed—just as she always had, even if she hadn't given herself credit for it.

And what she needed was to make sure Jake's relationship with Sam was okay.

You want to take Sam this weekend? she'd texted.

I wish I could. Out of town. But—maybe soon.

She hadn't quite realized that there were degrees of heartbreak, that something cracked could fall apart into shards, that the shards could be ground down into powder. She'd thought she'd lost what there was to lose already. But it turned out she could feel worse, because Sam's loss amplified hers. He'd been mopey since Jake's departure—even all the Lego-building with Aaron hadn't seemed to snap him out of it, and when Aaron was out of earshot, Sam had told her that running races with Aaron was fun but that *dads were better,* and *I want a special fun day with my dad soon, Mommy, okay?*

She might have to march downtown and strangle Jake with her own bare hands if this continued, because he could break her heart and stomp on the shards, but he'd sure as hell better not break Sam's. And she didn't believe Jake— didn't believe *maybe soon,* didn't believe *wish I could.* What she believed was his walking away, which she could still see in her mind. His shoulders slumped, his head bowed.

Something in her calling out to him, *Come back!*

For now, though, she knew there was nothing she could do except go after what mattered, which was taking care of Sam.

Hence today's trip to the park.

Sam had been all obsessive this morning, starting in before breakfast about how he wanted to go to Discovery Park and play pinecone baseball and if she didn't want to take him could he call Jake? It had made her feel like six different kinds of crap, but she said no because she'd burned her last scrap of wounded pride in the text where she'd invited Jake to do something with Sam, and there was no way she could do it again so soon. Besides, the idea of being face-to-face with him was too overwhelming. She had no idea what she'd do—if she'd yell at him for being an idiot, or be all calm and icy (which was what she was hoping), or grab the sides of his face and start kissing him the instant she laid eyes on him (which was what she suspected). And she had even less idea of how he'd react to any of those things if she actually did them.

It would be easier to catalog the things she *did* know than the ones she didn't. She knew taking care of Sam wasn't as much fun when he wasn't there. Because a day in the park, a visit to a tourist attraction, cooking dinner, ordering takeout, sitting on the couch—all the ordinary moments of her life—were drabber without him in them.

She knew that in destroying her fantasy of what it would be like for Sam to have a father—the fantasy of rescue, of being yanked out of the rut and into a dashing romance, an easier, safer life—she had found something she hoped could be even better. A tease, a hint, of the possibility of companionship, partnership, contentment.

Not that there hadn't been sizzle, too. There had been abundant sizzle. But it was real sizzle. The friction of coarse bark and inconveniently placed buttons, of artificial limbs insinuating themselves into movie moments, of a kid's questions instead of a long, leisurely morning lounging over breakfast in bed. And Jake himself, not the unmarred perfection of a bigger-than-life Army Ranger, not twenty and idealistic, but who he was: rough himself, inconvenient even, sometimes. Troubled, troubling.

She knew that she could never settle for less now. That she owed it to herself to find someone who made her feel that way, rough, messy, sizzling. Poised at the edge of danger and, strangely, *safe*. Someone like that who also loved Sam as much as she knew—knew in the depths of her heart—that Jake did.

And she owed it to Sam to never settle for less—not for herself, and not for him. Even if it meant that it would be just the two of them. Because there were way, way worse things than the feel of Sam's little hand in hers, the contented sound of his humming.

She and Sam walked past the big open field, the grass and wildflowers. *Oh, shit*, she'd forgotten his inhaler, an oversight she'd been committing more and more recently as it approached the two-year mark since his last attack. There was enough pollen in that field to make her nose and eyes itch, but Sam seemed unfazed. Maybe he had outgrown his asthma.

"Mom, can I run in that field?"

Her immediate impulse was to say no.

Jake would say yes.

Jake's not here, though, is he? Doesn't matter what he thinks.

The voice in Mira's head sounded a little like Opal, warm and giddy. Someday, maybe, her own good sense would catch up with the situation and that voice would be her own. For the time being, she was grateful anyone was talking reason in there.

"Mom."

"Let's go up to the playground," she said, and he trotted

after her obediently. He was a good kid. She'd done a good job.

There were some other kids climbing on the play structure and she almost told him not to go too high, but then she didn't. Instead, she turned away so she didn't have to see him perched up there, above the world, and she thought about things.

Last weekend, Opal had taken Mira out for some retail therapy—shopping for skimpy dresses and lacy underthings —because she had insisted that whether or not Mira was interested in dating again, she had to dress up at least once a week like she was too hot for Jake's sorry ass. They'd spent hours at the mall, until the pain in Mira's chest had quieted to a bearable ache and it had seemed possible, maybe, that it wouldn't always be the loudest thing she felt. Maybe.

Unfortunately, though, whenever Mira looked at the lacy underthings in her lingerie drawer, all she could feel was that deep sadness. Because Jake would have appreciated them so very, very much, right before he ripped them off, got bossy all over *her* ass, and then held her and talked to her for hours. But that was never going to happen.

So someone else—someday, when she was ready—would have to appreciate the new purple demi-bra and practically nonexistent thong.

Sam and the other kids had climbed down from the structure and Sam was demonstrating pinecone baseball to them. They were developing an actual game, with home plate and several bases, and it looked like they were dividing into two teams. She watched closely for a moment, but they split without visible trouble into two groups, and Sam's team lined up near the improvised home plate to bat.

Sam was up first. He turned around where he stood, as if searching for something he'd lost. But he hadn't brought anything with him. He caught her eye and looked away.

Squirrelly.

She frowned.

Sam swatted at the ball and somehow beat the throw to first. He jumped up and down and tried to catch her attention. "Did you *see*?" he called.

"That was great!"

Sam craned his head and looked around, and she followed his gaze, and then she saw Jake.

He was striding up the path toward them, purposeful and even, his shoulders big enough to support a house. He was still a good distance away, and she got to watch him narrow the distance between them, figuring it out as he approached —he and Sam had plotted this, that squirrelly boy—and then swooning a little under the rush of pleasure that brought— *they'd plotted this because he was coming to tell her he'd been an idiot*, although her underwear was all fucking wrong, white cotton top to bottom.

He was carrying a cooler and wearing a T-shirt and jeans, and seriously, she was having these intense, unstoppable fantasies about peeling him out of his clothes and riding him while he lay under her, staring up at her in worship.

Um, that was the opposite of bossy.

But they could do that too, right? Because here he was, and he was *smiling*. Smiling!

Only then he wasn't. He was frowning, and he was hurrying off the path toward the baseball game, and she turned to see Sam bent over, and—

She ran.

31

Sam was beside himself. "I *ruined* everything," he said.

"You did *not*," Mira said.

They sat on opposite sides of Sam's gurney in an ER triage room. He was fine, breathing well, though a little hyper from the steroids they'd given him. They were waiting for the pediatrician on staff to see and discharge him.

Jake and Mira had reached Sam's side at the same moment, and everything had happened *fast* after that. They'd tried to get him calmed down, tried to get him to relax and just breathe, but it had been a long time since he'd had an attack and he'd lost the knack. No one around had an inhaler, and Mira vowed that when this was over, she was going to strap one permanently to Sam's arm.

Without discussion, they'd split the tasks. Jake had used every inch of his physical presence and every ounce of his natural command to make the crowd back off to give them more space. Mira had coached Sam to relax and breathe, and when it became evident that wasn't going to happen, Jake had scooped him up and run him toward the parking lot as Mira ran alongside, dialing 911. By the time they reached the parking lot, Sam's breathing was a little less labored, and minutes later, the ambulance arrived. Mira rode in the back with Sam, and Jake drove Mira's car to the hospital.

Now was the first moment she'd had to consider the events of the last forty-five minutes, and her emotions were in an uproar. They'd been in an uproar before Jake had showed up and rearranged the topsy-turvy world once again. Before Sam had been, if not in mortal danger, scaring the shit out of her. Before Jake had been exactly the father Sam needed, the man Mira wanted.

But parenting was parenting, and she wasn't going to get any time to think or sort things out. Sam was crying.

"Jake had a whole plan. He had a picnic and wine and he was going to tell you he was sorry and he wanted to spend lots of time with us, and then he was going to kiss you, and I ruined it *all*."

She looked over at Jake, and he nodded to confirm Sam's story. That was it, just a nod, but her hope winged, a rustle of feathers, an unwinding of the dread and sadness she'd carried with her.

"I ruined the picnic and now you won't get back together and Jake will never live with us and you will never ever ever ever ever get married like a *normal* mom and d—"

"Sam," Mira said. "Honey. You didn't ruin anything. You're not in charge. You don't have the power to ruin things. Your dad and I are in charge. We're the only ones who can ruin things."

Startled, Jake looked up and met her gaze. She gave him a small, tight nod. *That's right, you heard right. You and I. We.*

"I think sometimes I've made you feel like you have to

take care of me," Mira said to Sam, leaning down over the bed and touching her lips briefly to his forehead.

She sat up and looked pointedly at Jake. "But you don't. I'm really, really good at taking care of myself."

She held Jake's gaze, and she saw a reflection of her own hope in his eyes. "Although," she said. "Wow, it was good to have you there. In the park. Thank you. For everything. You were . . ."

There didn't seem to be an adequate word to describe what it had felt like in that moment, having a partner, having someone who cared as much as she cared and who could do what had to be done. Or how easy it had felt to let him, how right.

Her father had implied that Jake was like her mother, unable to love, but that wasn't true. She knew it wasn't. She saw it in how thoroughly, how much, he loved Sam. And she'd seen it every time they'd been together, every time he'd opened up and spilled himself out to her, in words or kisses or touches, rough or gentle, overflowing everything he'd ever held back in any other part of his life.

"You're a good dad," she said.

Sam had stopped crying. "You *are* a good dad," he said.

"Well," Jake said. "It's easy, because you're a good kid."

Then he reached over Sam and took her hand, and her body buzzed with the contact. "And you are a *great* mom."

Her heart was warily listening. Responding with a tentative opening, a curious willingness to risk itself. She wasn't sure, though, about what he was saying, whether it was enough. Because it was one thing for him to have made a picnic, one thing for him to fully accept the mantle of fatherhood, to praise her in her maternal role. Even if he had come with an apology and a kiss—those were good things, but until she heard what he had to say, they weren't enough. Because she was done risking Sam, done risking herself, unless he could tell her that he would never again walk away from a moment of truth between them.

She knew what she wanted, and she wasn't going to let any man take it away from her. She smiled, a secret, internal smile, and took her hand back. Gently.

"Can we still have the picnic?" Sam asked.

"Let's see what the pediatrician says, okay?"

"If he says it's okay?"

She looked over at Jake. "If the pediatrician says it's okay, we can have the picnic. And the apology and the wine. I'm going to reserve judgment on the kissing, though."

THEY STOOD side by side at the rail of the ferry to Bainbridge Island, Puget Sound rolling out beneath them, the Seattle skyline straight ahead. They were at the back of the boat, so there was no wind and no spray, only the sound of the engines and the wake fanning out behind. Sam was counting the holes in the grid under the rail, standing several yards away.

Jake felt flayed. There had been all the anxiety leading up to the picnic excursion, the shock of watching his son double over, the outright *terror* he'd felt when he heard Sam's labored breathing, the relief of hearing the ambulance's siren.

The tsunami of hope he'd felt when she'd called him a

good dad, and the realization that it wasn't enough. It wasn't all he wanted to be, wasn't all he *needed*.

What he needed was to be Mira's family.

He had no idea if that was even a possibility she was still willing to entertain, but the fact that they were here, that she had agreed to this outing, was something. A *big* something. He had never been confident that he could win her with a picnic, that he could woo her back with promises. He had known, when he secretly enlisted Sam's help with the plan while Mira was at work, as he made sandwiches and packed napkins, as he took the bus to Discovery Park, that he might get sent home with his tail between his legs. And he wouldn't blame her for it, not at all. He'd had his chance—two chances, in fact, and both times he'd let fear, not love, rule his heart.

This time, though, was different. This time, one way or another, he'd make her see. That he wanted to live, not just partway, but all the way, and that he wanted to do it with her by his side.

But just as he was about to speak, she said, "Was that all true? What Sam said? That you were going to apologize and say you wanted to spend time with—us?"

This was it. His moment to grab the bull by the horns, or life by its balls, or whatever he had to grasp onto to commit himself full force to what he wanted most in the world. "He got the gist," he said. "What he didn't tell you was that it's not just that I want to spend time with the two of you. I want to spend it with *you*. I want to *be* with you. The way we were, before I fu—screwed it up."

Her eyes were wary.

"You have every right to be hurt. Mad. I should have—I

should have, I don't know, shoved Aaron around and beaten my chest and slung you over my shoulder."

Her eyes got big, wide with surprise, and she smiled. "Well, yes, possibly. Why didn't you do that?"

"Some wrong reasons. Some right reasons. I wanted to be the kind of guy you deserved. And I knew I wasn't."

Her hand flew to her mouth. "You were, you idiot. You are. You always have been."

"No. Listen. I didn't—I didn't handle it well, Aaron's proposal. I should have stepped in, and I should have said, 'You can't marry him. I want you to marry me, but you can't marry me now—I have things to sort out.' But I didn't see all that yet. I was making the same mistake I always make, panicking because I felt—"

The words backed up against his throat.

"Felt too much," he finished.

Her eyes were shiny with tears.

"I've never learned to trust the way I feel. I don't know. Maybe because my role models were shitty, or maybe just because. I didn't that night at the lake. I should have trusted the way I felt about you, talked to you about it. But I didn't. I went against my gut, which was what I did with Mike, too. I should have—"

His voice splintered, and something in his chest, too.

"If I'd trusted my gut, I would have sent Mike home. But I would have talked to him first. Made sure there was a network in place at home, people for him to go home *to,* a plan in place for getting him back in action. But I didn't trust it and I couldn't talk. And it was the same with Aaron, and then—"

He had to stop to catch his breath and pull himself

together, because he had more to say, and he was going to say it this time. All of it.

He drew a breath that rasped against his raw throat and hurt his chest, but the steadiness and warmth of her gaze gave him the strength to keep going. "But it was true, too. I *didn't* deserve you."

She started to protest, but he shook his head. "Maybe that's the wrong way to put it. Maybe it's more right to say I wasn't ready for you.

"I came back from Afghanistan alive, but without really choosing to be alive, if that makes any sense. Just—I had no choice. Mike died, I lived; that was the way the chips had fallen.

The sympathy in her eyes was killing him. And giving him the strength to keep going.

"It was actually Sam who made me see. That day he showed up at my place. He made me see I was scared. Scared of how complicated things are. Not like in the army. Things in the army are—maybe not black and white, but at least shades of gray. Not Technicolor, like you and Sam. And I was scared of living halfway, too. So scared that it was easier not to live at all. I didn't want to do something half-assed that wouldn't feel like it meant something, so I wasn't —I was along for the ride. And I wanted more than that for you and Sam. I wanted you to have a *man* in your life, someone who was here. Really here, not just getting up in the morning. So—I did a few things. I went to see Mike's wife."

"Oh, *Jake*," she said, her voice warm, his name sweet on her tongue.

"I should have done it weeks ago. Months. But I did it.

And she was great. I mean, she's a mess. The kids are a total mess. But she hugged me and told me it wasn't my fault."

"It's not," Mira said, and she touched his cheek, a gesture that almost undid all his tightly held self-control, the governance that held both his tears and his sex drive in check. There was so much still to say, and Sam's gap-counting was bringing him closer and closer to where they stood, so now was not the best possible time for either crying or kissing.

"I still think it was my fault," Jake said. "I'll probably always think it was. It's something I'll always carry with me. But talking to her helped a lot. I realized that part of what I was doing was refusing to live this life because Mike couldn't. I think you kind of said that, that night at the beach, but maybe I wasn't ready to hear it yet. Maybe I heard it as much as blame as an absolution at that point."

"It's not your fault," she repeated. "I'll say that as many times as you need to hear it."

He had to stare out at the skyline for a moment to regain his composure.

"Anyway, I applied to the University of Washington and a few other schools. I'm going to get my bachelor's degree, and then I'm going to apply to get a master's, probably in prosthetics and orthotics, but maybe in physical therapy, depending. In the meantime, I'm going to organize and lead some workshops and support groups through my own prosthetist's office." He had a couple set up already, one focused on finding an outlet through competition and exercise, and the other on helping people decide whether to embrace and reclaim their old lives or strike out on a new path. The kitchen table in his apartment was strewn with notes—on his own discoveries, as well as bits and pieces of conversations he'd had with other vet amputees. Every time he saw the mess of papers, he felt a surge of fresh pride.

"But . . . I thought you wanted to go back to active duty. You told me, you told your mom—"

"I thought I did. But everything's changed. You, Sam . . ."

"I don't want to be the reason you're not fighting." She said it flatly, in that no-nonsense voice that he knew now from personal experience meant she'd dug in.

"You're *not*," he said, with heat. "God, it's the opposite. You're the reason that makes all the other reasons make sense."

"But—"

"I've thought about this a lot," he said, and the thing was, as deep as she could dig in, so could he, and that was one of the many things he loved about her, that at the most primitive level, they *matched*. "I've thought about my motives, what I want to do, where I want to be. And when I say it's about you and Sam, I don't mean I'm giving it up because I feel like you need me to or expect me to. I mean because of what I've learned since I've—*re-met* you. When I first was injured, I didn't want anything. I was empty. Nothing."

She nodded. She'd first seen him at a pretty low moment, and that hadn't even been the worst of it, because the moment he'd seen her in that physical therapist's office, she'd opened a chink in the dam and life had begun seeping back in. Slowly at first, then in a rush, until—

"And then you guys—being with you, getting to know you, falling for both of you—made me alive again, even if I didn't realize it or even want it. Even if it wasn't something I was ready to choose. That day, when Aaron proposed, all I could see was that he had so much more to give you than I did. That's why I didn't fight for you. And then when I'd lost you—when I thought I'd lost you—that's when I saw it. What living means now. What I'm fighting for now. For you. To be the best man I can in the world, *for you and Sam*."

She was crying. He reached out and brushed the tears away and then, because he could, and she let him, he put his fingers in her hair and loved the feel of it. Loved her damp eyelashes and slightly quivering lower lip—which he badly wanted to kiss—and the way she was staring at him like he was something she could commit forever to memory.

"And right now, for me, being the best man doesn't mean going back to the war. It was the right fight for me, then. It was a fight that had to be fought, and I was good at it. I was the right man for it. But things are different now. When the phone rings and it's you saying, 'Can you get Sam?' Or 'Sam needs'—or '*I* need,' I want to be there to answer it. Every time."

"God. Jake."

"Every. Time."

Her hands were clenched together at her throat, but he reached for one and wrapped it in his, and she made a choking sound. She smiled at him as tears ran down her face, a smile that collapsed and re-formed, breaking through like a rainbow every time.

"Daddy," Sam whispered, from under Jake's elbow.

It was the first time Sam had called him that, and Jake had to catch his breath before he could answer. "Yes?"

"You made her cry."

"No. No, he didn't. He made me very, very happy." Mira stroked Sam's hair. "Sometimes grown-ups cry when we're happy."

Sam glared accusingly at Jake. "When are you going to say the 'I'm sorry' part?"

Despite their best efforts to keep serious, they both laughed a little, and Sam made a face of confusion and hurt.

"He did," Mira told Sam. "He said a very nice 'I'm sorry.'"

"Does that mean you'll kiss and make up and he can live with us all the time?"

Jake dared to glance at Mira, and she was looking right back, an eyebrow raised. Not a *yes*, exactly, but definitely not a *no*. A bright Christmas-in-July gladness settled on him.

"That's something your dad and I will talk about and it will take time to figure out," Mira said. "You have to be patient with us. Grown-ups are slow about making decisions."

"But in the meantime," Jake said, "I would be happy to visit you whenever I can, as long as it's okay with your mother. And no matter where I live, I'm your dad, and that's never going to change."

Sam nodded thoughtfully, then said, "There are two hundred and fifteen spaces between there"—he indicated —"and there."

"Did you count those?" Mira asked, pointing at the most distant panel.

"No," said Sam, and skipped off.

"You made a good kid," Jake said.

"*We* made a good kid," she corrected.

He grinned at her. "I was just the sperm donor."

She slugged him in the arm, and he grabbed her fist and tugged her close, so close he could feel her warmth. Another inch or two . . .

But he had one more thing to say. The most important

thing. "I love you, Mira. And I'm sorry it took me so long to tell you that."

Her eyes got, if possible, brighter, and her lower lip trembled. "I'm glad it took you so long, because I had to get my head sorted out. I had to realize that I was trying too hard to be someone I already was. I wanted to be an adult, as if it were a test I had to pass. But in the end, I realized that growing up is a lot about deciding. Deciding to *be* who you want to be. Not letting anyone else dictate the terms, and not getting stuck in old ways of seeing yourself. And I owe you an apology, too."

"Does it come with wine and kissing?"

"No," she said. "Maybe chocolate and blow jobs?"

Jesus. All the blood in his entire body had just screamed into his dick. "Okay," he said. "I'm good with that."

"I didn't fight hard enough for you. I was so busy trying to prove something—I don't even know exactly what—to myself, about my independence and whatever, that I missed what was going on."

"What was going on?"

"I was falling in love with you."

"Oh," Jake said, the words springing to life in his chest. Because maybe he'd known, but there was nothing, *nothing*, as good as hearing her say it. As seeing it there on her face, her eyes shiny with it, her cheeks glowing, as if the way she felt about him was beaming out from the inside.

"I love you, Jake. I kept not *wanting* to. Because it seemed like I went straight from being my father's baby to being my baby's mother, and the last thing I wanted was another role like that. Jake's girl. Someone's—someone's wife."

"I never thought you were anyone's anything," Jake said quietly.

"I know."

"Except your own you."

"I know."

"Who I love. Because you are spectacular. Bold and bossy and beautiful and an amazing mother and completely, insanely sexy . . ."

A flush had risen in her cheeks, and he wished like mad they weren't on a boat with Sam mere feet away, but later on, he was going to have the best time demonstrating *vividly* to her just how much he believed what he was saying. In the meantime, he would get a start on things . . .

He took her in his arms and lowered his mouth to hers, savoring the last moment before contact, when it felt like the world was going to catch fire and burn them up yet he didn't care, because she was in his arms, heat and light and *his Mira*. A tiny whisper of a groan escaped her just before he slid his tongue into her mouth and his hands into her hair.

"Kissing!" said Sam, and he felt Mira's laugh vibrate through his lips, in his heart, in every cell of his body.

32

S am fell asleep in the car on the way home and was still out cold when they arrived.

"Let me," Jake murmured. He hoisted their sleeping son into his arms and carried him up the stairs while Mira followed behind, overwhelmed by the sight of Sam's cheek against Jake's shoulder. Jake laid their son into bed and drew the covers up to his chin, as Mira watched and tried to ignore the tightness in her chest. Jake stepped back to make way for her.

As she bent to kiss Sam, Jake stood at her shoulder, quiet, breathing. Foreign and familiar. As if he'd been there hundreds of other nights holding vigil like this.

She kissed Sam's forehead and cheeks, nose and chin. Her son stirred and burrowed farther into the pillow.

"Your turn," she whispered.

Jake slipped in front of her and stood over Sam. Sam looked so peaceful.

She guessed Jake hadn't seen many kids sleeping. She'd seen a few besides Sam, friends' kids, and they all looked like this, as if they'd thrown themselves into sleep's arms, worries abandoned.

Jake was big in Sam's room. The room was small to begin with, and Jake filled it, making the corners shrink in on her.

She was pretty sure he'd been clean-shaven this morning, but now there was five o'clock shadow clinging to his jaw and chin. It was an unnecessary reminder of how masculine he was. Overkill, to throw a stubbled jaw on top of the way his shoulders and his scent filled the room, crowding her and making all the invisible hairs on her body stand on end.

"Will I wake him up if I kiss him?"

"No." *But you might break my heart. In the best possible way.*

He bent over the bed, and she heard him whisper something, but she couldn't hear what it was. It didn't matter. The fact of the whispering, the fact of his leaning in close, his cheek so close to Sam's, was enough to make her want to cry.

He kissed Sam's face. He kissed him three times, once on the forehead and once on each cheek.

"His cheeks are so soft."

He lifted his head and showed her his reverence. She felt full, her heart swollen with her love for him and for Sam. Her eyes brimming with it. "I think I know how the book is going to end."

"What book?"

"The one I'm writing. Do you want to see?"

She brought him into the living room and gave him a frosted glass full of beer and went to get her paintings. She came back and laid the pages in his lap.

"You've been having all these revelations about what you want to do with your life," she said. "Well, I have, too. I'm not quitting my job or anything—not after I've practically killed myself this summer to keep it—but I definitely need some kind of other outlet. Something creative. So—yeah. Here it is."

She'd been painting almost every night since the day Jake had rescued Sam from the babysitter's whack-job ex.

He lifted the pages one by one, examining them in that way he had, as if she'd disappeared from the room, as if the world had dropped away and there was only her work to take in. Drinking it in.

She leaned over so she could see the paintings too, because she was so happy with them.

Jake and Sam. Only not exactly.

A man with a robot leg.

A man and a boy, playing pinecone baseball.

A man and a boy, running, side by side.

Racing. Winning.

Like him and Sam, only bigger. A whole story she was telling the world.

"I haven't written the words yet," she said. "But I know exactly how it starts."

"How does it start?"

"'My daddy lost his leg in the war.'"

He made a sound, a sharp exhalation, and she touched his cheek. "Is that okay?"

"Yes. God, yes."

He touched his thumb to the paper, smoothing over the place where Mira had drawn his hand on Sam's hair. "This is amazing."

"Thank you."

"You said you know how it ends?"

"I think I do. I hope I do."

"Yeah?" he asked, laying the paintings on the coffee table and reaching for her hands, pulling her down on the couch next to him. He touched her hair reverently, as if it were some semiprecious substance instead of ordinary, sometimes flyaway, blond hair. He looked at her and she leaned into him, into his strength, his heat, and rested her head on his shoulder.

"'And then my Daddy came home to live with us.'"

"That's a good ending."

"I thought so."

EPILOGUE

FIVE YEARS LATER ...

Mira admired the view as Jake slipped into his wet suit. The suit clung tight—to boost his speed—and his taut, well-muscled torso gleamed with the lube he'd used so the suit would slip off easily after the swim.

The crowd was cheering like crazy. Even though Jake had been running triathlons for years now, big throngs still turned out to support their local hero. And today was an even bigger deal than usual, since all the proceeds and sponsorships from the race were going to support Jake's new project, R&R, a retreat for wounded veterans. Ground had been broken just a few weeks ago on the site of the new retreat, several hundred miles south near the Oregon coast. As Jake strapped on his swim leg and changed his clothes, people approached him to congratulate him and thank him and tell him how inspiring he was. Mira could not have been any prouder of him.

Even her father was puffed up with pride over what Jake had accomplished. Mira had to give her dad credit; from the moment she and Jake had moved in together five years ago, he'd gone out of his way to be considerate to Jake. And Jake, for his part, while not ready to embrace her father as his new best friend, had settled on a tone somewhere between civil and warily friendly. Since then, they'd grown to genuinely love each other. Of course, Sam had helped dispel the last lingering tensions, since neither his dad nor his granddad could resist indulging him, and he wanted his dad *and* his granddad to do *everything with him all the time.*

She knew Jake wasn't sure how he felt about all the people clamoring to congratulate and praise him. He didn't think of himself as a hero. He believed he had a lot to tell people and plenty of good ideas to share, but he wasn't crazy about the idea of people viewing him as someone special. He did the triathlons because they made him feel alive. He had gotten his bachelor's degree and was getting his physical therapy degree so he could do the job he wanted to do. He talked to other soldiers who were wounded, traumatized, or just plain lost, because he wanted them to have the benefit of his experience. And the retreat? He liked to say he was only doing what he needed to do to find his place in the world and help other guys find theirs.

"I understand," she'd told him, last night after they'd had bone-melting pre-race sex. Since the research was split on whether sex before a race improved or inhibited performance, they always erred on the side of orgasm. Afterward, limbs intertwined, he brought up how uncomfortable it made him when people fussed over his accomplishments. "But I think you have to accept that no matter how you see yourself, there will be some people who choose to look to you as a hero or a role model. You don't have celebrity status, but you do have a certain public face, and there's not a lot you can do about it."

The black neoprene suit emphasized the breadth of Jake's chest and the narrowness of his hips, and Mira's stepmother, who was standing beside her with Sam on her other side, said, "He's a fine specimen, honey."

Mira laughed. "He *is* a fine specimen, isn't he?"

"Ew, Mom, really?" Sam demanded. At twelve, he was often still the same wise and goofy child he'd always been, but sometimes was also very much the teenager. And displays of affection between his parents were his least favorite thing these days. Which made Mira laugh and want to cry, too, thinking of how Sam's romantic streak had once been so instrumental in getting her and Jake back together. At her and Jake's wedding three years ago, Sam had been the ring bearer, his earnest nine-year-old face beaming over the top of the little satin ring cushion. He'd taken his role so seriously, it had made her tear up (for the hundredth time that day).

"We should do a tri, Mom," Sam said thoughtfully. "With Dad. I mean, he'll kick our butts, obviously, but it would be fun anyway. Or we could do it as a team."

"That would be fun!" Mira said. "As long as it's after I turn in the next book. I don't know if I'll have time to work, finish a book, *and* train for a triathlon."

The three-book contract for *My Daddy's Leg* had launched Mira's children's book career, and she turned out at least one book a year. She was also working on a young adult novel about a teenaged boy whose father had come home from Afghanistan with an above-the-knee amputation. She liked to think she was writing to keep up with Sam. She guessed when he graduated from college she'd start writing for adults.

The swimmers climbed out of the water, and Jake peeled himself out of his wet suit and began swapping legs. He always lost time doing the swap, but he was philosophical about it. "You can argue all day long about whether prosthetics give athletes a natural advantage or a disadvantage," he'd once told a group of veteran parathletes. "I just train as hard as I can, use the equipment God and John Harwood gave me, and pray."

The bike portion of the race, which wound twelve and a half miles over the island on hilly terrain, would terminate at the high school track, so Mira helped Jake's mom and his sister back to their car, then herded Sam and her parents into her own car and drove them to where the final sprint of the race would take place.

It was a small field of runners, a couple hundred, and Jake arrived at the track sixth. He lost a lot of ground swapping legs for the last time—not a change he could possibly avoid.

Mira was cheering so loudly it hurt her throat. Beside her, Sam jumped up and down, yelling, "Daddy! Daddy!" his tween dignity forgotten. All around them, she heard a chant beginning to rise. "Jake! Jake! Jake! Jake!"

He came out fast, and she could tell from watching him that he wasn't winded at all. You couldn't undo years of conditioning and a powerful will to triumph, and when you layered that with rigorous but careful training, well, you got *Jake*. Even so, a 5K gave him very little time to make up lost ground. He passed one runner after another, head down, arms churning, and she cheered and cheered and cheered for him, his parents and his family beside her doing the same.

He wasn't going to win, or even place in the top five, but he was kicking ass and inspiring the hell out of people, and she could not have been more proud of him.

After the race everyone came back to their house—not the Ballard house where Mira had lived when she and Jake had reunited, but a new house with a slightly bigger yard in the Seattle suburb of Issaquah. Mira and Jake had gotten into the habit of hosting a lot of picnics with friends and family, and pretty much any holiday, occasion, or sports event could be the excuse. Jake split off to shower, then rejoined Mira at the food table. He needed three paper plates to support the food he heaped on his plate.

"Hungry much?" she asked, eyebrows raised.

He smirked. "In more ways than one."

"I could help with some of those. If you're asking."

"I'm always asking."

Their eyes locked and Mira felt the same old heat smack her in the belly. She figured it would always be that way. He reached his hand out and took hers, their fingers intertwined. An overwhelming sense of peace and contentment settled over her. She surveyed the friends and family who'd gathered with them, feeling like she had everything she needed to be happy.

She spotted one of Jake's friends, a young army grunt with gold hair that glinted in the sun and the swagger of a guy who could get away with anything. "Is that the guy you got drunk with after that talk you gave at UW?"

"Nate," he affirmed. "Super nice guy."

She surveyed the territory. Broad shoulders, pecs that filled out the black t-shirt Nate wore over well-loved jeans. He couldn't hold a candle to the guy beside her, but he was definitely built to make any woman happy.

"Yeah," said Jake with a smile, following her gaze. "He doesn't have any trouble getting laid."

Nate crossed the lawn and approached a cute, dark-haired woman who was sitting in the grass. He bent to speak to her.

"Hey. Is that Alia from your PT program? She's the one you like?" Jake had told Mira that if there was one person in his program he'd want to have as a colleague someday, it was Alia.

"Yeah. Huh. Interesting."

As they watched, Nate set his plate on the lawn. He sat cross-legged beside Alia. She was an athletic woman, strong and graceful in a sports top and cropped leggings, but next to Nate she looked tiny. They exchanged a few words and shook hands.

"They'd make a cute couple," Mira mused. She squeezed Jake's hand.

Jake gave her a look. "Don't even."

"What?" She batted her eyelashes innocently. "You think they're both good people, right? And objectively, they look cute together."

Jake shook his head. "Nate falls for women *because* they're beautiful and then doesn't understand why he can't make relationships work. And Alia—" Jake sighed. "She just has no idea how great she is."

Mira was only half listening. She watched over his shoulder. Nate and Alia were smiling. Laughing. Talking animatedly, hands in motion. She shrugged. "They look like they're having a pretty good time."

Sam ambled over, football in hand. "Dad?"

With a last squeeze of her hand, Jake trotted off to throw spirals with their son.

A blond woman was approaching the couple on the grass. She was tall and slim with classically beautiful features and the kind of perfect body that could make a woman despair. Mira willed her to take a different path. *No! Go get some food. Or, come over here!* If she had known the other woman's name, she would have called it out, but instead she watched Nate and Alia both turn their attention to the newcomer. They rose to their feet and Alia made introductions.

Mira thought she saw irritation in Nate's posture, a look thrown Alia's direction, like he hadn't wanted his time with her to be interrupted. But he politely turned his full attention on the newcomer and smiled at her.

The next thing Mira knew, Alia was walking away, leaving Nate and the blond woman together.

Nooooo! Where are you going? He's into you!

It was like watching the characters in her favorite TV show self-destruct for sweeps week. She caught Jake's eye. He shrugged as if to say, *You see? I told you.*

Mira wasn't ready to give up. She watched as Alia served herself from the potato salad. Alia kept her head down, concentrating on her plate, then peeked over at Nate. Alia's gaze was wistful. The instant Alia looked away, Nate's attention flickered from the woman beside him and toward the table where Alia stood. Their eyes just missed meeting.

It's not over yet, Mira thought, and smiled.

Then she gave her full attention to her gray-eyed boys,

spiraling the football back and forth. They were beautiful in the sun, one tall and rugged, one shorter, slimmer, as lanky as a colt. She took a deep breath, filling her lungs with the sweet summer air.

She did. She had everything she needed.

ACKNOWLEDGMENTS

Thank you first and foremost to my husband, who every day and in so many ways, supports my writing, and to my children, who have appointed themselves my cheerleaders. Thank you to Amber Belldene, Shelley Ann Clark, Ruthie Knox, Amber Lin, Mary Ann Rivers, Jessica Scott, and Samantha Wayland for reading, loving, and burnishing this book. Thank you also to brainstorming buddies and morale officers Jessica Auerbach, Rachel Grant, Samantha Hunter, Ellen Price, and Charlene Teglia. Many other writer and reader/reviewer friends helped in countless other ways along the way, and I'm deeply grateful.

Thank you to Dan Knowles and Jessica Scott for offering generous amounts of input about army matters; Jess also contributed insights about amputations and prostheses. Any factual errors in the book are strictly my own.

Thank you to my fabulous agent, Emily Sylvan Kim of Prospect Agency, and to Sue Grimshaw and Loveswept, this book's first editor and publisher.

Because this book is a re-release, I also have quite a few

additional people to thank, people who have been instrumental in helping me get this book back out in the world (and/or in saving my sanity in the process): Karen Booth, Sarina Bowen, Cheryl Cain, Kate Davies, Christine D'Abo (with sugar and post-its on top), Gretchen Douma, Nicole French, Rachel Grant (again), Molly Hays, Gwen Hayes, Gwen Hernandez, Sierra Hill, Christy Hovland, Kris Kennedy, Claire Kingsley, Jaycee Lee, Kathy McGowan, Alexa Rowan, Ellen Schroer, Jessica Scott (again), Lauren Seilnacht, Sierra Simone, Darya Swingle, Skye Warren, the attendees of Seattle Unconference 2018, the members of Emerald City Author Chicks, the members of Living the Dream Mastermind, and about a bajillion other people. I hope I'm not forgetting anyone, but I might be, because there are so, so many generous authors out there willing to buoy each other up, and everyone I turned to during this process gave their time and support generously.

Also, extra thanks to the best (and sexiest) tech consultant ever, the inimitable Mr. Bell.

Every book is a collaboration. This book is my most collaborative so far, and I would not have wanted to do it without any one of you. Hugs.

ALSO BY SERENA BELL

Returning Home

Hold On Tight

Can't Hold Back

To Have and to Hold

Holding Out

Tierney Bay

So Close

So True

So Good (2021)

So Right (2022)

Sexy Single Dads

Do Over

Head Over Heels

Sleepover

New York Glitz

Still So Hot!

Hot & Bothered

Standalone

Turn Up the Heat

ABOUT THE AUTHOR

USA Today bestselling author Serena Bell writes richly emotional stories about big-hearted characters with real troubles and the people who are strong and generous enough to love them. A former journalist, Serena has always believed that everyone has an amazing story to tell if you listen carefully, and she adores scribbling in her tiny garret office, mainlining chocolate and bringing to life the tales in her head.

Serena's books have earned many honors, including an RT Reviewers' Choice Award, Apple Books Best Book of the Month, and Amazon Best Book of the Year for Romance.

When not writing, Serena loves to spend time with her college-sweetheart husband and two hilarious kiddos—all of whom are incredibly tolerant not just of Serena's imaginary friends but also her enormous collection of constantly changing and passionately embraced hobbies, ranging from needlepoint to board games to meditation.